New Beginnings

JM Dragon & Erin O'Reilly

Affinity E-Book Press NZ LTD

New Beginnings
2011© JM Dragon & Erin O'Reilly

Affinity E-Book Press NZ LTD
Canterbury, New Zealand

ISBN: 13: 978-615563107
ISBN: 10: 0615563104

Editor: Nancy Kaufman
Editor: Jo Atkins
Cover Design: Helen Hayes
Photo Credit: The Omega Nebula by Venom82

Acknowledgments

Thank you to all the women in the background who helped get New Beginnings to this point. Nancy and Jo—you are the foundation that keeps us grounded and out of editing trouble.

Dedication

For Teresa Luis

Book One

Gentle Sunset

Chapter One

The sun creeping over the horizon made the woodlands appear surreal. Eventually, beams of light filtered through the trees and resembled spotlights, lighting the way for early morning travelers. Lauren smiled as she lazily watched a doe and her fawns quietly grazing on tender new shoots of grass. Bird songs greeted the new day as the river babbled the harmony. Unlike the mess that was her life, the scene was one of peaceful tranquility—something she hoped would last for the entire two weeks of her vacation.

The lush green forest gave Lauren the necessary seclusion to rethink her life's plan. Her drive to excel and to achieve in all that she undertook guided everything that Lauren undertook. Although, she was finding that once she attained her goal, the luster quickly faded. Work no longer held the excitement of discovery it once had; her thoughts were turning more and more toward finding a special someone and settling down. Lauren was tired of solitary meals and nights when her only companion was her pillow. The singles scene, along with many one-time dates that went nowhere, made her wonder if she might spend the rest of her life with only her research. Overall, Lauren had found herself hard pressed to find suitable companionship. It had never been high on her list of priorities to settle down. But now that she realized that it was what she wanted, it seemed out of reach. Her career, and the time her research demanded, left little opportunity to develop any type of lasting relationship. What free time Lauren did have her mother requisitioned in a relentless attempt to control her life. It would take a serious life change if she were ever to find the happiness and love she longed for. It was the reason she sought refuge in the small cabin and in its surroundings. There she always found the peace she needed.

"Well, at least I have the wildlife to keep me company." She chuckled. "See you later. I'm going to have breakfast too."

The doe raised her head, giving her a fleeting glance before she nudged her family to move deeper into the forest.

∞

Coffee and a book in hand, Lauren returned to the small porch and slumped down on the well worn rocker. She always enjoyed reading but with all the demands on her time, she rarely finished more than one or two books a year. Now, she had the newest novels by Patricia Cornwell and James Patterson in the queue, along with a frivolous romance novel titled *Love Found.* Lauren brushed back the lock of light brown hair that had strayed over her forehead and partially obscured the words. She looked at the romance's cover and sighed. *If I can't experience love for myself, at least I can read about it.*

After pushing her glassed up her nose, she began reading chapter seven of *Carolina Moon.*

"God damned mother fucker."

When she heard a loud curse coming from the direction of the river, Lauren dropped her book and stood up while her mind was rushing through possible scenarios. *The worst case—someone is drowning.* Although she realized she might be putting herself in danger, she didn't hesitate to jump down the three steps and begin a full out run to the river.

Lauren was only about half way to the river when she suddenly realized that all she was hearing was the sound of her own footsteps along the pathway. She stopped to listen.

Nothing.

There was nothing. She didn't hear a bird, the wind through the trees, or any sound from the person in the river. A chill shot up her spine as she became aware that she might be too late. With a renewed urgency, she drove her five foot four inch frame quickly toward the river praying to God, that it wasn't an escaped convict or someone equally as dangerous. When the river came into view, what Lauren saw astounded her.

∞

Maggie Sullivan paddled furiously against the increasingly strong current. The river that had started out as calm and rolling was rapidly turning into white water. She was in real trouble. *Shit. What an idiot I was to think this was a good way to find out if I still have what it takes to rise to a challenge.* Her experience in difficult waters was limited, at best. The little knowledge she possessed did not include manipulating a canoe through swirling eddies or around jagged rocks. Arms screamed in pain. Maggie was certain that her depleted energy was no match for the danger she was in.

Short dark hair matted on her head and rivulets of sweat and spray obscured her view. She dared not brush them away. She needed both hands and all her concentration to try to steer the small vessel to safety on the riverbank. *Where is help when you need it? Shit!*

The rapidly moving water reached out and captured Maggie in its grip. The canoe rocked with abandon and Maggie feverishly dug the blade of the paddle deep into the water using 'j' strokes to keep the canoe upright. She was winning the battle until a jutting rock appeared and she pulled the paddle out of the water to push off it. The sudden motion was too much for the tenuous balance of the small vessel and Maggie found herself pitched from the canoe. As her body was about to hit the water, she let out a piercing cry that sent startled birds squawking from their nests before everything became a swirling mass of icy, foaming water dragging her under. Scraped and bruised by rocks and the river bed, Maggie fought her way back to the surface. She sucked in deep gulps of air as the empty swirling canoe continued down the stream. The nearest bank was ten feet away. Tired and weary arms protested each stroke that Maggie took toward the safety of the shore. After she clawed her way up the bank, she dragged her battered body onto the soft grass where she collapsed.

Maggie lay there collecting her thoughts while she gently moved her limbs to assess the damage. Relieved that her limbs seemed to be intact and functioning, she clenched her teeth and willed her tired, aching muscles to stand. She stretched her five feet seven inch body gingerly to work out the knots as she took stock of the numerous welts and cuts on her arms and legs, as well as a couple of painful slashes on her breasts that were no longer covered by her badly ripped shirt. Her wet shorts clung to long, tan legs. In one fluid motion, she shook the moisture covering her body away much as a dog shakes itself after a bath. Maggie looked up and found expressive hazel eyes gazing down at her.

∞

Lauren stood with her mouth opened wide. The shout that had drawn her to the river had come from a beautiful woman who was obviously in need of help. Lauren could see angry, bloody cuts and contusions over much of the woman's body."Are you okay? Of course, you're not. Can I help you? What are you doing out here?"

"I thought it was a nice day for a swim. What the hell does it look like?"

"Sorry, that was a stupid question. You look banged up. Can I do anything to help?"

Maggie looked at the woman and smiled inwardly at her obvious nervousness. *She is kind of cute.* "Well, if you could lead me to a phone, it would be a big help."

Lauren nodded and pointed through the woods. "My cabin is over that way. I have a cell you can use. Can you walk?"

Maggie grimaced as she stepped gingerly, in an effort to keep the tatters of her clothing from rubbing against the painful lacerations. Lauren screwed up her face and she gave the woman a fleeting smile. "Right behind you."

Lauren's heart was pounding. Her rule in life was *caution first*, and yet she was leading a stranger to her secluded cabin in the woods. *Just because she's a woman, doesn't mean she can be trusted, does it?* She looked over her shoulder and watched as the taller brunette wipe drops of water from her eyes. It was clear from her scowl that she was not only in pain, but very angry. "What happened?"

5

"Happened? That's a stupid question. Haven't you got eyes? The canoe dumped me into the goddamn water and I was lucky to get out in mostly one piece."

Lauren felt her face burning. "Hey, those remarks are completely uncalled for. In case you hadn't noticed, I'm trying to help you. Sorry I asked."

Maggie looked at the retreating back, kicking herself for taking out her frustration on the only person who was in a position to help. The woman didn't deserve it. Too late to take the words back, she sighed heavily as she squished along, relieved when a cabin came into view. *Great, now I can get out of this horrible wilderness and go home to a nice hot shower, warm clothes, and my own bed. So much for trying to prove to myself that I can still rise to a challenge. The faster I get out of here, the better.*

Lauren opened the door and left it ajar for the other woman. She walked purposefully toward the table and her phone. *I may have come here for solitude, but this brief intrusion has certainly been interesting. If the woman wasn't such a bitch, I might have liked getting to know her better.* She watched as her visitor braced herself against the door jamb and took off her shoes. She didn't expect that. Once the woman was inside, Lauren handed her the cell phone.

"Thanks," Maggie said softly as she accepted the phone.

"You're welcome." Lauren, still miffed over the woman's rude behavior, spoke coldly. "Just in case you need to leave a call back number, here it is." She handed over the slip of paper before turning her gaze away from her unexpected guest.

Maggie punched in her friend Gale's number and waited impatiently for her to pick up. As the ringing

6

continued, Maggie paced in the small area. "For God's sake, woman, pick up!"

Although Lauren had moved to a discreet distance, she smiled when she heard the pent up frustration in the woman's voice. *Now might be a good time to make coffee.*

The phone buzzing in her ear, Maggie considered how quickly the day of intended personal discovery had gone so sour. Not only had she nearly drowned, but she was now stuck in the middle of nowhere and soaked to the skin with her clothes in tatters. If that wasn't bad enough, she had no money or car keys to get home and Gale had picked that moment, her moment of need, to not be home. Maggie snapped the phone closed and turned around to see Lauren entering the cozy room with two steaming mugs of what she hoped was coffee.

"Hi…hmm, I'm sorry, I don't know your name. I thought you might like some coffee. I can vouch for it warming you up."

"I'd love some. I am pretty cold after the dunking I took. The name is Sullivan…Maggie Sullivan."

"I wasn't sure how you took your coffee, so it's black."

"Just the way I like it, thanks." She hesitated a moment while she rearranged her attitude. "And, thanks for being so kind to me after I took my bad day out on you. I'm sorry."

Lauren responded, "Don't worry about it. I probably would have done much the same if I had gone through what you just did. I'm Lauren…Lauren Walker. Welcome to my home away from home, Maggie Sullivan."

"Thank you. I couldn't raise my friend to come pick me up. Guess I'll have to try and make it back to the parking lot where I left my car and get some help there to get downstream and try and retrieve my canoe."

Maggie's statement was calm enough, but Lauren saw the exasperation in the woman's face. "Sorry, my Land Rover is being serviced or I'd offer to take you home. You can stay here if you want, until we can get you some transportation. I have the room. I think I can find you something else to wear. Not that your outfit isn't attractive, in a primitive kind of way," she said with a teasing smile. "Still, I bet you would feel better with a hot shower and dry clothes."

Maggie smiled. "That sounds wonderful." In another time and under different circumstances, she might have asked the women to join her, but this just wasn't the time. "If it isn't too much trouble."

"No trouble at all. Follow me to the bathroom and I'll get you some clean towels."

∞

Lauren rifled through the dark oak chest in the extra bedroom, trying to locate something for the woman in her shower to wear. She was hoping one of the visitors to the cabin over the years had left behind clothes that would be close to the right size—so far her search had come up empty. She heard the water shut off before she found something suitable. Near the bottom of the trunk, she finally came across just what she had been looking for and pulled them out of the drawer. *Yes, sweats.*

Lauren found Maggie sitting in front of the fire with only a towel around her. To her surprise, the fire was crackling. A small smile edged over her lips as she noted the look of pure pleasure on Maggie's face

8

as she thawed out in front of the fire. It looked…romantic and inviting.

Reluctant to move past the moment, Lauren nevertheless cleared her throat, when Maggie turned to look at her, she held up the clothing. "I found you some sweats to wear, and a pair of wool socks." With a smile, she handed the items to the woman seated by the fire. "How did you get that fire going? I tried forever this morning and nothing, and here you have it well on its way to blazing. What's your secret?"

The woman laughed. "You had it all ready; I just struck the match." She took the offered clothes and smiled. "Thanks."

Lauren's return smile froze into shock as Maggie, without modesty, peeled off the towel to reveal a muscled torso with perfectly proportioned breasts. The nipples, a dark shade of brown in contrast to the creamy breasts, were peaked from the change in temperature. Lauren turned her eyes away, but they kept drifting toward the nude body. In her medical practice, she had seen naked woman, plenty of them, but to have one so attractive standing in her living room caught her totally off guard. After Maggie tugged the shirt over her head she ran her hand over the tightly clinging fabric.

Lauren's heart was racing and she was having difficulty catching her breath. She was amazed at her reaction, unable to recall when, if ever, she'd had such a strong response to seeing someone's naked body. *Have I been alone that long?* "Sorry that the clothes don't fit better," she offered.

"Hey, no problem. They're better than what I was wearing, don't you think?"

"Considering what you had on, I would say it's a vast improvement." Her voice went from playful to serious. "Would you like me to look at the scrapes and cuts you got? Some of them looked pretty nasty. It's been a while since I dressed a wound, but I'm confident that I remember how."

"Are you in the medical profession, Lauren?"

"Yes, I'm a medical doctor. Right now I'm on the research side, specializing rheumatoid arthritis. I rarely have to treat injuries. What do you do, Maggie?"

Maggie deliberately ducked the question. "I would appreciate you looking at some of them When the water from the shower hit them they got my attention."

"Fortunately, I always keep my medical bag with me when I come to the cabin." Lauren smiled. "Just in case I ever need it…you're the first. Be right back."

"A doctor who takes her little black bag on vacation …isn't that some sort of sin?"

Lauren laughed. "Yes, it is, so please don't report me to the AMA," she said as she left the room.

Maggie looked around the homey cabin. There was the door to the bathroom, two partially opened doors that she supposed were bedrooms, and off to one side was a small kitchen. The furniture was typical cabin décor with a well worn couch, two arm chairs, and a maple coffee table along with two end tables. Tucked away in one corner she saw a round oak dining table and four chairs. There was something special about the ambience place. It said, *"Welcome, you're home."* A sense of peace that she hadn't had for some time washed over her.

"Okay, I have the bandages and antiseptic. Shall we take a look?"

"You will be gentle, won't you?"

"I haven't had anyone complain about my technique yet, but I'll let you be the judge." Lauren found the thought of touching Maggie very appealing and somewhat frightening. "So, tell me, Maggie, where does it hurt?"

"Actually, I think the ones on my breasts are the worst, although when I showered, I did notice a bad scrape on my leg."

"Okay, take off the shirt and let's look at those first."

Maggie pulled off her shirt, grimacing at the pain. "I want you to know that I appreciate everything you're doing for me. When you're done I will call my friend again and be out of your hair soon."

"I...I don't mind, really I don't. It's nice to have the company." With trembling hands, she gently wiped a betadine solution over the nasty looking cuts. It was impossible not to notice the swell of the nipples. Nothing in her experience had prepared Lauren for the emotional upheaval she was feeling. *God, what is going on with me? Am I so lonely that I'm trying to reach out to someone...anyone?*

Maggie was finding it difficult to keep her hands to herself. Lauren's touch was gentle and it wasn't much of a leap to imagine the skilled hands roaming over her body. *I wonder what it would be like to make love with her. Those hands could touch me anywhere, anytime.* She consciously reined in her libido. *Get control of yourself, Sullivan. You'd think you were some horny kid.*

"These cuts aren't all that deep. I'm going to put some butterfly bandages on them to minimize scarring. When you get home, you should contact your doctor and have them looked at. Considering where you were when you got them, there's the

11

possibility of infection no matter how much I've cleaned them out. You'd be amazed at how one small bit of dirt can begin to fester weeks later." Lauren's attention turned to Maggie's leg. "The cut on your leg will probably need stitches. I can put a butterfly on it, or I can sew it up for you—your choice.

"How many stitches do you think I'll need?"

"Three or four at the most, the cut is deep rather than wide."

"Then stitch away. I am yours to do with as you please." Maggie closed her eyes, mentally chiding herself for the wayward thoughts running through her mind. Half an hour later, Maggie's leg had a neat row of four stitches.

"Did I hurt you?"

"You have a very gentle way, Lauren. You can be my doctor anytime. Thanks for taking care of me. I really appreciate all that you've done today."

Two pair of eyes—one hazel, one blue—locked. Silence pervaded the room for a few minutes until the women heard a rumbling sound, like the beginnings of a thunderstorm.

Lauren's eyes rested on Maggie's growling stomach.

Maggie pressed her hand to her stomach in hopes that the sound would stop, but the growling got louder. A self-conscious smile along with a rising blush colored her face.

"Would you like something to eat?" Lauren offered with a grin, her eyes twinkling.

"Oh, did you get my subtle hint? Thanks."

"Was that your stomach? I'm shocked. I thought it was about to rain." Lauren winked at Maggie before she laughed. "Why don't I fix us some dinner? I have steak, potatoes, and broccoli." Still chuckling, Lauren headed for the kitchen. *This is turning out to be fun. Strange how life works.*

Maggie grimaced slightly at the word *broccoli.* "Sounds wonderful. Do you need any help?"

∞

The kitchen was too small for the both of them, so Maggie set the table and tended to the fire as Lauren prepared dinner. Glimpses of the small woman in the kitchen brought unfamiliar warmth to Maggie's heart. *This is turning out to be a fabulous day.*

Lauren had a satisfied smile on her face as she looked at the meal on the table. "You ready to eat?" she asked her house guest who was standing by the fire.

"Yes. It sure smells good." Maggie made the short journey to the table. "Where do you want me to sit?"

"Right here will be good." Lauren patted a chair and smiled. "Name your poison—you have a choice of coffee, tea, soda, or beer.

"Beer sounds good." Sitting at the table, Maggie swallowed the broccoli as quickly as possible. *With the day I've had, why not the one tasteless vegetable I really hate. The rest is great, though.* While picking up her glass of beer, she discreetly looked at Lauren.

Lauren was gazing back at her. "May I ask what brought you and your canoe to Warwick and this particular stretch of river? I can't recall anyone ever coming this far down; the rocks are extremely dangerous here." Her eyebrows scrunched together. "Didn't they warn you about the rapids?"

Maggie was tempted to answer sarcastically. But as she looked into the friendly, interested hazel eyes, she changed her mind. "I had a free weekend before I start a new job. Probably won't have much time for anything but business after I start in five days. I just found an access and put my canoe in the water. I didn't see anyone else. Guess that should have been my first clue."

"I thought they had warnings posted all along the bank." Lauren shrugged. "What does your new job involve? Do you live near here?"

Maggie didn't want to share any specifics about her life with Lauren. *Maybe she wouldn't want to know me if she knew what I do.* She ducked the questions by posing one of her own. "How come you're out here alone? It is a little desolate." She gave Lauren an appraising glance. "I'd think you'd be here with a husband or boyfriend, or a significant other."

Lauren decided to ignore the comment. "The cabin belongs to my family. I make it a practice to come here for two weeks every year to renew and recharge."

"Ah, the Thoreau experience."

"You tell me. Did the river remind you of Walden Pond? Seriously, this year there's a twofold reason to be here. My uncle died recently and left me his business. I decided to check it out before I sell it."

"Do you want to sell?"

Lauren laughed before she let out a long sigh. "My mother wants me to sell. She said it's not the business for me. It has been in the family for as long as I can remember, though. My uncle was very special to me and partly responsible for my decision to go into medical research. He had rheumatoid

14

arthritis and I really wanted to find a cure and end his suffering."

"Why not make up your own mind about selling, then? Life is too short, Lauren. Regardless of what your mother says, do what makes you happy."

"I'm trying to decide what that is."

"What kind of business is it?"

"Would you believe it is one of the oldest, continuously operating, general stores? The place is disorganized, but if you want something, you would most likely find it there eventually. My uncle prided himself on having anything and everything. And, he did."

Maggie saw the wistful look on Lauren's face as she spoke lovingly of the store and her uncle. "I would like to see the store. Is it in town?"

"Yes you can't miss it since it is the only one in town."

"From the picture you paint, it sounds like a wonderful store. Why on earth would you want to sell it, Lauren? Sounds to me like you ought to keep it."

"My mother would be livid if I didn't sell." Lauren knew as she said the words, what the other woman would think. The biggest mystery—why she was telling a complete stranger about the store or her mother.

"Mommy's girl, huh?" Maggie couldn't stop her condescending words. In a fluid motion she got up and walked the few steps to the fireplace refusing to look in Lauren's direction.

The tone and delivery and not the words made Lauren see red. After scraping back her chair, she walked briskly over to the other woman and spun her around. "What the hell would you know about it?"

"I know enough to know you don't want to sell."

"Maybe I don't, but it really isn't any of your business."

"When you told me about the store, your mother and selling it became my business. It is obvious you don't want to sell your uncle's store so why are you?"

Lauren sucked in a breath. "Sometimes it is easier to go with the flow than cause upheaval."

"At what cost, Lauren?"

With her shoulders slumping, Lauren sat in a nearby chair. "My mother and I have had an adversarial relationship for a very long time." Her eyes met Maggie's. "I haven't a clue why I'm telling you this."

Maggie rubbed her chin. "What do you mean?"

"Because, you are a complete stranger and never in my life have I ever told even those closest to me about me and my mother."

"Perhaps it is time to let it go. I'd like to hear about why you want to sell the store that obviously means so much to you."

For a long time Lauren's eyes watched the flames dancing in the fireplace. "You're right I don't want to sell my uncle's store. I love him and that store." She shook her head. "My mother will keep on me until I sell and there is nothing I can do to stop her."

"You can stand your ground, Lauren. I don't see you as someone who compromises."

A slight smile wreathed Lauren's lips. "I'm not."

"Except when it comes to your mother?"

"Yeah, something like that. If you met my mother you'd know what I mean. She is not someone who…,"

The intrusive sound of a cell phone ringing had both women looking in its direction.

Drawing a deep breath, Lauren got up and walked toward the small table where her cell phone was. "That's probably your friend." She flipped open the phone, "Hello." She smiled and handed Maggie the phone.

"Hey," she said softly. "Yeah, it was quite an adventure. My canoe capsized. I was lucky to get out in mostly one piece. ... Wait I'll find out. Lauren what road is near here?"

"Fifty-one."

"It's highway fifty-one. ... That close? ... How soon? ... What do you want me to do, sprint in the dark? ... Yep, I'll be there. Bye."

Maggie closed the phone and glanced at Lauren. "That was my friend Gale. She already passed the road and has to turn around. Her best estimate as to time was that she didn't know."

"Why don't you call her back and I can give her directions?"

Maggie shrugged. "She's not all that familiar with this area so it will be easier for her if I wait for her on the highway."

"It gets pretty dark out here at night. Let me get a flashlight and I'll walk with you to the road and then wait until your friend arrives."

Maggie looked at Lauren. She didn't want to leave. There was something in the way Lauren spoke about her mother that compelled Maggie to want to know more. "Lauren, when I get home, can I call you? I'd like to thank you for rescuing me. Maybe we can go to dinner."

Lauren looked into the cool, focused blue eyes, and smiled. "Sure, I'd like that. Right let me get the flashlight while you put your shoes on."

Maggie retrieved her shoes from the porch, pulled them on and waited by the door. The cold dampness surrounding her feet made her shiver.

"I've got the flashlight. I think you should call your friend back so I can find out where she is and give her landmarks so if she gets there before we do, she won't drive past by the dirt road that leads to my cabin."

"Sounds like a good plan to me."

Lauren took a notepad from a drawer in an end table and jotted down her number. "Here's my number if you want to call."

"Count on it." Maggie held up the paper. "Now I have it twice."

Lauren rolled her eyes. "Right I gave it to you before didn't I?"

∞

Maggie squished as they walked along the path to the highway. "This is awfully narrow to be a driveway."

Lauren laughed. "You're right but my Range Rover gets me to the cabin." Lauren handed the woman her phone. "You need to call your friend."

"Okay." Maggie took the phone and dialed Gale's number. "Where are you now? ... Yeah, sounds good. The woman who rescued me wants to talk to you so you'll find me. ... Okay here she is."

"Hi, Gale, I'm Lauren. Where are you exactly? ... Good that means you are exactly five miles from the road to my cabin. ... You will see a mailbox that looks like a fishing boat. That's where we will be. ... We should be there before you. ... Okay see you then."

"I take it she is close by."

"Yep." Lauren focused the beam of light from the flashlight ahead of them. "There's the road and she's five miles away. Great timing."

While they waited, Maggie paid no attention to the road and kept her gaze on the woman next to her. "I will call you."

Lauren smiled. "I hope you do, Maggie." Her eyes saw the glow of headlights. "That must be your friend."

When Maggie saw Gale's SUV, she frowned. *I sure would like to stay here and talk with Lauren more.* "Yep, that's her." Just as the vehicle rolled to a stop, Maggie leaned in and kissed Laruen's cheek. "Thank you for everything. I'll be in touch."

As the SUV moved away, Lauren placed her palm on her cheek. "I hope you do call."

Chapter Two

Water was still seeping out of Maggie's shoes as she settled into Gale's SUV.

"Hi, Mags, you look like you could do with some heat," Gale said after giving her friend the once over.

"Ya, think? First, I found myself dumped in the cold river where I feared for my life. Then, I look up to see this hot chick staring at my mostly naked body. I probably would be wondering around in the woods freezing to death if she hadn't come to my rescue."

"Guess you've had better days." Gale grinned. "Lauren, is that the woman who you kissed?"

Maggie smacked Gale's shoulder. "I kissed her on the cheek you dumbass. That hardly qualifies as a kiss."

"Get her number? If you didn't I have it on my phone.

"Give it a rest, Gale." Maggie winked at her friend. "And, yes, I did get her phone number."

"Is she going to be your *honey* for the time we are here?"

"No," Maggie said sharper than she meant to. "Unlike others she is a class act and seems to be a really nice person.

"Do I hear Mags talking? No, it can't be. She doesn't ever refer to woman as *nice*. It's usually in the terms of *hot piece of ass*."

Maggie glared at her friend. "She is definitely hot but…"

"But what?"

"She's different. After I got out of the water, she was there and I was my usual bitchy self. But that didn't matter. She welcomed me into her cabin, let me take a warm shower, gave me clean clothes to wear, doctored my injuries, and made me dinner."

Gale laughed. "I was going to mention your new fashion statement—too small."

"Stop."

In all the years of their friendship, Gale had never heard the tone Maggie was using now when she described her relationships or conquests, or anyone. "You really are taken with this woman aren't you?"

"I don't think so. How ridiculous would that be? I've only just met the woman."

"Come on, Maggie, be honest for just a moment. Are you interested in this woman or not?"

"Lauren is different from anyone I've ever met before. Hell, I don't even know if she'd be interested in me…she could be straight for all I know."

"Don't give me that. You have the best gaydar of anyone I know."

Maggie looked away. "Even if she is family she's way out of my league."

Gale snorted. "When have you ever thought any woman was out of your league, Mags? The look on your face and the tone of your voice tells me you're attracted to her."

"Her last name is Walker, Gale."

"Oh. Not good."

"Exactly."

"I guess that means you won't call her then."

"I need to give her back these clothes."

"That's a convenient excuse."

Maggie only shook her head.

"If you're truly interested in the possibility of a relationship you better come clean with her, Mags. Why you're in Warwick isn't something she should find out on her own."

"And, she owns the general store."

"You're kidding."

"I wish I was." After each of her affairs had dried up almost as quickly as they had begun, Gale had always been there for her. Now Gale was speculating about a woman Maggie had only just met.

"What are you going to do?"

"Do? We just met, Gale. I'm going to call her and arrange to give her back her clothes. That's it. That's all there is."

Gale pulled her vehicle in front of the bungalow that her friend rented while they were in Warwick. "Mags, I've known you long enough to know the difference between lust and a genuine interest on your part. Part of my job as a lawyer is to read people and right now, I'm not seeing this woman as some roll in the hay to you. What I hear is that this woman you just met is different."

Maggie rubbed her hand over her face. "Maybe you're right. The only thing I know now is that I don't have a key to get into the bungalow."

Gale laughed. "Fortunately for you, my friend, I do."

∞

In her return walk to the cabin, Lauren's mind was dizzy with thoughts of the woman that just left. She realized just how excited and alive Maggie's presence had made her feel. *Like I'm scratching at my skin trying to itch what I can't reach.* The arousal building in her body at the thought of seeing Maggie again made her catch her breath. Surprised, she shook her head at the way her body was reacting. *Don't be stupid. She's here on business, I'm here on vacation.*

22

Still, the thought of a short term affair with Maggie did have its appeal. *Does it ever.*

Her thoughts turned to the situation with her mother. *Will I ever find some happiness, or will I end up just going along with what mother has planned for me.* She shook her head violently. *NO! I'm not going to marry some guy to make my mother happy.* She laughed bitterly. She and her mother had been close at one time but that had changed and she wasn't sure why. *Wouldn't mother be shocked to know how turned on Maggie makes me feel.*

Her purpose in spending time alone was to come to some conclusions about where her life was going. Granted she was successful, well respected, and her life held great promise, but there was something fundamental missing. The brief encounter with Maggie not only turned her on, but it gave her a glimpse of what life outside of work could be.

Lauren opted to drop into the worn rocking chair on the porch instead of going inside. She was back to where her day began before Maggie Sullivan came into her life. There was a new sense of purpose in her life. *Do I really want that?*

∞

The next morning, Gale dropped Maggie off at the parking lot where she left her Jeep. Once she said goodbye to her friend she looked at the empty rack on top of her car. "I wonder if my canoe is salvageable. A smile crossed her face as she thought of Lauren Walker. "Yep, that's just the excuse I need to go back to the place where I lost my canoe. And just maybe I'll run into Lauren again." The arousal she felt the night before reemerged tenfold as she unlocked her car, got in, and started the engine. As she drove the short distance, she turned up her radio and sang along as Melissa Etheridge belted out *I'm the Only One*. When she turned down the dirt road that seemed to disappear into the trees, she squirmed in an attempt to squelch her arousal.

Maggie felt foolish, but at the same time at ease, as she parked her Jeep and slowly made her way toward the cabin door. Gale had been wrong—she did want to bed Lauren. *The sooner the better.* If there were something more, like a relationship, that would have to wait. Right now, her body wanted satisfaction.

After nearly drowning, the intense emotion of surviving turned to lust and desire when she first saw Lauren. Maggie knew she could cajole her into bed without much objection. But then something unexpected happened and she'd allowed other emotions to take over. Now, with every step that took her closer to the cabin, the anticipation of seeing Lauren again made her feel more than sexual arousal. Yet, the imagine that taking Lauren invoked made the tempo of her heart increase. In the space of less than twenty-four hours, Lauren had invaded her mind and body. All she wanted now was to see her, touch her, hold her, and the growing need for release.

∞

Once again Lauren was sitting in the rocker in the morning light as she tried to get a grip on the feelings of hollowness and sadness that filled her life. She had come to the cabin to find answers only to have a stranger enter her life and add to her confusion. If she was honest with herself, the only confusion about the woman was how to get her in bed. *How idiotic is that? Is my life so barren and without affection that I'll take whoever comes my way to my bed?* The arousal she was feeling answered *yes.* "But what does that mean to the rest of my life? I don't want one night stands or brief affairs. I don't want to be alone."

Her arms pushed up and off the rocker. "If she does call, she'll want to know about her canoe." The least Lauren could do was to see if it was nearby or had drifted off down river. It didn't take long for Lauren to spot the canoe once she arrived on the river's bank. The small vessel nestled between two rocks near the opposite bank had a gaping hole in the skin. "It will be cheaper to buy a new one."

"My thoughts exactly."

Lauren jumped. She turned around and saw the twinkling blue eyes that had pervaded her thoughts staring at her. "Oh, you scared the shit out of me!" She eyed Maggie and had to dampen her surging arousal.

"No one answered at the cabin. I thought you might have gone to get your car." Maggie couldn't stop the smile that plastered itself on her face. "I see you had the same idea as I did." She pointed her chin toward the damaged canoe. "Looks like a goner."

For a moment, Lauren was speechless. *She came back.* "Hmm, I think you are right." *How lame.*

Maggie's senses surged with her desire to kiss the woman. "Any suggestions on how I get over there to get it?"

Lauren turned so she was facing Maggie. "If you're up for an adventure and a bit of a hike, there is a spot several hundred yards up stream where we can cross."

Maggie raised an eyebrow. "I seem to remember that exact spot. I thought when my paddle dug into the rocky bottom that the river was no challenge at all."

"Yep, that's why they posted the big signs."

"I swear I never saw them."

"How could you miss them? They're the size of a small billboard."

"Why don't you show me?"

"Why don't I fix us breakfast first?"

"Lead the way. I hope that offer includes …"

It was Lauren's turn to raise an eyebrow.

Maggie wiggled her eyebrows. "Coffee of course. Whatever else did you have in mind?"

"Whatever indeed."

∞

Breakfast had been easy and pleasant and after it was finished, both Maggie and Lauren went back outside and began hiking along the river's bank. At a shallow area of the river, they crossed it and retrieved the canoe. In tandem, they worked to portage it back to Maggie's vehicle. Once they had it secured to the top of the Jeep, they stood awkwardly.

"Would you like to come inside?"

Maggie just kicked the dirt, refusing to look at Lauren. "I…I want you to know something."

Lauren braced herself for what was to come. "What's that?'

"I'm attracted to you."

"You are?" Lauren asked.

Maggie rubbed her eyes with her thumb and forefinger before looking directly at Lauren. "Yes."

"What do you mean?"

Maggie reached out and caressed Lauren's cheek. "I want you."

Lauren covered Maggie's hand. "Funny thing is—I want you too."

Kisses became caresses, and caresses became explorations, until both women wanted more. In the feverish excitement, fingers found their way to skin.

Maggie's lips kissed Lauren's ear before she whispered, "Let's take this inside."

Lauren reigned in her emotions that threatened to take over completely and pulled away slightly. "I can't do this." She saw the frustration on Maggie's face. "I don't want to rush into something that we might both regret later. Can we take this slow?"

Beyond frustrated, Maggie exhaled sharply and removed the hand that had snaked its way under Lauren's shirt. "Yeah. Okay. If that's what you want." She gave Lauren a brief hug and then stepped back.

"I would like nothing more that to make love with you, Maggie. God knows I have thought of little else since you left last night. I'd like to know you a little more before we have a quickie. If we met in a bar there would be seduction before we went to bed." The disappointed look on Maggie's face had Lauren reconsidering her stand for a moment. "What do you say we get to know each other first?"

Although Maggie's body was screaming for release, she recognized the wisdom in Lauren's words. If her initial feelings about Lauren were right and there was the possibility of more than a one night stand, she'd take it. They needed a stronger base than sex. "I want that too, Lauren."

∞

They spent that afternoon sitting on the porch, talking about their lives, and taking the first steps towards getting to know each other.

"Tell me about Maggie. Where exactly is home? Where do you live, what you do, where you work? You said you were starting a new job, didn't you?"

Maggie wanted to take Lauren in her arms and hold her tight as she revealed what her new job was. Gale had warned her that the moment would arrive and would be a defining moment in their fragile relationship. She took a deep breath, then said, "I have a home in Stafford, but I just rented a bungalow in Warwick. That's where my job will be."

"Warwick? That's where my uncle's store is. What sort of job is it?"

"Have you heard of Preston, Moser, and Sullivan?"

"The construction and development group?" Lauren's eyes widened. "You're *that* Sullivan?"

Afraid that Lauren might tell her to leave, Maggie's heart was beating rapidly. "Yes, I'm afraid so."

"Why would you want to come and change a lovely old town like Warwick? Your company made millions when you modernized Westfield and Grover. Wasn't that enough money for you? Look at the countryside." She gestured around. "Do you think it needs more traffic or people? Do you have any idea what your plans will do to this town?" Anger tinged her passion.

"Lauren, this isn't personal; it's business."

"It's personal to me, Maggie. This is my hometown. The place where I grew up. It's bad enough that my mother keeps badgering me to sell the store. I just don't understand why, Maggie. Doesn't anyone care about roots anymore?"

"I understand what you're saying, but there's a proposal on the table and my company needs to see it to a conclusion." Relived that she was still there, Maggie took Lauren's hand. "Tell you what, why don't we go into town and have some lunch, and then you can show me Warwick through your eyes. What do you say? Does it sound like a doable plan to you?"

Lauren looked at Maggie and felt the love for her town warring with her bourgeoning feelings for Maggie. Her lonely heart spoke. "You make everything sound so easy. Let's try your plan. I think you'll like my town, just the way it is."

∞

Later that afternoon, after the service station dropped off Lauren's vehicle, the two women headed out to see Lauren's hometown. As they drove along the country road, Lauren pointed out all the historic sites. One that particularly interested Maggie was an old gristmill that was used for grinding grain and was built in the early eighteen hundreds. "This is an amazing place, Lauren, are there tours? Can we go inside and explore?"

"I can do better than that, my Uncle Jeb owns it. You're in luck, Ms. Sullivan, you are about to have a personal tour." She stopped the car in front of the building. "Come on, let's check it out."

"Are you sure?"

"Yep, come on." Lauren opened the car door, jumped out, dashed around to the other side, and opened Maggie's door. She laughed when she saw the surprise on Maggie's face. "Hey, you wanted to see it, right?"

Maggie looked quickly at the mill, then back to Lauren's hopeful eyes. "Yes, I...I was wondering if your uncle is here."

Lauren leaned into the car slightly. "Why?"

"Maybe he'll wonder why you're bringing a stranger around."

"Not to worry, Maggie, I won't let him bite you if he shows up." Lauren laughed and grabbed Maggie's hand and pulled her out of the car. "Let's go around back. Have you ever seen a waterwheel up close?" she asked enthusiastically as she led her toward the swiftly flowing water.

Maggie looked around in wonder as she watched the massive wooden wheel with water laden paddles turning lazily in the bright sunlight. "It's still operational?"

Lauren shook her head and laughed.

Maggie added, "Duh, its turning."

Lauren lightly cuffed Maggie's shoulder before she turned, took at the entire site, and inhaled deeply. "Actually, just because the wheel is turning, it's not necessarily grinding anything."

"Guess I should rephrase my question. Do they still mill grains here?"

"Yep. We grind our own special varieties of flour and cornmeal. The general store is the exclusive local vendor for what is produced here."

Maggie's face scrunched as her business mind kicked in. "That can't be very profitable."

"Actually, we have quite a lively business. Our products are also offered on our website." Lauren laughed. "It seems people today want home ground organic products and are willing to pay a premium price for them."

"Amazing. Absolutely amazing." Maggie ran her hand over the wooden exterior of the building. "This is fantastic. I had no idea that places like this still existed." Her eyes searched Lauren's. "Can we go inside?" A magnificent smile was her answer.

Lauren took Maggie's hand. "Up here," Lauren said as they climbed the six steps up to a landing and entered the mill.

"Oh, wow. I can't believe this." Maggie, eyes wide, looked around the clean smelling building. "I don't think I've ever been in a structure like this that didn't smell like cows, horses, or hay." She looked up at the series of long, slanted, dark wooden chutes coming from the upper parts of the loft. "What are those?"

"Those are used to transport the grain." Lauren turned and found Maggie standing close. "What do you think?"

"This is fabulous." She squeezed Lauren's hand. "Thanks for indulging me."

For what seemed like minutes, their eyes locked.

"You're welcome."

Maggie pulled Lauren closer and gently kissed her cheek. "Want to show me more of this wonderful mill?"

∞

They returned to the car an hour later. "Hey look, there's my uncle, do you want to meet him?"

"Uh, Lauren, mind if we do that later? I want to get to know you before you introduce me to the

31

family." She laughed heartily when Lauren gave her the once over.

"Why, Ms. Sullivan, I do believe you are on the same wavelength as I am." Lauren wiggled her eyebrows in a suggestive manner. "Of course we can meet the folks after we *know* each other better."

A shiver made its way through Maggie's body at the thought of holding Lauren again. "I'll hold you to that, my dear."

While driving to Warwick, Lauren asked, "Where's your bungalow?"

"On the corner of Walnut and Maple. Don't suppose your family owns that property, too."

"No, silly, but we have properties right down the street." Trying to suppress a grin, she reached out and took Maggie's hand. "Hey, if I move to Warwick, we could be neighbors."

"I'm not interested in being your neighbor, Lauren."

Afraid she had overstepped, Lauren said, "Sorry. You already have a home in Stafford. Don't you?"

Maggie let an indulgent smile wreath her lips. "Yes, I do."

The woman remained quiet as Lauren guided her car into the town that she loved. She hoped that Maggie would see its charm and convince her to recommend that her company abandon the plans for modernization.

Lauren pulled the SUV into a slanted parking slot in front of Maxwell's General Store, "Ready to see my town?"

"If it's anything like the mill, I can't wait." Maggie thought for a moment before looking over toward Lauren. "When I come to a town, I usually walk the streets, visit all the stores, speak with the residents, and make a judgment. I don't think I've ever taken the time to appreciate fully others' points of view. It has always been about business." Her eyes took on a distant look. "I wonder how many of those places I never really saw."

Lauren gently touched Maggie's cheek. "We all do things that hindsight makes us question. It's life, teaching us a lesson."

Maggie emotions were raw and she quickly pushed them down and smiled. "You're right." She looked at the rocking chairs sitting in front of the general store. "I bet if we sit there," she pointed to the rockers, "you can tell me all about the town."

Lauren opened the vehicle's door and hopped out. "I can try."

Once seated in the comfortable chair, Maggie automatically began to rock. She smiled when she heard the requisite squeak. "This is nice."

"Yes, it is. I'll duck inside and get us a drink. What would you like?"

"Tea would be nice." She watched as Lauren disappeared into the store, then scanned the street. The main thoroughfare had a friendly, hometown feel that said, *come sit a while and make yourself to home.* She watched as a young mother pushed a stroller, with a little girl walking closely by. A man stood in front of the bank and vigorously swept the sidewalk. *When would you ever see that in the big city?* She noticed that many other people were out caring for their businesses as well.

"Here you go," Lauren said as her hand held out the drink.

"It seems like everyone here takes pride in the town," Maggie said.

"Yes, they do. It's been here since before the Revolutionary War. Down the street is the heritage center that has an impressive collection of artifacts from the early days of Warwick." A swell of pride filled Lauren as she scanned the buildings and people. "Look over there." She pointed down the street. "That's Mr. Jenkins. He was my fifth grade teacher." She laughed softly. "He was old even then."

Maggie watched the variety of emotions that crossed Lauren's face. The one that was the most frequent was love. The woman clearly loved the town and all that it represented. "Do you think that the building project will help the local economy?" she asked, genuinely interested in the answer.

For several minutes, Lauren tapped her fingers on the armrest as she pondered how to answer the question best. "The unemployment is about one percent and most of those are people that really don't need to work." She pursued her lips before continuing. "When I drive you around the town later, you'll see that there really isn't anything that could be considered substandard housing." She went silent as her eyes focused on a little boy with his dog.

"And?"

"See that kid over there walking with his dog?" Lauren waited for Maggie to nod. "You don't see that in cities or towns that are all built up because it's considered a dangerous thing for kids to do. The crime in Warwick is mostly to out-of-towners speeding." She turned toward Maggie. "We don't need your project. It will ruin the ambience of this lovely, peaceful little town to promote a prosperity we already have."

Maggie recognized the truth of the words. "Why don't we visit that heritage center?"

34

Lauren's face lit up. "I'd love to."

∞

Six hours later, the two women arrived back at the cabin in the woods. Lauren had given Maggie the grand tour of the town, as well as some of the lesser known places that the typical tourist might not find. She hoped that Maggie had seen the area as she did and would change her mind about the development. That was business, though, and time would tell what would happen on that front. For the moment, she was content just to be with Maggie and get to know her.

"Shall we sit out here on the porch, Lauren? It looks like there's going to be a wonderful sunset tonight."

"I love sunsets. What do you say I make us some hot drinks, and then we can head out along the trail to the west? There's this perfect spot for watching sunsets that I found years ago. I've never taken anyone there with me, but I'd like to share it with you."

Maggie's smile was dazzling. "And I'd love to share it with you. Thanks for asking."

Fifteen minutes later, they were walking out of the woods at the top of a hill overlooking the valley below. In the distance, the sun was hovering on the horizon, spraying pinks and purples across the sky. They sat on a blanket with their shoulders touching as they watched as the sun gently slid below the horizon. The array of colors gave the sky an ethereal glow.

Lauren's mind always tried to create a stairway in the low clouds. "What a beautiful sunset. They never fail to disappoint."

"Yeah, it's beautiful," Maggie agreed.

Lauren looked at Maggie, who was clearly looking at her, the sunset going unnoticed. "Oh, Maggie, you're not looking at the sunset. Please do. It's so relaxing."

"I'm looking at my own sunset; it's called Lauren. And to me, she is as much of a natural beauty and just as wondrous." The words flowed easily from Maggie's lips and she had to pinch herself mentally at the words. *I never say anything like that.* All her life she was the one in control in both business and personal affairs. Yet, for some reason she was allowing feelings for Lauren emerge and did not intend to tamp them down. *Damn.*

That night back in the cabin, they kissed passionately before agreeing not to go to the next level until they were both sure that is what each wanted. One-night stands held no appeal for Lauren. The opposite was true of Maggie— promiscuity colored her past.

Chapter Three

Over the next week, Maggie and Lauren explored not only the town and the area surrounding it, but each other. Maggie had spent several nights at the cabin and they had both found it difficult not to take their physical relationship to the next level.

They had spent the evening in each other's arms, talking about the day. Lauren listened as Maggie recalled the first time she drove into Warwick. Her eyes focused on the woman's lips before moving down to fix on the peaked nipples. She moved closer to Maggie and began running her fingers up and down her arm. It wasn't long before eyes locked and, as was the case over the last several days, a primal message passed between them. This time, though, there would be no denying what both women felt, needed, wanted.

Desire was in control as Lauren's hand moved from Maggie's arm to begin a slow exploration of her body. It wasn't long before lips captured lips in fervent kisses. Maggie's insistent tongue parted willing lips and began its exploration of Lauren's mouth. Greedily Lauren sucked in Maggie's tongue, delighting in the sensations that were filling her body.

Maggie's body was on fire and allowed her body to melt into Lauren's.

Hands groped as both women tried to free flesh from its confines.

Maggie's experienced hands tugged gently but insistently at the shirt tucked securely in Lauren's jeans. She could feel the woman tense. Nimble fingers slid under the waistband of the jeans as the shirt came free. Maggie sighed as she encountered warm, soft flesh. Her hands trailed lightly over the slight swelling of Lauren's abdomen, and she smiled into the lips she held with hers.

Lauren's body arched as Maggie's soft touch continued the exploration.

Maggie's fingers moved gently higher, feeling the generous swell of the breasts captive in the gauzy bra. The touching was tantalizing Maggie, and she trembled in anticipation.

Lauren, enthralled by the incredible feelings that enveloped her as Maggie's mouth trailed delicate wet kisses along her jaw line gasped. With exquisite gentleness, small kisses found her neck, causing her to moan in appreciation. She slipped her hands under Maggie's shirt. As she felt the smooth, muscled flesh sliding beneath her fingers, the sensation of touching Maggie's skin sent shivers through her body. She lost herself in feelings that seemed unexpectedly familiar.

Maggie's sure fingers moved around and unclasped the bra, which, along with the shirt, was quickly disposed of.

Lauren moaned as wonderfully warm hands caressed her breasts.

At that moment, nothing could have dissuaded Maggie as she slowly caressed the nipples and smooth breasts. Her tongue teased the tip of a waiting nipple as her lips encircled and captured the delightful morsel. She slowly sucked the nub in deeper and deeper, causing Lauren to arch toward her mouth as her hands held Maggie's head captive. The need inside Maggie was growing beyond her control. After moving her head slightly, she gazed into glazed hazel eyes. "Lauren, would you make love with me?"

Lauren's mind vied with her senses and heart to determine the answer. She knew that she was powerless to do anything but make love with

Maggie—it was a strange sensation but one that felt right. As she stared into Maggie's eyes, Lauren knew she was lost, if only she would let herself be lost. Her need for the woman was building with every second and fulfillment was what she wanted. "Yes. Oh please, Maggie, yes." Her voice sounded strange to her ears, but the words conveyed her desire.

Maggie gently picked Lauren up, carried her into the bedroom, and laid her on the bed. Her eyes never left the smaller woman as they devoured every inch of her. "You are so beautiful." Her passion surged as her eyes feasted on the large, pale breasts. Maggie's mouth hovered close to Lauren's, teasing her lips with her tongue. Warm wet lips captured her tongue and pulled it deep into Lauren's mouth.

Lauren's fingers rested on the edge of the Maggie's open shirt before sliding it aside. Her breath caught as she stared at the puckered aureoles. The nipples looked ready and willing. Lauren pulled Maggie down a little so her lips could place feather light kisses on the tempting breasts. As she trailed from one to the other, she could feel Maggie arch into her mouth. The sensual explosion made Lauren ache for satisfaction. Her lips captured the closest nipple, and Lauren was satisfied, for the moment, by the breath that Maggie sucked in.

Maggie was dying an exquisite death. Her nipples pulsed with the need to have Lauren's mouth on them. Eyes half-closed with desire, Maggie watched as the smaller woman sucked on her breasts, then she covered Lauren's breasts with her hands and gently squeezed. She massaged and stroked them teasingly, avoiding the nipples until she heard a moan. The next few moments were a frenzy of shared passion and pleasuring, until Maggie needed to feel more flesh next to hers. Her fingers unzipped jeans and tugged them down, quickly casting them aside. Slowly, she guided the panties down as Lauren looked at her, silently pleading.

Lauren was trembling with desire. Finally, long tapering fingers tangled in soft dark curls as they lightly touched her inner thighs. Burning with desire, Lauren wanted to feel those delightful fingers deep inside of her. Lips claimed hers again in a kiss of insatiable passion.

Maggie mustered what little control she had left and offered Lauren the chance to retreat, if she wanted. "You want this, don't you, Lauren?"

"I want you, Maggie."

Maggie placed a tender kiss on the side of Lauren's mouth and gently glided one finger along the velvety smooth recess between the curls.

Raw passion and desire swamped Lauren as she allowed herself to relax and enjoy the moment. Her hips were moving, slowly building a tempo in time with the finger that was making small circles around her center. Long slow strokes combined with the circles and sent Lauren to greater heights. She sucked in a deep breath as she felt Maggie's lips trail along her abdomen and down to the apex between her legs.

Maggie felt the tremors in Lauren's body and knew that it wouldn't be long before she reached her release. She slid two fingers deep inside and began to move them in rhythm with Lauren's movements. Her lips moved to capture Lauren's center, sucking the engorged tip as gyrating hips rocked in time. Maggie's fingers built up a rhythm to match the movement and Lauren moaned in ecstasy. As she felt Lauren begin to tighten around her fingers, she knew the orgasm was close, very close. Maggie increased

the tempo of her fingers and tongue, and brought
Lauren to a powerful climax.

Maggie marveled at her responsiveness as she
kissed Lauren's clit reverently before making her way
up toward her mouth. They shared a kiss tinged with
the taste of the smaller woman. Her fingers remained
inside until the spasms ceased and Lauren settled
against her with a satisfied sigh. Maggie cradled her
in her arms and kissed her gently. *This feels like
nothing I have ever known.* "Are you okay?" Maggie
asked quietly. She watched the glazed expression
leave Lauren's face and a wide smile take its place.

Lauren turned slightly so she could make eye
contact. "Mmm, oh yes, much more than okay. Thank
you."

"For what?"

"I didn't know it could be like that, Maggie. No
one has ever made me feel... It was amazing, utterly
amazing."

"Mmm, I think you're the amazing one, Lauren."
Maggie smiled as she looked into the warm gaze of
the woman. Although her heart was singing, her
feelings of tenderness for Lauren confused her. Her
rule had always been to love 'em and leave 'em, but
what she was feeling for Lauren was different from
those one-night stands.

Lauren's hand began to wander over Maggie's
sweat slick abdomen as she delighted in her feelings.
Over the years, she had dated many women, kissed
her fair share and did some heavy petting, but never
took the final step of making love. Her fantasies about
what that would be like exceeded all her imaginings.
She focused on the texture of the skin beneath her
fingertips, wanting and needing to make Maggie feel
all the sensations she had just experienced. Lauren

rose up, situated herself on top of Maggie's larger frame, and smiled seductively. Slow deliberate small kisses worked down her neck and nipped at the skin.

Maggie moaned at her lover's advances.

∞

The early morning sun crept into the room through the opening in the curtains, setting the stage for the dust motes to dance. Maggie awoke with a start, unsure of where she was. As she gazed at the woman next to her, a smile of pure delight crossed her face. Never in all her liaisons had making love been so intense and gratifying. She quietly slipped out of bed and shivered as the cool morning air hit her. She headed for the bathroom and a hot shower picking up her clothes along the way. Then she would make a fire and some coffee. *I wonder if Lauren likes breakfast in bed.* Maggie smiled. *Damn, I feel good.*

The smell of freshly brewed coffee wafted through the air, waking Lauren from a tantalizing dream of…Maggie? *Coffee? Who's making coffee?* A satisfied smile crossed her face as she recalled the beautiful woman who had ravished her late into the night.

Just at that moment, Maggie came through the door with a tray. "Hey, sleepyhead, you think you might like some breakfast?"

"You must have been reading my mind. It smells wonderful. I can't wait to sample it."

"Wait until you taste my cooking. You may want to reconsider eating it."

"Not to worry, I have a cast iron stomach."

Maggie bent over and gently kissed Lauren. "Good morning. Did you sleep well?"

"Mmm. Better than I have in years. It's all thanks to you. So, let's see what you made us for breakfast."

Maggie's eyes twinkled as she grinned. "I was going to make *you* for breakfast, but…I thought you might need real food first."

Lauren smiled and winked at Maggie. "I'll have you for dessert, then."

Both women laughed as they shared cooking horror stories over breakfast in bed. Lauren found it necessary to lick some jelly off Maggie's lips, and that led to making love.

∞

Maggie contemplated her day ahead as she watched Lauren who had dozed off. She was to meet with her partners at the café in town before they addressed the Warwick town council to discuss the plans for renovating and rejuvenating the town.

When the firm received the proposal for development, Maggie was in California putting the final additions on a project there. Once home, she received the preliminary reports and keys for the bungalow in Warwick so she could do her standard scouting of the area. Her first impression of the town remained, especially after spending several days with Lauren getting to know the area. The same question kept coming to mind. *Why Warwick?* From what she observed, the town simply did not meet any of the typical criteria for development. The population was not large enough to sustain the type of changes they would make. Then there was the biggest problem: all the roads leading into the town were two lane highways. Before they could even begin thinking about development, road improvements were needed.

That in itself was a major undertaking. She hoped to understand more about the site selection when she met her partners for breakfast.

Slowly and silently, she edged out of bed. Just as her feet hit the floor, a hand grasped her wrist and a sleepy voice pleaded, "Don't go."

"Aw, baby, you know I have to go to work. I can't be late today."

"Please, Maggie, I need you."

Maggie had no choice. She slid back next to the warm, naked body waiting for her. Her reward was a tender kiss that rapidly turned passionate.

As their tongues danced, Lauren rolled over and slipped her thigh between Maggie's legs as the warm, wet smoothness began to grind against her. Soon both their bodies were moving as one. Heat and intensity grew with each movement. Moans of pleasure accompanied the touches of hands that roamed over familiar bodies. Maggie's tongue retreated as Lauren's searched for it. How she loved kissing that way. It was like being lost in a cavern and trying to find a lost treasure.

It wasn't long before Maggie's lips captured Lauren's tongue and sucked it deep into her mouth before their tongues met again.

Lauren's lips engulfed a waiting, peaked nipple as her teeth gently bit and pulled up.

Maggie's fingers slid between Lauren's thighs and began to stroke the velvet wetness that awaited her.

The insistent ringing of the phone drew both women out of their fever pitched passion. "Lauren, I thought you turned that off."

"Maggie, I'm a doctor. I can't just turn my phone off. I have several patients that I asked my associate to call me about if there was a problem. That's the hazard of experimental medicine—you never know when a discovery will happen, good or bad. I'll only be a moment, promise."

"Mind if I keep reminding you that I'm here?" Maggie began sucking on a tempting nipple as Lauren answered the phone.

"Doctor Walker."

Maggie felt Lauren go stiff and she heard the coolness in the voice of her lover.

"Mother, what do you want? ... No, I can't have lunch with you. There must be something important you want if you are asking me to lunch. ... You know, Mother, if I had taken this tone with you once in a while fifteen years ago, maybe I wouldn't be little more than your puppet now. ... Just tell me what you want. I have things to do. ... Stop badgering me about the store, it's mine to do with as I please and is really none of your business. ... I will use any tone I want, Mother. For your information, I plan to keep the store. How do you like that? ... Forbid me? You don't have that kind of power anymore, Mother. Goodbye."

Lauren slammed the phone down before grabbing Maggie and giving her a savage kiss. She worked her way down to the neck, where she bit and sucked with such force she could taste the blood. She would mark Maggie for all to see that she belonged to her and her alone. *Keep away, she's mine.* It wasn't until Maggie had her by the shoulders and shoved her away that she heard the words.

"Lauren, I said stop it."

"I know you want this, Maggie. Why are you pushing me away?"

"I don't want *this*, Lauren."

"Yeah, right." She moved in on the tantalizing lips again.

"Lauren, no!"

For a moment, Lauren was confused. *Is Maggie turning her down? Are we over already?*

"Lauren, I don't want to have sex with you. I can get that anywhere. I only want to make love with you. Do you understand that? Taking your anger at your mother out on me isn't fair, Lauren. It isn't right."

The tears welled and then overflowed. "Oh, Maggie. I am so sorry. I don't know what got into me. Please forgive me? I'm so ashamed." Lauren, sobbing uncontrollably, buried her head in the pillow.

Maggie wrapped her arms gently around Lauren and held her close. "Shh, it's okay. I've got you."

Tear filled eyes looked at Maggie. "No, what I did was completely unforgivable. I am so sorry, Maggie."

"Want to tell me about it?"

"Where do I begin? My mother wasn't always so controlling and nasty. We actually had many good times together. We both loved Uncle Max, and I spent summers in Warwick helping him out at the store. Then one summer, it seemed that everything changed, including my mother, and we never came back here. She started telling me what to wear, which friends I should have, who to date, and tried to run my life completely. I defied her by going to medical school instead of law school. But she did forgive me when I graduated top of my class and obtained a residency at Johns Hopkins. What I don't understand is why she is so insistent on my selling the store. She really loved the place at one time."

"I don't know the answers, but I do know that together we can work anything out. Why don't we put

46

this to rest for a little while and we can talk about it later on." She tugged Lauren closer. "What do you say?"

"Maggie Sullivan, do you know how much I adore you? Thank you for understanding. I'm so sorry." She hung her head.

"Hey," Maggie lifted Lauren's chin. "It's over, let's get past it." She smiled fondly. "I will always try to be there for you, no matter what. You can count on that."

Lauren gave Maggie a soft kiss. "And I'll always be there for you." She pulled back slightly before gently caressing the beautiful face before her. "I'm falling in love with you."

Maggie took Lauren's hand in hers. "I know the feeling and it scares me."

"Me too." Lauren's eyes focused on the bedside clock. "Oh my, God. Maggie, look at the time. Isn't your meeting at nine? It's eight fifteen now. If you hurry, you can just make it."

Maggie scrambled out of bed and headed for the shower as Lauren set out her clothes and started the coffee. Lauren smiled as she opened the bathroom door. *I need a shower too.*

Chapter Four

The best word to describe the approach into Warwick was 'lovely'. A hand carved sign welcomed travelers, proclaiming they were home. The tree lined street was dotted with sprawling old homes complete with carriage houses and barns. It was as if one was stepping back into a time of gracious living and friendly people.

The center of town was full of quaint shops not seen in the bigger cities. Off to one side was Maxwell's General Store. It retained the original wooden sidewalk that had once connected the entire town. A large porch containing several rocking chairs welcomed customers to sit a spell and visit with neighbors and friends. The store itself held a conglomeration of anything and everything from groceries to nails. If the populace needed anything, Maxwell's would have it.

Parking her car in front of Ruth's Café, Maggie once again wondered, *why Warwick?* Entering the café, she saw Gale, her best friend and the company's lawyer, waiting for her. As was typical, her partners were late, for which she was grateful, because she wanted to talk to Gale privately.

"Hi, Mags, how is everything going for you?"

"Absolutely fabulous. Now I am waiting for the other shoe to fall."

"What do you mean?"

"I can't recall a time when I've been this content and happy. My life experience tells me that won't last."

"Do you want it to?"

Maggie hesitated. "Yes. Yes, I do."

Judging by the size of the hickey on your neck, I can tell that your backwoods woman must be very physical." Gale winked and then began to chuckle.

"Shit, I forgot about that. Quick, let me use your scarf."

"My scarf? I will have you know this scarf *makes* my outfit. It screams of success, money, and breeding to all who see it. I can't possibly let you have it, Mags. It just wouldn't be right."

"Come on, Gale, this is serious. I can't go into a meeting with potential clients like this. Please."

Unable to contain her amusement any longer, Gale began to laugh heartily. "Here, take it. If this weren't business, I would let you suffer the stares you'd surely get. My God, that is the biggest hickey I have ever seen."

As Maggie arranged the scarf, the waitress brought coffee and menus. Maggie was sure the woman was eyeing her neck.

Once the waitress left, Maggie asked, "Gale, what do you know about the proposal for this town? I have some serious questions about the venture. I don't understand why this town was even considered."

"I really don't know too much myself, Maggie. I just finished litigation on the Miller proposal Friday and didn't receive the preliminary reports on Warwick until late yesterday."

"Something isn't right here, Gale, and I intend to find out what that is. Hey, try the blueberry pancakes here. They're the best. Everything is homemade and the blueberries are local."

Ben Preston and Hank Moser came into the café and greeted the two women with smiles and kisses. Over ten years, they built a successful business and were well known and respected for their integrity. Maggie had made a substantial investment in the company five years earlier and joined them as co-owner. Not too many companies had the reputation for standing behind their word, but Preston, Moser, and Sullivan always did. That gave them the edge in many business deals.

"Late as usual. Do either of you own a watch?"

"We got lost, Maggie. Took a right instead of a left and found ourselves in the middle of nowhere. From now on, I'm using the GPS to heck with Ben's map reading skills. It smells good in here. I'm starving. Great day for deal making, don't you think?" Hank always brimmed with enthusiasm.

As usual, Ben had a ready excuse. "Hey, I can't help it if all the roads only go right."

With breakfast finished and the small talk done, it was time to get down to some serious business. Maggie wanted her question answered before meeting with the mayor and the village council.

"As you both know, I have been in Warwick for a week doing some preliminary scouting of the area. Frankly, I can't see any way this would be profitable for us or good for this town. It is eight miles along winding roads to get here from the main highway. There's no industry to speak of, and I can't see any reason for someone to come here, unless it would be to visit that general store. My question to both of you is why? Why are we here?"

Ben was the first to speak. "Maggie, this town is a diamond in the rough, just waiting for a company like ours to bring it into the Twenty-First century. If we build it, they will come."

"Ben, I'm in no mood for bullshit. I want answers and I want them now. We have a great reputation, and I will not have that jeopardized by some stupid, baseless venture. What do you have to say, Hank?'

Hank nodded. It was time for straight talk. "While you were in California, we were approached by a lawyer and his client with a proposition to develop Warwick. Our firm is to get a ten million-dollar bonus. We had to make a decision immediately or they were going to go elsewhere. I know we can make this work for all concerned, Maggie, and it will be highly profitable too."

"You had to make this decision so quickly that you couldn't pick up a phone and call me?"

"Maggie, I studied the preliminary reports the lawyer had and it looked too good to pass up. Let's hear what the mayor and council have to say before we make up our minds. If there's a problem, then we'll walk. I'm telling you, though, the town is going to proceed with their plan whether we do it or not. The lawyer made that very clear."

"Are you telling me that the leaders of this town are the ones who sent the lawyer? They want this to happen?"

"No, it was the lawyer's client. I have the name here somewhere. Here it is…the name is Walker, Victoria Walker."

Maggie was silent. *No wonder good old mom wanted Lauren to sell the store. But the question is…why?* Touching the mark on her neck, she wondered if she should call and let Lauren know, or wait and see how it all played out. "Well then, let's find out what these people have to say. Ten million? That's a hefty sum. What do you think, Gale?"

"Mind if I reserve judgment until after we meet with them? I'd like to talk to their lawyer and this

51

Walker woman. From the prelims I read, everything seems to be on the up and up, but something doesn't ring true. Let me do my thing and see what I can find out. We have an hour before the meeting, I'll make some calls."

"Thanks, Gale. Ben, Hank, why don't you look around the town before the meeting." She looked at her watch. "You've got a little under an hour before the meeting starts."

"Sounds good to me," Ben said as he stood up. "We'll see you there."

"I'm going to make some calls," Gale said as she too stood up."

Maggie laughed. "I see the three of you have stuck me with the bill again."

Gale chuckled. "Why do you think we keep inviting you to have breakfast with us in every town we go to?"

∞

Maggie had been in a hundred council rooms, and the one word that always came to mind was "wood." Wood floors, wood paneling, wooden table, and the ever popular, high back wood and leather chairs. The Warwick town council chamber didn't disappoint.

She saw a tall, distinguished looking man standing at one end of the long table. He had graying hair and a well-trimmed beard, and was dressed in jeans with a polo shirt and a sports coat. He was no doubt the mayor. Talking to him was a very pretty smaller woman, probably in her early thirties, dressed casually. The body language said something definitely was going on between the two.

Directly across from her, near the windows, were two men and a woman. The older man, dressed in boots, overalls and a plaid flannel shirt, looked like he had just come from mucking out the barn. Maggie guessed he was probably the richest man in town. The other man had sandy blonde hair and a thin moustache, was probably in his forties, and was dressed in tan slacks and a blue shirt. The woman was heavy set, dressed in a navy suit with her hair pulled back in a severe bun.

At the far end of the room, Gale sat at the table with Hank and Ben. As she walked toward them, the older man stopped her.

"Ain't you the gal I saw around town with little Lori Walker?"

"Lori? Oh, Lauren." Maggie recognized the man as Lauren's uncle. "Yes, I know Doctor Walker."

"Thought so. The name's Jeb Maxwell, I own a farm right outside of town."

"Pleased to meet you, sir. I'm Margaret Sullivan. Maxwell? Do you own the general store?"

"Nope. That'd be my brother Zeb. He died a while back and left the store to our little Lori. Surprised she didn't tell you that … you being friends and all."

"It was nice meeting you, Mr. Maxwell. I need to join my partners now."

"Listen, missy, not everyone wants this fancy stuff. Just thought you should know."

Once Maggie reached her business partners, she looked back and saw the person she thought was the mayor in what looked like a heated conversation with Jeb Maxwell. *Interesting.* "Hi, Gale. I hope you have some information for me."

53

"Hi, yourself. Well, it's all preliminary, but I'll give you what I have so far."

"Shoot."

"Victoria Maxwell Walker and Steven John Walker are lifelong residents of Warwick. They went through school together, except when she went away to boarding school at age fifteen. She returned after graduation and went to Vassar, where she graduated with honors. She went on to Harvard Law and worked for some time in the DA's office in Boston before going into private practice. She is currently a district court judge, and the buzz is that she's next in line for a state Supreme Court position. Steven Walker went to Harvard for both his undergraduate and graduate degrees. That's where he and Victoria met again and fell in love. He is renowned as a law professor and lecturer.

"There were three pregnancies with one birth. Her daughter, Lauren Elizabeth Walker is thirty-five years old and a research physician. She is a Rhodes Scholar and graduated from medical school first in her class. Her residency was at Johns Hopkins, where she specialized in rheumatoid arthritis research. She is by all accounts the top researcher in her field. Several of her patients seem to be improving on an experimental regime she has developed.

"That big ranch you pass on the way into town is theirs, as well as a home in the state capital. Between them, they own about sixty-five percent of the town and the surrounding area. Their net worth is approximately six hundred million."

Maggie scratched her cheek. Gale's description of Lauren's mother didn't stack with the impression she had from the way Lauren spoke about her mother. She wasn't exactly sure what she expected but it wasn't the woman Gale described. "You said six hundred million?"

"Yep, give or take a few mil."

"That makes no sense, Gale. Why would this Walker woman want to see something like this happen to her town? The question still remains, even more so now ... why Warwick?"

"Why indeed."

"Is she here? Do you know what she looks like? Hey, Hank, did you meet the Walker woman when you met with their lawyer?"

"Yes, I did. Why?"

"Is she here?"

"No. I heard she was held up in court, but will be here in a little while."

∞

The meeting proceeded in the usual manner, with Ben and Hank pitching their ideas with their usual flair. They were surprised to learn that the Walkers donated all the land for the project.

Just one more puzzle in the mystery for me to solve, Maggie thought as she keenly observed the people sitting around the grand table. Jeb Maxwell was definitely not happy as he listened to the proposal. In fact, except for the mayor, no one seemed particularly enthralled with Ben and Hank's ideas.

Just as they were about to delve into the issue of road development, the door to the council room opened and in walked a stunning woman. She was the type of woman whose presence made other women squirm. Maggie found herself instinctively tugging at the scarf around her neck and straightening her suit jacket. The woman had stylish, dark blond hair and was dressed in a simple but very expensive gray suit. The rings on her fingers were unpretentious, as was the gold heart locket around her neck.

The mayor stood as he welcomed the visitor. "Victoria, I'm glad you could make it. Please, come and sit by me."

"Thank you, Bill, but I will sit next to my uncle."

The look on Bill Westerly face at the refusal was not lost on Maggie.

The newcomer walked toward Hank and Ben, holding out her hand. "Mr. Preston and Mr. Moser, nice to see you again, I hope you are enjoying your visit to our town."

Ben beamed—he never missed an opportunity to appreciate a beautiful woman. "Thank you, Mrs. Walker. May I introduce our partner, Margaret Sullivan?"

"Ms. Sullivan, I've heard much about you. I believe we have a mutual friend, Thomas MacDonald. I spoke with him several weeks ago and he asked that I let you know he was asking about you."

Maggie, taken aback for a moment at the woman's charm, tried to once again match the impression of the woman that Lauren gave her and that of what she now witnessed. "Yes, thank you. May I introduce our company's legal representative, Gale Bailey?"

"Ms. Bailey, so nice to meet you. Weren't you an assistant DA in Memphis? I did a stint in a DA's office myself. I look forward to speaking with you later."

As the woman made her way to the seat next to Jeb Maxwell, Gale leaned over and quietly said, "Looks like she did her homework, too."

"It would seem so."

After the presentation concluded, Hank spoke. "Thank you all. At this time, Ms. Sullivan would like to speak with you. Maggie."

Maggie walked to the middle of the room so she could make eye contact with everyone there. "Thank you, Hank. As is customary, one of us will come into a town and spend a week or so just looking around and getting to know the area. In the last week, I have seen many sites and spoken with some of the residents. I have learned a number of things. I have eaten in many restaurants around the world, and I can tell you I would be hard pressed to find any better food than right here at Ruth's Café. Maxwell's is the most unique store I have ever been in. It is a treasure you should all hold dear. What I don't understand, and to be truthful, haven't since I first arrived, is why you would want things in Warwick to change." The remark engendered a gasp from the gathering.

"Do any of you have any idea the impact something like this will have on your town? The unemployment in Warwick and the surrounding area is non-existent. That would mean you would have to find workers, and that would lead to new housing developments and more traffic. The list of changes is endless."

The mayor stood up. "Who the hell do you think you are, coming in here and saying such things?"

From behind Maggie, a voice said, "She's the expert you hired to come here and make a proposal. She is giving you her expert opinion, Bill."

Maggie turned around to see Lauren's beautiful hazel eyes shining at her. Despite the setting, she fought the urge to take Lauren in her arms.

"Warwick has been my home most of my life. Although I don't live here now, you should know that I will be as soon as I can set up practice and take ownership of my store."

"Ownership of the store? Victoria, you said she would sell." Bill's face was red with anger.

Victoria remained calm and cool but Maggie thought she saw fear in her eyes.

"Surprise, Bill, it's not going to happen," Lauren spat.

"The council will come to my office, right now. We need a private session immediately." The mayor stormed out of the room. The remaining council members just sat there with mouths agape, not knowing what to do. Eventually they began collecting their belongings and, with Maggie, began to file out of the room. As Jeb left, he gave Lauren a thumbs up and winked at Maggie.

Mouthing a "thank you" to Maggie, Lauren approached her mother.

Maggie smiled a reassuring smile and received one in return before she exited.

∞

"So, Mother, care to tell me just why you were trying to manipulate your own daughter by insisting I sell the store."

"How dare you talk to me in that tone? What has gotten into you?"

58

"How dare I? How dare you? I'm not going to let you push me around anymore, Mother. I can't believe you would do this to me."

"Lauren, may I remind you that I have always had your best interests in mind."

"Oh, really, Mother? Like the time you said I couldn't go to the prom with Robbie Miller since he was beneath me. Or when the only friends I could have, were the ones you chose for me. Or when you forbade me to go see Uncle Zeb at the store. Was all that for *my* own good, or yours?"

"Lauren, please, don't do this. You have no idea what will happen if you do."

"Perhaps you should start explaining it to me, or you'll find yourself without a daughter."

"I can't explain. You just have to trust me."

"No chance of that, Mother. My days of trusting were over when you tried to sell me out to that sleaze Bill Westerly."

"Lauren, please."

"Not good enough, Mother. Goodbye." Lauren made her way toward the door and her new life that she hoped would include Maggie. The idea of her lover brought a smile to her face and her anger began to abate. *Yes, I'll go to Maggie and everything will be okay.*

"Lauren, wait. Please. Can I come and see you tonight? I'll explain everything then."

Lauren turned around, looked directly into her mother's eyes and saw fear. "Why not now, Mother?"

"I have some things to work out first. Will you please give me until then?"

"Be at the cabin at seven. I'll be there with my friend. We can talk then."

"I will not talk in front of a stranger, Lauren."

"I'll see you at seven, Mother. Goodbye for now." With that, Lauren left her mother standing in the room alone.

∞

Lauren reached her Land Rover, surprised at her upbeat mood. Normally a bout with her mother generated resentment and anger, followed by a deep depression, but not this time. She felt good about herself and her resolve where her mother was concerned. Slipping her hand in her pocketbook, she dug around for her phone. Dialing, she smiled as she heard Maggie's voice. "Hey."

"Hi. Is it all over?" Maggie asked.

"Yep, the battle is done and I came out unscathed."

"Good. I was worried about you."

"Are you at your bungalow?" Lauren asked.

"Yes."

"Why don't I pick you up and we can go out to the cabin and I can tell you all about it."

Maggie chuckled. "I like the sound of that. Should I bring my toothbrush?"

"Well, yes, I think you should bring your toothbrush if you don't want to use the one you already have there."

"You got it, babe. I'll be watching for you."

"Okay, I'll see you soon. Oh, Maggie?"

"Yes."

"I love you." *There. It's said.*

"I love you, too," Maggie returned.

"I know you do. I'll be right there. Bye."

After starting the car and preparing to merge with the traffic, Lauren noticed her mother and Bill

Westerly in front of the courthouse in an intense argument. The mayor grabbed her mother's arm, and from the looks of it, Victoria was in immediate danger.

Moving out into the street, Lauren pulled her car up beside the combatants and lowered the window. "Hey, Mom, are you ready to go? We have that appointment in five minutes."

Victoria looked gratefully at her daughter, fear clearly etched on her face. "I'm coming right now, Lori."

"We're not done here," shouted Bill, his voice shaking with anger.

"Yes, we are. Goodbye, Mister Mayor."

"It's not over yet, Vicky, not by a long shot. Do you hear me? Not by a long shot."

Victoria walked quickly over to the waiting car, hoping that the deranged man would not come after her. She opened the door, got in, and slammed it shut. "Let's get out of here quickly."

Lauren pressed the gas pedal and moved them away from the mayor, who was still shaking his fist.

"Lori, I want to thank you for the rescue. I know things haven't been very good between us lately, but I hope you know how much I love you."

"Mother, we need to talk." She glanced over at her mother before returning her eyes to the street ahead. "What the hell is going on between you and that bastard?"

"I will tell you, but first, can we get further away?"

"We're going to pick up my friend and then we're going to the cabin. We can talk there."

"I am not going to bare my soul in front of some stranger, Lauren."

"I trust her. It will be fine."

"Who is this person? No, don't tell me, it's that Sullivan woman, isn't it? I've heard all about you traipsing around town with her."

"She does have a first name. It's Maggie."

"How long have you known her?"

"Since she almost drowned in the river by the cabin," Lauren said casually.

"Drowned? She's not going to sue, is she?"

"Mother, everything doesn't come down to money. No, she isn't going to sue us. She's very special to me. We've become very close."

"Exactly how close is that?" Victoria already knew the answer but she had to hear from Lori to give it validity.

"I'm falling in love with her, Mother."

"Does she make you happy?"

"Yes. Here we are, I won't be but a minute, and then we can get going."

Lauren jumped out of the car and started toward the bungalow as Maggie came out to greet her. They hugged, and Lauren clung to her a bit before kissing her soundly on the lips.

Pulling away, Maggie looked toward the vehicle. "Hey, what's your mother doing with you?"

"Something is going on, and you and I are going to find out what it is."

"Does she know?"

Lauren nodded. "Yes."

"Should I take my toothbrush back inside?" Maggie asked, only half joking.

"No. I need you with me, Maggie, now more than ever."

Maggie pulled Lauren into her arms and whispered, "You have me."

Chapter Five

The drive back to the cabin was uneventful although Lauren had the distinct feeling she was being followed. Every glance in the rearview mirror reflected only Maggie's face. It wasn't until they finally turned off onto the road to the cabin that she was certain no one was behind them. Lauren's focus turned to her mother. *I will get answers and won't let her leave until she tells me.*

Inside the comfortable cabin, Lauren felt her stomach churn over what her mother had to say. "Why don't you both get comfortable? I'll make us some sandwiches and then we can talk."

"I'll go get some wood and start a fire. The radio said it's going to get quite cold tonight. Besides, I know that you are fire-starting challenged." Maggie chuckled and headed outside to the woodpile.

Lauren watched her from the window.

"You certainly seem taken by that woman, Lauren."

"Don't start, Mother."

"Start? What am I starting? I was merely mentioning that you look like a lovesick kid when you look at her. I'm sure I brought you up with better values than that."

"What values, Mother? To look down my nose at those who are different from me? To kick dirt in someone's face when they're down? Are those the values you are talking about, Mother?"

"How dare you speak to me like that? I am your mother and you will treat me with respect. You certainly have developed a backbone lately. Did you get it from that woman?"

"That's it. You're out of here. I'll take you back to town. Whatever mess you have yourself in with the good mayor, you can get out of it all by yourself. I was an idiot to think I could have anything but an antagonistic relationship with you."

"What do you know about anything, Lauren? Everything I have ever done has been for you, and this is how you repay me."

"I never asked you for anything, Mother. Since I was a teenager, all I ever wanted was to be out from under your thumb. You've pushed it too far this time, and now I'm done with you. No more, never again. Now get out."

"You don't mean that."

"Oh yes, I do. Collect your things I'm taking you back to town." Lauren couldn't remember a time when she had ever seen her mother cry. Yet, there she was weeping like a baby seemingly broken and defeated.

"Lori, no. Please don't. I am so tired, so tired of fighting this alone. Please help me…please."

Although her mother had infuriated her once again, Lauren's heart went out to her and she put her arms around the older woman in comfort. "Mom, why don't you sit here on the couch while I get us something to drink. How about some coffee, tea, or a soda?"

"How about a Scotch?"

"You've got it."

∞

Once the shouting inside had died down, Maggie thought it would be safe to enter the cabin. She'd had to clench her fists and walk toward the river when she first heard the raised voices. Everything inside her wanted to go to Lauren's defense, but she knew it wasn't the right time. She had learned early in life that you must pick the battles you want to fight—this wasn't one of them.

"Here's the wood. I'll have a fire going in a moment. Judge Walker, do you enjoy fires as much as your daughter does?"

"What? Oh, the fire," she said. "Yes. I do enjoy a nice fire on a cool night. It's rather relaxing, I think. We used to come out here, Lori and I, just when the leaves were turning. We'd bring hotdogs and marshmallows and just sit in front of the fire and tell ghost stories. Do you remember that, Lori?"

Lauren returned from the kitchen and placed the sandwiches and drinks on the coffee table. She smiled. "Yes, yes I do. Whatever happened to make that all change?"

Victoria looked into the now flickering fire with tears welling up in her eyes before the ran down her cheeks. "I'm afraid that it's a rather convoluted story."

Maggie looked at Victoria and then at Lauren. "Would you like me to leave? After all, this is family stuff."

"No, you stay, Maggie, please," Lauren replied quickly.

"Yes, please stay, Ms. Sullivan. It's always good to have an impartial participant."

"The name is Maggie." She held out her hand to the trembling woman.

Lauren's mother took Maggie's hand and managed a small smile. "My friends call me Vicky." She took a deep breath. "Shall I begin then?"

"Yes, Mother. It's time we cleared the air."

∞

"The summer I was fifteen, my girlfriends and I went over to Westfield to the fair. It was a day just made for a fair. Blue skies and a gentle breeze. We made our way to the midway and began playing some of the games. I noticed one of the guys working at the ring toss booth looking at me, so I went over to play the game. Many games later, he and I made a date to meet the following day at the fair. He was one handsome fellow, and I think my adolescent heart fell in love with him the moment I saw him.

"The next day, my parents wouldn't allow me to go back to the fair, saying once was enough. I pouted for a while and then went to my Uncle Zeb's store and whined about not being able to go to the fair. Zeb was always a sucker for my tears, and away we went to the fair. While he was off looking over the livestock, I went to meet Rob. I was walking on air the whole time, and when Uncle Zeb found me, I introduced him to my new friend. Rob said he was tired of traveling from town to town and wanted to settle down with steady work. Wouldn't you know it my Uncle Zeb offered him a job and a place to stay. I was so happy.

"I spent the entire summer at the store, just so I could be with Rob. Finally, late in August, he started to get restless and talked of leaving. I cried and begged him not to, but he said he just wasn't a roots kind of man. I packed a bag and went with him. I thought I was in love."

Taking a long sip of her Scotch, Victoria stared into the fire. "I never meant to be mean to you, Lori. I only wanted to protect you from making the same mistake I did." A lone tear made its way slowly down her cheek. "Anyway, I followed him from one town to the next, in search of the perfect sunrise, the meaning of life. Whatever it was, we were looking for it. On my sixteenth birthday, I found out I was pregnant. Rob took us to his brother's home in the Midwest, where we stayed until our daughter was born."

Lauren kept shaking her head, finding it hard to believe this was her mother speaking. "What's her name? Where is she now?"

"We called her Baby Girl. We couldn't come up with a name, so the hospital put that on the birth certificate until we could think of one. I wanted to be a good mother. I tried so hard, but Rob had to move on. So one morning, we told Rob's brother, Harry, that we were going, and leaving our baby with him. He protested, said he couldn't do it, said the baby didn't even have a name. Rob said, *Yes she does...name her after you.* Then we left, never to see either of them again.

"We made our way across the country doing odd jobs then caught a steamer to Europe, where we hiked everywhere. Our last trip was to the Alps. During a climb, Rob lost his footing and fell to his death. There I was with the love of my life gone, penniless, and alone. I had sent my parents the odd postcard from time to time to let them know I was still alive, but they were frantic to have me safe and home once again. So when I called my parents to tell them about Rob dying, my father immediately flew to get me. Apparently, they had told everyone I was abroad at boarding school, so my reappearance fit into their plans perfectly. When I got home, my mother arranged for me to take the GED, and then go on to her alma mater—Vassar.

"The only person I ever told about the baby was my Uncle Zeb. Years later, he unwittingly betrayed me to that bastard Westerly. I could never forgive him for that, not even when he was lying on his deathbed. Westerly dug around enough until he found out everything, and he's been blackmailing me ever since." She turned teary eyes toward her daughter. "I want you to know that I regret giving my little girl away."

"Why didn't you go back for her, Mom?"

"I was too ashamed. And I told myself that she was better off without me. Once you've turned your back and walked away, there really isn't any going back." The tears were flowing freely as if they were cleansing her soul of the long held secret.

"You know the right thing to do is to go and find your daughter and let her know her mother still cares about her. You have to do it, Mom. If not for her sake, then for yours."

"I can't, Lori. I can't."

"Yes, you can. You have to."

"You don't understand anything at all. I can't risk it...I can't risk you," Victoria finished on a choked sob.

"What? I don't understand."

"You have to understand that everything I've done has been for you, Lori. Westerly threatened to kill you, and her, if I didn't cooperate with him." Victoria sighed deeply when she saw the look of shock on her daughter's face. "Don't you understand? I abandoned her once; I couldn't take the chance he would actually kill either of you. I needed to protect my daughters in any way I could."

Maggie was horrified at the revelation. "I think we need to call the police, Vicky. This is far too dangerous for both you and Lauren."

"No. We can't."

"Why, Mom? I don't understand. Does Daddy know?"

"No, your father has no idea. At first, Westerly wanted speeding tickets fixed, and then I had to support him for mayor. After that, I told him it was enough. About five years ago, Bill came to my office and said I should take him seriously. He shoved a newspaper article in front of me about a pregnant woman who died in an automobile accident. He said that my daughter was supposed to be in that car but she wasn't so all he got was her partner." Tears were streaming down her cheeks. "After that, I was afraid he might go after you."

Lauren and Maggie stared at her in disbelief.

Maggie excused herself to go to the bathroom. After she closed the door, she pulled her cell out of her pocket and rapidly dialed a number. "Hey, it's me. I've made contact and the job that needs your special touch is going down now." Returning to join the two Walkers by the fireplace, she smiled. "Why don't I make some calls? I have connections that can get information about the good mayor ... information he may not want anyone to know."

Victoria shook her head and managed a weak smile. "Thank you, I would appreciate that."

Chapter Six

Clouds hung low and threatening over the village of Warwick. A tempest was brewing and residents were scurrying about, making ready for the imminent storm. Even though it was early in the day, the streets took on a deserted look as winds picked up, causing leaves to dance on the air currents.

It had been two days since the disastrous council meeting, yet Bill Westerly was still upbeat about the prospects for the town. He had five hundred thousand dollars in cash in his briefcase, and he would have another five when the construction began. There were some loose ends, but he could easily tie them up. He needed to get Victoria Walker back in line by reminding her who was in charge and what the consequences would be if she didn't cooperate. *I need to deal with that annoying Sullivan woman.* She wasn't as greedy as her partners were and that surprised him. But he would resolve that, no problem there. He would see to it that the good Dr. Walker didn't keep the store. Once he was owner, he could search under the floorboards for the fortune his grandfather had told him about. Life was good.

Insistent knocking on the door sent him scrambling to hide the briefcase. The last thing he needed was for someone to uncover his plans. After straightening his shirt, he slowly opened the door. Two men who looked like cowboys stood on his porch. "Yes, what can I do for you?"

"Mr. Westerly?" the taller of the two men asked.

"That's me. Who are you?"

"Sir, my name is Ed Blake and this is Frank Robinson." He took a badge out of his pocket and flashed it in Bill's direction. "We are with the Texas

Rangers and we need to ask you to come along with us."

"Like hell I will. Let me see that badge again. How do I know you are who you say you are?"

Frank Robinson nodded and produced the badge again. "Sir, we have a warrant for your arrest. It would go easier on you if you cooperate."

The statement shocked Bill. *It's a mistake and they have me mixed up with someone else.* "My arrest? For what?"

"Conspiracy to commit murder."

"What? You're kidding me. I think you have the wrong person"

"No, we don't, sir. Now will you please come with us?"

"Not without my lawyer." Bill pulled out his cell and rapidly dialed a number. "Get over here right now, I need a lawyer ... I don't care what you're doing. ... There is no one else to call. Who? ... I'll call him, but you get your ass over here as soon as you can, if you know what's good for you." After punching in another number, he drummed his fingers on the doorjamb. "This is Bill. Come to my house right now. I need a lawyer." Bill smiled. "My lawyer should be here soon. Please, gentlemen, come in, sit down and I'll get you some coffee."

"Sir, we really need you to come to the police station with us. Your lawyer can meet us there."

"I am the mayor of this town. I am not going to run away. As soon as my lawyer gets here, we can clear up any confusion and you can both be on your way. Now, what can I get you to drink?"

Ten minutes later, there was a knock at the door and Bill casually walked over and opened it. The man who entered was an elderly gentleman with snow white hair. He was a fair facsimile of Mark Twain. As he shuffled across the room, Bill could see the amusement on the faces of the rangers. *Good, I can see they are wondering about my lawyer. Wait until my ace in the hole gets here. They'll be singing a different tune then.*

Storm clouds swirled in the sky.

"Gentlemen, this is my lawyer for the moment, Claude Claiborne." Bill winked at Robertson and whispered, "Don't let his appearance fool you, he never misses anything."

Robinson grabbed Bill by the arm, and his cold dark eyes bored into Westerly. "Neither do I."

Bill wrenched his arm away and walked over to Claude, trying to quell the fear he felt. The ranger had accomplished something not many had—the mayor was terrified. He spoke quietly to Claude. "Stall for time 'til she gets here. These yahoos won't know what hit them then. If you know what's good for you, Claude, you won't let me down."

"I won't, Mr. Westerly. You can count on me."

The quiver in his voice was not lost on Bill. "Claude, would you like some coffee?"

Robinson was quickly tiring of this man. "It's time to cut the pleasantries, Mr. Westerly. Your lawyer is here and we need to get down to business."

"Just a minute there, I need to consult with my client first. May I see the warrant, please? Bill and I will talk before he says anything to either of you. Is that clear?"

Hank grudgingly, replied, "Yes."

"Good. I'm glad we all understand each other. Now if you will excuse us."

Robinson and Blake stepped to the other side of the room while the other two men consulted.

∞

The shrilling of the cell phone brought a smile to Maggie's face. "Do you ever turn that thing off?"

"Oh. How else would I aggravate you? This is Dr. Walker. ... Hi. ... We're just coming into town now and should be there in about five minutes. I hope we get there before the storm. I'll be careful. Okay, bye."

"Your mother, I take it. I'm surprised she didn't call about an hour earlier." Maggie winked at Lauren, a lascivious smile crossing her face.

"Yep. She said she needs to talk to us as soon as possible."

"Good, I hope she'll like the news I have about the good mayor."

∞

Entering the judge's chambers was always an awe inspiring experience for Lauren. The rich look of the interior with the huge wooden desk, the big comfortable leather chairs, and the bookshelves filled with law books. The whole room looked and smelled powerful. Rising, Victoria smiled brightly at both women.

"Thank you so much for coming. Westerly called and told me he needed a lawyer and to get over there, if I knew what was good for me."

"What did you tell him, Mother?"

"I told him I couldn't get away right now, and would be there as soon as I could. I don't want to go, Lori. It doesn't feel right."

"I don't see where you have a choice right now, Vicky," Maggie interjected. "Just go there, find out what's going on, and make sure you do everything by the book."

"I have always followed the letter of the law. Even when he wanted me to fix tickets, I would just pay them myself. Have your sources found anything out yet?"

"Yes. There seems to be a connection to organized crime, but I won't know anything for certain until later this week. I'm sorry. It's the best they could do in two days."

"Just knowing that something is being done makes it easier to bear, Maggie. Thank you for everything you're doing for me." She turned her attention to her daughter. "Lori, are you serious about keeping the store?"

Lauren tersely asked, "Why?" *I can't believe her. What is she up to now? I thought we were past this.*

"No. No, Lori, you don't understand. I want you to keep the store. I don't trust Bill. If you are keeping it, you need to go over to that mess of an office and find the original deed."

"You don't have it? I thought you were the executor."

"I looked. Zeb had a filing system that was all his own that I just don't understand. I thought maybe you two could give it a go."

Lauren glanced at Maggie and received a slight nod. "We'll go while you're at the mayor's. When you're done, why not come over to the store and help us."

"Sounds good to me. I need to be home by four. Your father and I have a charity fundraising dinner to attend tonight. I guess I'd better be on my way. I wouldn't want to keep the bastard waiting too long, would I?" She gave Lauren a loving hug. "Thank you for giving me another chance."

Lauren wrapped her arms around her mother and whispered, "Mom, I'm so glad to have you back in my life. I'll do whatever I can to help you in any way. You're worth it."

Victoria wiped away a tear before giving Maggie a quick hug. "Wish me luck."

"Shall we go too?" Maggie headed toward the door, only to feel Lauren grab her wrist.

Lauren's eyes were sparkling with merriment and lust. "What's the hurry? Ever done it in a judge's chamber … in a big overstuffed chair?"

Maggie gave the smaller woman a once over. "As a matter of fact, I haven't. What exactly did you have in mind?"

"Actions speak louder than words. Come with me and I'll show you. I promise you won't be disappointed." Slowly unzipping Maggie's jeans, she pointed to a large brown leather chair. "Just sit yourself down and I shall see if I can get a confession out of you."

"Mmm. I think I might like your approach to getting information. I'm all yours, but I must warn you, it will take a lot of … oral persuasion to get me to talk." Maggie pasted a stubborn look on her face.

Lauren pushed Maggie into the chair, lowered the jeans to Maggie's ankles, licked her lips, and knelt. "Shall we get started?" Just as she began spreading Maggie's knees, a loud harsh bell sounded.

"What the hell is that?" Maggie blurted. "I can't believe this."

"Shit, it means someone is in the courtroom. They installed that years ago when someone came through that way to murder a judge." The door to the room squeaked open as the clerk entered. Lauren quickly sat on the arm of the chair in an effort to hide her partially clad lover.

"Oh, Lori. I didn't know you were here. Where's your mother?"

"Bea, she had to go out for a little bit. She should be back after lunch. I'm going to see her later, want me to give her a message for you?"

"No, it's nothing that can't wait. Are you going to introduce me to your friend there?"

Maggie laughed before peering around Lauren and waving to Bea. "Hi, Bea. I'm little Lori's friend Maggie. I'd get up, but I seem to be somewhat indisposed at the moment."

"My, dear, do you need a doctor? Are you hurt?"

Lauren was beet red and at a loss for words.

"Bea, that is so kind of you. As you know, little Lori here is a doctor and she can minister to any of my ailments quite capably. Thank you, though."

"Right, okay then, I'll leave you two to whatever it is you need to do. Nice to meet you, Maggie, and please, Lori, don't be such a stranger." Bea left the room shaking her head.

Once the door closed, laughter erupted from Maggie as she pulled Lauren down into her arms and kissed her soundly. "Well, that certainly was a mood breaker."

"I can't believe you. I'll *little Lori* you. *She can minister to any ailments* ... how on earth did you come up with that?" Lauren returned the kiss before she got up from the chair. "Shall we go over to the store? It should be more private there. Did I ever tell you Uncle Zeb lived above the store? There are two bedrooms that we will need to check out thoroughly."

"Lauren, that's just what we need. To be in a bedroom making love and have your mother walk in."

The smirk on Maggie's face told Lauren they would be doing more than searching for a deed at the store. "Let's hurry. The wind sure is kicking up out there."

Maggie stood and pulled up her jeans, then took Lauren's hand and walked out of the courthouse.

They fought the strong wind as they crossed the street.

∞

The rumblings of the approaching storm were louder as Victoria climbed the steps to Bill's porch. *Is this how the people I've sent to prison feel when the cell door closes behind them? This can't be happening to me. How did everything get so out of control that I've reached this point?* She knocked on the door hoping for a miracle that would rescue her from her nightmare.

"It's about time you got here," Bill snarled.

"Nice to see you too, Bill."

"Gentleman, may I introduce Judge Victoria Walker, my other lawyer." Bill beamed at the look of confusion on the rangers' faces. "Vicky, these are Rangers Blake and Robinson."

She shook their hands. "Nice to meet you. I'm afraid, that Bill has misunderstood my role. My position as a sitting judge precludes me from acting as his lawyer. I can provide him with any personal advice I may have, but I cannot act as his lawyer." By having the upper hand in a legal situation involving Westerly, Victoria felt in control for the first time.

Bill shot daggers at Victoria.

In the distance were the rumblings of thunder.

"What exactly is the situation involving our mayor, Ranger Blake?"

"Judge, we have a warrant for his arrest. The state of Texas is charging him with conspiracy to commit murder. Would you like to see the warrant?"

"Yes, thank you." Victoria took the document and perused it quickly. "Everything looks to be in order." She cocked her head and then turned to Blake. "Would you mind explaining the details to me? Once I have a clearer idea of the circumstances, I can advise Bill."

"Certainly," Blake said. "On September eleventh, six years ago, a man named John Henry Brown was involved in an accident wherein his truck broadsided a BMW, wrapping it around a lamp post and killing the male driver and a pregnant woman. Two witnesses came forward supporting Brown's claim that the driver of the other car ran a stop light."

Robinson picked up the story. "Several months ago, Mr. Brown was arrested for selling guns to terrorists. In his attempt to save himself, he disclosed that a man had hired him to kill the people in that car six years ago. He received fifty thousand dollars and he alleged that the witnesses were also paid. The name he gave us was William Westerly, Warwick's mayor. Since Westerly was mayor of a small town thousands of miles away, we doubted Mr. Brown's story. Still, we checked with the witnesses. They both admitted to being paid for their testimony."

Robinson could see the disbelief on the faces of the other occupants in the room. "There's more. We had each person meet individually with different sketch artists to describe the man that paid them. Here are the drawings. As you can see, they are all roughly the same and all bear more than a passing resemblance to Mr. Westerly."

The winds howled as the storm bore down on Warwick.

Victoria's mind flashed back to the newspaper article Bill had given her years before. *What did he say? I should take him seriously, because he could make this happen to Lori, too.* With her legal mind working at full throttle, she allowed herself a small, satisfied smile. *Gotcha, Bill.* "Thank you, gentlemen. This certainly is convincing evidence. Will you give me a minute to confer with Mr. Claiborne and Mr. Westerly?"

With a nod, the rangers retrieved the sketches and the warrant, and removed themselves to a spot over in front of the door.

"Claude, I think you should advise Bill to go with these men and not fight extradition. Since I have personal knowledge of this situation, I am compelled to share the information with the court and therefore I am unable to continue any dialogue with either of you about this issue."

"Who the hell do you think you are, bitch? I own you, and you will do as I say," Westerly growled in warning.

"No, you don't, Bill. It's over, as of now." Victoria rose from her seat and moved toward the two rangers to offer a statement.

Bill screamed, "No! I will not allow this! This will not happen."

Claude couldn't believe the outburst. "Bill, settle down. This isn't helping. Let's sit down."

"Shut up, old man. You're nothing but a drunken has been. Vicky, you'll be sorry if you open your mouth. I promise you that."

"Is that a threat, Bill? You do realize these men are witnesses to that statement, don't you? I would suggest you listen to your lawyer, and sit down and shut up." The crazed look on the mayor's face reminded her of a cornered animal ready to fight for its freedom. His rage was not lost on the others in the room either.

Bill had moved across the room and opened a drawer. No one had time to react before he pulled out a gun and pointed it in Victoria's direction. "Who are you to tell me anything, bitch? If I go down, you go with me. I can see the headline now: *Judge Walker Abandoned Firstborn to Follow Lover Around the World*. Did you know that, Claude? She isn't as pure as everyone thinks. She's a slut and a child abuser. She was willing to sell out her own daughter so I could get that damn store. Do you have any idea what a scandal that will bring to our town? She's an abomination, a blemish that needs to be eradicated, and I'm just the man to do it." He leveled the gun at Victoria's body as he bellowed, "Get ready for hell, bitch."

Blake and Robinson drew their weapons and stood with their feet apart, arms outstretched their guns at the ready. "Put the gun down, Westerly," Blake demanded. "Drop it now!"

The electrically charged air added to the tension. Suddenly, lightning cracked through the air and there was the sound of a loud explosion. Then, all was deathly still.

∞

Maxwell's store was like going back to a time when profit wasn't king and family meant everything.

Suspended from the ceiling were yokes, harnesses, sleds, and baby buggies. On a far wall, a cabinet with hundreds of small drawers containing everything from nuts to bolts. In another section were shelves with glass jars filled with flour, sugar, coffee, candies, and other edible items. The counter in front held an old copper scale. Throughout the store, stacked in helter-skelter fashion, was every item imaginable. On the wooden counter stood a cash register from the turn of the century, and a ledger that was a record of every sale.

From her precarious position atop a ladder, Ellie Hudson, a small frail looking woman, greeted the two women with a warm smile as they entered the store. "Lori, I am so glad to hear you are keeping the store. It would never have been the same if some other family had it."

"Thanks, Ellie. This is my good friend, Maggie Sullivan. I don't think you met her when I we were in last week."

Ellie scrambled down the ladder. "I saw the two of you the other day but that Joe Belier just loves to talk so I couldn't come say a proper hello." She smiled as she shook Maggie's hand. "Pleased to meet you, Maggie. Any friend of little Lori is a friend of mine."

"We'll be in the office if you need us. You be careful up on that ladder, Ellie. Can't have my best employee getting hurt."

"Lands sake, Lori, I've been going up and down that thing since way before you were born. Go on now, so I can get my work done."

Lauren took Maggie's hand and led her through the maze of shelves to the office in the back of the store. Once inside, the women were greeted with the smell of stale cigar smoke and musty papers.

"I think we need to open a window and air this place out. With all these papers stacked everywhere, it's no wonder my mother couldn't find anything. This must have driven her crazy. She doesn't like disorder of any kind." At the vision of what she knew was a look of horror when her mother opened the office door, Lauren chuckled. With a physician's need for precision, she had to admit she was much the same.

"How on earth are we going to find anything in here, Lauren? Where do we begin?"

"Why don't you start with the desk, once you find it," she said laughing. "I'll move things around some and see if I can find the safe that's supposed to be here."

After a half an hour of searching, Maggie walked over to Lauren and handed her an envelope with her name on it. "I found this on the desk, Lauren. Looks like your uncle left you a note."

As Lauren took the envelope, tears trickled down her cheeks. Memories of her beloved uncle flooded her mind. "I loved him so much. I wish you could have met him, I know he would have loved you." She turned the envelope over in her hand and was about to open it when the sound of sirens startled them both. "I don't recall ever hearing police sirens in this town in my life, except on holidays."

As if to accentuate the sound of the sirens, thunder and lightning streaked through the air and shook the old building. Ellie suddenly appeared at the door. "The sheriff just called looking for Doc Wilson. There's been a shooting at the mayor's house and

Doc Wilson is out at the Barnes' farm. They need a doctor, Lori."

Without any hesitation, Lauren and Maggie rushed out of the store and ran as fast as they could to Bill Westerly's home.

∞

The wailing of sirens reverberated throughout Warwick. There, in the home of the town's mayor, Lauren Walker sat on the floor holding the limp body of her mother. As she compressed the bloody wound with her jacket, sobs wracked her body. "Don't leave me, please. Not now. We were just beginning to understand each other again. Oh, God, please no." Lauren reigned in her emotions. Her mother needed a doctor not a crybaby. "Maggie, can you go to my car and get my medical bag?"

"Sure thing," Maggie said over her shoulder as she ran out the door. It was two blocks to the car and there was no time to waste.

The room was a bustle of activity as the small Warwick police force gathered to process the horrific scene. Bill Westerly laid dead, with a bullet hole in his temple and copious amounts of congealing blood seeping into the floor around him. A dumbfounded Claude Claiborne was sitting with the two rangers on the couch.

Steven Walker entered the house, scanned the area quickly, and walked briskly toward his wife and daughter. He gently touched his daughter's shoulder and knelt down. "Sweetheart, what can I do to help?"

"There's so much blood; I can't seem to stop the blood." She looked at the door and was relieved to see Maggie returning.

"Lauren, here's your medical bag. There's a medivac unit on the way."

"Daddy, put your hand here and apply as much pressure as you can. That helicopter needs to be here now! Elevate her feet, Maggie, then go to Doc Wilson's office and bring his nurse back to assist me. Tell Dolly we need two IV setups and two bags of Ringers, and make sure you get lots of bandages and material to pack the wound."

"Back in a flash." Maggie, ran out of the door and down the street to the doctor's office. She turned the knob only to find that it wouldn't turn. With winds swirling around her, Maggie began pounding on the door. "Dolly, there's an emergency! Open up."

Dolly opened the door and looked at the woman whose clothing showed spatters of blood. "What's wrong? Are you hurt? Who are you?"

"I'm Maggie Sullivan, a friend of Lauren Walker. There has been a shooting at the mayor's and Lauren needs you there. You need to bring so…."

"I know what to bring, dear. Give me a minute to get the supplies and we can go." Dolly gathered the necessary items and returned to the entryway. "Who's hurt?" she asked as she opened the door.

"Judge Walker."

"Oh no, poor Lori!" she exclaimed as they rushed out of the office, fighting the blowing winds all the way.

As Lauren and Dolly did their best to keep Victoria alive, Chief Miller questioned Claude and the rangers. "Just who are you two, and why are you here."

"My name is Ed Blake and this is Frank Robinson. We're contractors that Mr. Westerly contacted about the building project here in town.

From what I saw, he invited the judge here to try to convince her not to veto the project. When she refused to see it his way, he screamed out something about being ruined and took a gun from that drawer there and shot her before he shot himself."

"I see. Is that what happened, Claude?"

Claude didn't know what game the two strangers were playing, but the bottom line was he did not like the mayor. Westerly was a cruel man who enjoyed lording his power over everyone. His death was no great loss to anyone. "Why yes, it is, Tom."

"Just why were you here anyway, Claude?"

"You know how Bill liked to order people around. He called me and said he needed a lawyer and to get over here. I did what he told me to, just like everyone else in this town does."

Robinson looked casually at Blake, relieved that the old man hadn't felt the need to share the entire story with the sheriff. If he had, they would have had a hard time explaining why they were there and how the mayor had really died. As it was, they would continue to play their roles and then contact their boss with their report.

"I'll need statements from all of you. Be in my office in an hour. Eddie, get some sort of blanket over this body. No one needs to be gawking at it." Chief Miller walked over to Lauren and her father. "How's she doin', Lori?"

"We need that helicopter here now. She won't last much longer if we don't get her to the hospital."

"I'll check on that right away. Eddie, get the ETA on that 'chopper." He offered his hand to Steven Walker. "Terrible business, Steve. That Bill was a rustin' gun waitin' to explode. If there's anything I can do for you, let me know."

85

"Thanks, Tom. If there's any way you can get that helicopter here sooner, that would help. I hope this weather won't be a problem."

Everything outside went silent and the wind ceased to blow.

Maggie stood in the background watching the events unfold. *How did everything go so wrong? Things weren't supposed to happen this way.* She heard the helicopter in the distance, and then knelt down beside Lauren. "The helicopter is coming."

The medivac team hustled through the door. "We need to hurry while the wind is calm otherwise we won't get out of here," one of the paramedics said.

"They're here, Mom. Hold on." Lauren noted the pallor of her mother's skin and the shallowness of her breathing. Lauren had done all she could and knew that time was running out for her mother. "It was now up to you, Mom." With tears streaming down her cheeks, she gently kissed her mother's head as she released her to the newly arrived medical team. *I love you, Mom. Please don't go yet. I need you.*

"Who put in this IV?" asked a woman dressed in a flight suit.

"I did," a shaken Lauren replied

"And you are?"

"Sorry, I'm a doctor, Lauren Walker, and this is Dolly Simpson, a nurse. The bleeding was profuse, so I started IVs in both arms and ran them wide open. We packed the wound and the bleeding seems to have subsided. The swelling of the abdomen worries me, as does the shallow breathing."

"Thanks, Doctor, I'll take over now."

Lauren stood up and walked the short distance to where Maggie was standing fell into her outstretched in her arms. For a few moments, she knew she was safe in facing the gravity of her mother's condition. "Will you take my dad and me to the hospital?"

"Why don't we see if we can get you both on the helicopter so you can be with her?"

"Thanks." Lauren looked over at her father who, to all outward appearances, seemed in control, but she knew different. "I need to go to my dad."

"Yeah. He looks like he could use a hug. Listen, I'll drive your car to the hospital and meet you there."

Lauren kissed Maggie's cheek. "Thank you." With a professional eye on the medics who were lifting her mother on to a stretcher, she stood by her father's side. When his arm went around her waist, she leaned into his strong body. "She's going to make it, Daddy. I just know it."

Steven kissed his daughter's head. "If we're going with them, we need to get in the helicopter now."

As Lauren passed by Maggie, she gently squeezed her arm before she left with her father.

"I'll be right behind you." Maggie watched, as the helicopter lift off grateful that the wind remained calm. *That's the only thing good to come out of this. How the hell did everything get so fucked up?*

∞

Maggie stood on the deceased mayor's porch watching the helicopter head in an easterly position. The clouds that had been dark and ominous were now an angry gray. A tap on her shoulder diverted her attention away from the menacing skies.

"Maggie, I wrote down the directions to the hospital in Westfield. It's about fifty miles away, but very easy to find. You pretty much stay on this

87

highway and you'll eventually reach it," Dolly's reassuring voice said.

"Okay. Thank you, Dolly." She glanced at the sheet of directions. "I think I can find it."

"You seem a bit dazed. Are you okay to drive? You won't be any use to Lauren or the Walkers if you get into an accident."

"No. I'm good, Dolly. I'll be fine."

Maggie went down the stairs and up the street to where Lauren parked her SUV in front of the courthouse. Once inside the car, she shook as tears streamed down her cheeks. She turned the ignition key and started down the highway toward the hospital.

Chapter Seven

After she had driven about twenty miles, Maggie pulled the SUV into the deserted parking lot of an abandoned shopping center. Waiting for her arrival, a man stood outside a black limousine parked there. She opened the door and got out of the Land Rover before walking over to the long, dark vehicle. Her eyes scanned the area before she nodded to the man, opened the door, and got in.

A dark figure in the car spoke. "Sweetheart, it's so good to see you."

Maggie was shaking with anger and disgust over what happened to Victoria. "Just what the hell happened? No one was supposed to die. All you needed to do was scare the bastard so he would leave the judge alone. Now Westerly is dead and Victoria Walker is fighting for her life. How did this get so fucked up?"

"Please, settle down. You only gave me two days to put this together. I didn't have the luxury of profiling the mayor to find out if he was a hot head. He's out of the way, and the problem is solved."

"Out of the way? He's dead. And I'm responsible."

"I talked with Robinson. He said the deranged mayor could have killed them all. We were just lucky we had time to take care of business before the police arrived. How can you be responsible?"

"Because I'm the one who set it all in motion and I'm accountable. If Vicky dies, how can I ever face Lauren?"

"Darling, you did nothing. I set up the sting, not you. This woman means that much to you?"

"I will do what's necessary to keep her and those she loves safe."

"I had to call in a lot of markers on this one, Maggie. You know that, don't you?"

"Yes, I know. I just feel like everything is out of control."

"Have I ever let you down?"

"No." Maggie shook her head. The gravity of the situation was still causing her intense concern.

"Let me take care of everything, darling. I'm here now, and I'll make sure things are set straight. I have the top surgeon in the area on his way to the hospital to handle her case personally."

"You always have an answer don't you."

"I have resources they don't, honey. Let me take care of this. Trust me. She'll be in capable hands. If anyone can save her, Dr. Green will. Come here, sweetheart."

All the pain and sorrow inside Maggie welled up and erupted in a flood of tears. She slowly moved across the seat and nestled against the broad shoulder. She sighed deeply as she found loving comfort in the one person she knew would always be there for her, no matter what.

"Everything will be fine. I will make it so."

Several minutes later, Maggie looked up into the loving eyes of her father and smiled weakly. "I know you'll try. What should I do now?"

"First, we need to get you to the hospital. I'll have Neal drive your vehicle and you ride with me." Maggie's father pushed a button and his window rolled down. "Neal, follow us to the hospital in Maggie's vehicle." He picked up his phone and tapped in a number. "Charlie, is the doctor there yet? Good. We're still about thirty minutes out. I want you to make sure everyone stays safe. That means no press, only the medical staff. Let me speak with Green. ... Phil, it's good to hear your voice. How was the trip? ... Have you examined the judge yet? ... I see. We should be there within the next half hour. And Phil, I expect to find her alive when I get there. ... Not acceptable. She must not die. ... Thought you would see it my way. I'll see you shortly." After closing his phone, the man turned to his daughter and smiled. "Sweetheart, everything is in motion now. Tell m ... is Dr. Walker in your life permanently?"

"I don't know, Dad. We just met a short time ago. I can tell you that we share a connection that is unlike anything I have ever known. Of all the partners I've had, Lauren fills a void in my life I never knew existed. For the first time, I want to settle down and get out of the business." She shrugged. "So, I guess the answer to your question is *yes* but it is too soon to tell for certain."

"We can discuss that later. For now, I want you to know that I consider her a part of our family, and she and her family are now under my protection."

"It's a little late for Vicky, isn't it?"

"It is never too late. You know what I can do. This isn't an insurmountable problem; I'll see to that. Now, as we drive, you might want to look over the documents we compiled about the daughter."

"I really don't care what you found out about Lauren. Nothing will change my mind about her."

"No. I meant Lauren's half sister, Harriet Aristides."

∞

The dark clouds were clearing as the limo pulled up to the front entrance of the Westfield Regional Trauma Center. Keith opened the door for Maggie and offered his hand as she disembarked from the car.

Maggie leaned back into the car and gave her father a brief smile. "Thank you for everything. I suppose you'll be lurking in the shadows, as always."

"Of course, darling, that's what a good spook does." He smiled fondly, his devotion clearly visible. "I will always be there to protect you."

Maggie gently kissed his cheek. "I love you."

"As I do you, sweetheart. They are in the private family waiting room on the third floor. Keith will go with you."

"Dad, I don't need a bodyguard. Those days are over."

"Indulge me, will you?"

Maggie looked at her father quizzically wondering if there was something more that she should know. *He rarely does anything without a reason.* "Sure, this time I will but I have a sneaking suspicion that this conversation isn't over."

"We will speak later."

After one last quick kiss, Maggie closed the door and went inside.

∞

A pretty, strawberry blond nurse quickly approached Maggie as she entered the hospital. "Are you okay?"

"Me? Sure. I'm fine. Why?" At the nurse's nod, Maggie looked down at her blood pattered clothes. "It's not my blood, but thanks for asking. I'm looking for Judge Walker's family."

"Oh, you were there. Are you family?"

Maggie had been to hospitals enough to know the answer to *that* question. She took a quick look at the nurse's name tag. "Yes, Naomi."

With a gentle hand on Maggie's arm, Naomi began guiding her toward the elevators. "Are you sure you're okay? You look rather shaky. Should I take you to your family? Is he with you?"

Maggie looked back at the waiting Keith. "Yes. Thanks for helping me. I really appreciate it."

Inside the elevator, Maggie felt the nurse edge closer. *In another time, she'd be mine for the night...perhaps even a week or two.* Her thoughts quickly went to Lauren. She needed to be with her lover to give her comfort. She heard the elevator bell's ding of arrival and sensed that Lauren was nearby. When the doors slid open she saw Lauren.

"Maggie." Lauren collapsed in her arms, sobbing.

"Shh, I know. I know."

Lauren held her tightly. "Don't leave me, please."

"I'm here now." Maggie gently soothed her, stroking her hair. Once they moved out of the elevator, they walked toward the waiting room, arm in arm.

Maggie frowned at Lauren's attire of hospital scrubs. "You didn't participate in the surgery, did you?"

Lauren didn't understand until she saw Maggie's eyes looking at her greens. "No, they let me wear these 'cause my clothes were covered with blood."

∞

Everyone was anxiously waiting for word from the doctors when a catering service arrived with enough provisions to feed them all. "Where did this come from?" Steven Walker asked.

"Don't know, sir. We received an order, and here we are. I'm not sure who sent it or who's paying. You're Walker, right?"

"Yes." He pulled out a twenty from his wallet and gave it to the young man. "Thank you." Steven turned to the twenty or so people providing support and prayers. "Looks like someone thought we needed to eat. Please help yourselves." He filled a plate and took it to his daughter. "Here, Lori, honey. You need to eat."

"I'm not hungry. You eat it."

Steven looked pleadingly toward Maggie for help.

"Lauren, you won't be any good to your mother if you end up sick. Come on. Please try to eat something. Tell you what ... we can share. Please, for me."

Lauren smiled and reluctantly took half of a sandwich.

The sun was setting with brilliant reds and purples streaking through the darker storm clouds. Gazing out the window, Maggie recalled the first evening she and Lauren had spent together. It was hard for her to believe that only a few weeks had passed. Looking down at the sleeping figure in her lap, she softly stroked Lauren's hair. *I do love you, Lauren. That is something I never expected to happen to me.*

When Dr. Green entered the room, Steven Walker stood.

A hush fell over the waiting room.

"Mr. Walker?"

Lauren sat up instantly and went to her father's side.

"Yes. How's my wife?"

"The bullet grazed the heart and then lodged near her spine. She lost a lot of blood, and we had a difficult time removing the bullet. Her condition is critical. I've had her heavily sedated. The next twenty-four hours will be crucial."

"May we see her?" Lauren asked.

"You are?"

"Her daughter."

"Oh, yes, Doctor Walker. Your initial response probably saved your mother's life. The immediate family can see her, but just for a minute. Then you should all go home and get some sleep. There's no reason for you to be here all night."

"Thanks for your concern, Dr. Green, but I'm not leaving my mother."

"Doctor Walker, there is nothing you can do for her by being here. Please trust me. She is in ICU, has her own nurse, and I'll be here all night. Get some rest. There are long days ahead of you."

Steven hugged his daughter close. "Honey, the doctor is right; we need our rest so we can be strong for your mother. Please. We can stay at the hotel down the street."

"Okay, Daddy. I'll rest for a little while, but will be back here after that. Let's go see her." Lauren found Maggie's eyes and held them. "Will you still be here?"

"Count on it. I'll get everything set up at the hotel, okay?"

Lauren gave a weak smile and placed a whisper of a kiss on Maggie's cheek. "I won't be long."

Maggie watched as the two walked away with the doctor before she turned and strode to the end of the room. She spoke softly to the man standing in the shadows near the window. "Thanks for sending the food,"

"No problem. There are rooms for you at the Heritage. Everyone will find changes of clothes and toiletries in their rooms."

"Thanks, Dad. Where will you be staying?"

"Something has come up and I need to leave for a couple days." His tone was low and ominous. "I have arranged for Keith to be in the room across from you. If you need anything, he will take care of it for you."

"What's going on? I know you; there is more going on here. Please tell me what it is."

"Margaret, you have always been curious about things that could get you killed. The good mayor was in deep to some thoroughly unsavory types who are very upset about a missing half a mil and the project in Warwick going south. Apparently, they were hoping that Warwick would be a good front to camouflage their illicit activities in seemingly legitimate enterprises. They want payback. The way they see it, your doctor is responsible, along with you. I have no intention of letting them get to either one of you." He smiled at his daughter. "Now are you satisfied?"

"Shit, what a mess. I'm sorry you were dragged into this."

"If it concerns you, darling, it concerns me. I'll handle it. Everything will work out. Doesn't it always?"

Maggie gazed at her father. "Yes. I love you, Dad." Hearing a commotion, she turned to see Police

Chief Miller talking with Jeb Maxwell. "Oh no. This could be trouble."

"Want me to take care of it?"

"No. I'll take this one. I think I can still remember what you taught me." She kissed her father before he disappeared further into the shadows.

While walking toward the circle of people, Maggie heard Jeb say, "I know you need to question her, Tom, but don't you think they've been through enough? We don't even know if Victoria will make it through the night."

"I'm just doing my job, Jeb."

"Tom, didn't you have witnesses to what happened?" Steven Walker asked as he joined the group.

The chief offered his hand. "How is she doin', Steve?"

"Thanks for asking. Right now, she's stable but critical. That's all we know, Tom. It's in God's hands now. Do you think you have enough information from the witnesses so you don't have to bother Vicky with questioning when she wakes up?" He lifted one shoulder. "... if she does?"

"No problem, Steve. Don't see any need to bother her with anything more when it's clear what happened. Is there anything I can do for you? I can give you an escort you back to Warwick if you like."

"Thanks, Tom, but we're staying at the hotel tonight. It's the only way to get Lori to leave the hospital. As soon as she finishes interrogating Dr. Green, we'll be on our way." Steve winked at Maggie. "She would have made one hell of a lawyer."

Lauren reappeared in time to hear her father's statement. "Now why would we want to unleash another Walker lawyer on the world?" Lauren quipped as she leaned into Maggie. "I don't know about anyone else, but a nice hot shower would feel really good about now."

"I have everything arranged at the Heritage. There is a room for everyone who needs one." Maggie wrapped her arm around Lauren. "Let's get you over there and see about finding something other than those attractive scrubs."

"Sounds good to me, let's go."

Chapter Eight

By the time the Walkers and their supports were ready to leave the hospital, rumors had spread like wildfire. The ever hungry news corps were eager for the story. Keith pulled the Land Rover up to a side door of the hotel so they could avoid the waiting press. Steve, Lauren, and Maggie hurriedly made their way through the thick mist that filled the night air. An eerie calm made the hairs prickle on the back of Maggie's neck. *I'm glad Keith is here. Wish I had a weapon. At least he does. I need to talk to Steve and let him know what's going on; it's only right.*

"Maggie, did you see that we have clothes here? I wonder where they came from." Lauren looked through the closet and the drawers. "Hey, whoever it was, they have good taste and thought of everything. Was it you, Maggie?"

"I guess in a roundabout way it was. Never mind about that now. You looked exhausted."

"I am. All of a sudden, I can't seem to keep my eyes open. What do you mean 'in a roundabout way'?"

"Come on. I've drawn a hot bath for you." Maggie took Lauren by the hand and led her into the bathroom. She removed the scrubs and carefully helped the weary doctor into the bathtub. "You can relax while I call room service. What would you like?"

"I'm too tired to think of eating, Maggie. This is so nice. Mind if I just close my eyes for a minute? Mmm, I think I'm in heaven."

"Enjoy yourself. I'll call your dad and see if he wants to join us for dinner." Maggie smiled at her beautiful lover. *Tempting. Nope, can't go there now, too much to do.* "Call if you need anything."

"You're not leaving, are you?"

"No. I'll just be in the next room. Please relax and let me pamper you."

"Anything you want anytime, anyplace, anywhere, anyhow."

∞

A knock at the door gave Maggie a start as she watched Lauren sleep curled on the bed. She opened it cautiously and saw Steven standing there with what smelled like Chinese takeout.

She gave him a broad smile. "Come on in, Steve. That smells good; I hope its dinner."

"Yes, its Lori's favorite. Kung Pao Chicken, along with lots of other goodies. Hope you girls are hungry."

Steve was a handsome man who stood about six foot two with salt and pepper hair. His smile was captivating. Maggie suspected he'd won many court cases with his demeanor alone. She liked him. When Lauren first introduced her to him, he had welcomed her to his family telling her, "*Love knows no gender. When it's right, there's no stopping it.*"

Now, she found herself in the uncomfortable position of having to tell him about the entire situation. *I wonder if he'll still welcome me once he knows the truth about what I did.*

"Where's Lori? She's all right, isn't she?"

"She's sleeping. After her bath, she just collapsed in bed and fell asleep immediately. Think we should let her sleep, or wake her to eat something?" She knew what he'd say, but wanted him to have the opportunity to take some control in an otherwise untenable day.

"She needs her sleep more than food. Would you join me, Maggie? I really do have tons of food here. Maybe we should call Jeb and the others."

"How about just you and me for now, Steve. I need to talk with you about something urgent." As Steve set the food out on the low coffee table, Maggie got two beers out of the refrigerator. After sitting down, she sucked in a deep breath, not really knowing where to start.

"Sounds to me like you need to just tell me what you have to say, Maggie. Usually if you do that it isn't as bad as you think."

His fatherly concern warmed Maggie's heart. *I can trust him.* "Bet you're one hell of a lawyer, Steve. Do you know anything about what's been going on between your wife and the departed mayor?"

"Yes, I do. Vic and I had a long talk that night she spoke with you and Lori. She told me everything, and that you offered to help us out. I want you to know I really appreciate all that you tried to do. At least it's over now."

"That's the problem. It isn't."

"What exactly is going on, Maggie?"

"It seems that Mayor Westerly's business involvement with Warwick included ties to the mob. Some rather unhappy men out there not only want their money back, but revenge, too. They see Lori as the main cause of the project's demise, and I run a close second. They mean business, Steve."

"I see." His brow furrowed as he debated what to do next. "Have you spoken with Chief Miller about this?"

"No. I don't think that would be wise. Right now we're being protected, and someone is working on eliminating the problem."

"*You* don't think it's wise? Just who do you think you are? My family is in danger. Who is protecting us?"

Speaking in a quiet but firm voice, Maggie said, "May I remind you I'm in danger too. Keith is here to protect us, and so are a few others who aren't as visible. Don't you think I'm scared too, Steve? Your daughter just came into my life and I don't want to lose her. I will do whatever is necessary to keep her safe."

"Exactly what is being done to, as you say, *eliminate* the problem?"

"Will you trust me, Steve? Tomorrow night I'll answer all your questions. Right now, Vicky should be our main concern. We're safe. I promise you that."

"Don't see that I have much of a choice, since you're the one with the information. You're right about one thing though, my wife needs us right now. I'll give you until tomorrow, and then I'll take steps of my own to ensure my family is safe. Is that clear?"

"Yes. I wouldn't expect anything else." She wanted to confide in him and tell him everything but she couldn't, not yet. First, she needed to tell Lauren and hope she would understand.

They both turned when they heard a voice say, "Is that my favorite meal I smell? I can't believe how hungry I am."

Steve's face brightened into a beaming smile at the sight of his daughter. "Yes, sweetheart. I brought you the works. Egg roll, soup, and Kung Pao Chicken."

"Thanks, Daddy. What are you two having? I'm not sharing."

For the first time since the morning, Lauren was smiling, which warmed the hearts of both onlookers.

Maggie pushed a carton and a plate toward Lauren. "Have at it and if that isn't enough, we can always get you more, right, Steve?"

"Absolutely."

∞

Sometime in the middle of the night, Maggie woke, the sheets soaked with her sweat. Lauren was stroking her hair and whispering to her. "Maggie, shh, I'm okay, and so are you."

Maggie looked into warm hazel eyes and a sense of peace filled Maggie. Something deep inside told her that with Lauren by her side, there was nothing they couldn't overcome. "I'm sorry. Did I wake you? Guess I was having a nightmare."

Lauren continued to sing softly to Maggie. "Let my arms hold you and keep you safe and warm. Nothing will harm you now, my love. Let me keep you safe and warm." She gently kissed the wet hair. "Sleep now, darling. There's nothing that we can't face together." She pulled Maggie even closer as she continued humming until her lover fell into a restful sleep.

The loud ringing of the phone woke the two sleeping women.

"Got to be your family, Lauren, they always have great timing." Then remembering where they were, and why, she fear that something happened to Vicky filled her. "Want me to get it?"

Lauren wrapped her arms tightly around Maggie. "Yes, please."

"I'm waiting for you, bitch. You owe me, and so does your dyke girlfriend."

The line went dead and Maggie began to shake.

"Maggie? Maggie, what's wrong? Is it my mother? Please talk to me."

"Lauren," Maggie pulled her close, "it wasn't about your mother. But we need to talk."

"Maggie, you're scaring me. What's going on? Talk to me."

Maggie shook her head. "What would I do without you? I can't lose you, Lauren. I just can't."

"You're not going to lose me, Maggie. Never."

"Lauren, we're in big trouble. Bill Westerly had some …"

The phone rang again, and the tension in the room escalated.

"Hold that thought. I'll get the phone."

"Lauren, *no!*"

"Hello? … Yes, Daddy? … She is? We'll be there as quickly as we can." Lauren hung up the phone and turned to Maggie. "My mother is conscious." Lauren could see the fear still etched in Maggie's face. She took her in her arms and held her tightly. "Maggie, nothing will ever come between us and I will never leave you. Now why don't you tell me what the problem is?"

"It'll wait." Though fear gripped her at the potential danger of leaving the safe confines of the room, she said, "Let's go see your mother."

Lauren could still feel Maggie's tremors and knew there was something terribly wrong. "Please tell me."

"Lauren, Westerly had mob connections and they want revenge, and you and I are the targets. That was them on the phone. They know where we are." Maggie looked deep into Lauren's eyes. "I will protect you. I will not let anyone hurt you please trust me on that. I love you. Never forget that." Gently kissing Lauren's forehead, she said, "Why don't you get dressed while I make some calls?"

"Why don't you fill me in on everything first? Dad will want some time alone with my mother. I have a feeling there's a lot more to this story, and you know what it is." After kissing Maggie soundly, Lauren took her hand and held it to her heart. "Do you feel my heart beating? It beats for you. You are my heart and soul, Maggie. Whatever is going on, we're in it together."

"I'll tell you everything, but first, let me make two quick calls." Her eyes searched those of her lover. "You may not like me much when I'm done. Are you ready for that?"

"Trust in me, Maggie."

"I do. Please trust in me too." Maggie picked up the phone and dialed the familiar number. "Hi, it's me. I got a call a little while ago. They know where we are and promised to get even. ... No, I didn't call Keith yet. I wanted to talk to you first. ... Yes. Okay, I'll wait for your call. Bye."

"Who did you call, Maggie?"

"My father."

"Your father? Just because you've never mentioned him isn't a reason to think that you don't have a father? Is he somehow involved in all of this?" Lauren was looking at Maggie realizing she really knew nothing about her. *Will what I feel for her be enough?*

105

"Where do I start?" Maggie's mind flashed over the last fifteen years, wanting to explain but not knowing how. "I'm thirty- five years old. Did you know that?"

"No, I didn't. Maggie, just start from the beginning and go from there. I promise not to interrupt you unless you ask me to. Is that fair?" She could see the turmoil in Maggie and wanted so much to just take her in her arms and tell her it didn't matter but she knew it did.

Maggie sucked in a deep breath and began. "After I graduated from... No, that won't work. Okay, how about this ... my last name isn't Sullivan. To tell you what it is would put you in danger, so I won't do it. My father is the head of a government agency that, shall we say, works in the shadows. His people are located all over the world, combing the gutters for the scum of society. For six years, I did that sort of work too, until my cover was blown, I was captured, and savagely beaten. My father rescued me. After two years of plastic surgery, I was physically ready to work again." Maggie could see the horror in Lauren's face and questioned the wisdom of continuing. "Do you want to hear more?"

"Yes. I want to know everything, Maggie. Maybe then, I can help you exorcise your demons. Please go on."

"Okay. I use Preston, Moser, and Sullivan as a front so I can discreetly gather information."

"Then they're a part of this too?"

"No. They know nothing and they never can." The next part would be difficult for Lauren to hear. *I hope she'll understand.* "About five years ago, your mother contacted the agency about the mayor's scheme. It was evident to her that he was planning something illegal. We've been watching, and the building project proved to be our foot in the door. Your mother put her career, and her life, on the line to help nail Westerly." Maggie could see the wheels turning in Lauren's mind. *Please, don't go there, love.*

"My mother knew who you were?"

"Yes and no. She knew someone would be here, but she didn't know who until we actually met." Maggie watched as thoughts warred in Lauren's head.

What a fool I've been. I don't know anything about her, and I just fell into her trap. God, what an idiot I am.

"Lauren, why don't you just ask me and be done with it."

"I don't know what you're talking about." She looked over to Maggie who was raising an eyebrow. "Okay, I will. Did you happen upon my cabin by accident, or was it arranged...a way of getting in touch with my mother? I must have been a good laugh for you and your cronies. Did you tell them everything? Do you have any idea how humiliated I feel right now? Do you even care?" She was trembling and tears began rolling down her cheeks. In an instant, Maggie was by her side, holding her face, wiping away the tears.

"Lauren, I want you to listen to me." The fair head nodded. "I had no idea about you or your cabin. Yes, I knew there was a daughter, but I thought she lived out of the area. Our meeting was fated. We were destined to meet don't you see that? Think of it. One different turn of the paddle and I could have sailed by your cabin. I thank God every day that I almost drowned and that it was you that found me. Please don't doubt me. Please."

"That isn't good enough. What do I know about you? You told me that you've operated in the shadows, so how do I know you aren't you doing that now?" Tears were flowing freely. "I trusted you, and it was all a ruse to get to my mother."

"That simply isn't true. I have always been honest with you; why would I change now? Can't you trust your love for me…our love?"

Lauren looked directly into Maggie's eyes and thought she saw the truth. *But how can I trust that?* "Maggie, I am so afraid that it was a setup and you were just stringing me along. Can't you see it from my point of view? I don't know what to think." She swung her feet off the bed and stood up. "I can't think about this now. I need to go see my mother."

Maggie caught Lauren's arm. "Don't think. Listen to your heart."

Lauren wrenched her arm away and made her way to a chair and sat down before putting her elbows on her knew and placing both her hands over her face. "I don't know what to believe. Not long ago I was settling in for a quiet two weeks and then you came into my life and everything changed. My mother is fighting for her life and the woman I'm falling in love with and I thought I knew is a stranger to me."

Maggie was off the bed and crouching next to Lauren. She placed her hand on her lover's leg only to have it batted away. "Lauren, please listen to me. I don't want there to be any secrets between us that's why I told you about my past. I was beaten and left for dead and it took a long time for me to heal both physically and mentally. I was on that river because I wanted to prove to myself that I still had what it takes to be an operative. Sure, I saw the warnings but they didn't matter I had to overcome my fear.

"The best thing in my life happened when I saw you for the first time. I had no idea who you were. I only knew I wanted to get to know you. Please believe that, baby."

"My heart wants to believe you but my head is screaming at me to run." Lauren lifted her face out of her hands. "I've never know anyone like you, Maggie. You make me feel special and alive. I want to trust you but right now, I can't."

Maggie ran a hand across her face. "Okay. I'm not going any…"

Without warning, the plate glass window shattered and a bullet buzzed past their heads. In one fluid motion, Maggie pulled Lauren to the floor before covering the woman with her body. "Shit! Stay down. Think you can low crawl to the bathroom and close the doors? I'm going to try and reach the phone."

"I'm not going without you."

Maggie rolled off Lauren. "You need to get into the bathroom and close the door."

BANG! Another bullet shot over their heads.

"Are you hit?"

"No, I'm fine. Come with me. There's a phone in the bathroom," Lauren said.

"Yes. Good thinking." Crawling into the bathroom, they slammed the door shut. "Lauren, get in the tub and stay down."

"What about you? We're in this together."

"I'll be right with you, as soon as I get the phone." Maggie pulled a robe from the hook on the door, she gave it to Lauren who was shivering. "Put this on."

Once Lauren was safely in the tub, Maggie grabbed another robe and found the phone. "Damn, it's only a house phone. Shit." Pressing the front desk number, she heard a voice say, "Front desk. May I help you?"

"We have someone shooting at us here. We need help *now*!"

"The police are on their way, ma'am"

Who called them? Something strange is going on.

A loud banging on the door startled them.

"Are you okay in there? This is the police."

Maggie put her finger to her lips, motioning Lauren to get down. She quietly crept out to the door. "How do we know you're the police? You got here pretty fast."

"Ma'am, is anyone injured?"

"No. We're fine."

Jeb Maxwell's voice sounded through the door. "Lori, it's safe to come out now."

Maggie stood up and cautiously opened the door. As the room swarmed with police, she returned to the bathtub, helped Lauren out, and held her close. "I will keep you safe, Lauren. I promise you that." *Damn. Just how am I going to keep that promise?*

The police officer introduced himself as Officer Owens and asked both women their names.

Lauren introduced herself. "My name is Lauren Walker."

The officer excused himself before he made his way woman in plain clothes and spoke to her.

After several moments, the woman came over to them. "Hello, ladies, I'm Marissa Blackstone, the detective in charge. Dr. Walker, I would like to speak with you."

"You can speak in front of Maggie. I have nothing to hide from her."

"I didn't think you did. I just wanted to get independent reports about what happened here. Sometimes each party has a different ... description of what occurred."

Maggie was furious at the woman's insinuation. "What are you after, Ms. Blackstone? Do you suspect we've done something to precipitate this?"

"Settle down, Ms. ...?"

"Sullivan. The name is Margaret Sullivan."

"Okay, Ms. Sullivan. I'm aware of the circumstances surrounding the shooting of Dr. Walker's mother, and I'm wondering if there's a connection here."

"You're the investigator; you tell us. Just how did you get here so fast?"

The detective checked her notebook, answered. "Someone named Preston in room one thirty-five called us and said there was a problem in the room across from his."

"Keith? Something is wrong. He should be here." Maggie didn't wait. She was out the door and across the hall before anyone could stop her. Keith's door was ajar and she pushed it open. Keith was lying on the floor, the phone still in his hand and blood pooling beneath him. "Oh, Keith...no ... no."

Detective Blackstone grabbed Maggie's arm. "Don't go in there. Let me do my job."

Lauren tried to look around the woman to see if could assess the man's condition. "Detective, do you want me to take care of him until the paramedics get up here?"

"I'll let you know." Detective Blackstone proceeded to the body while the two women waited at the door.

"Were you close to him, Maggie?" Lauren asked sympathetically.

"He's been with my dad for years. He was guarding us, keeping us from harm. What the hell is happening, Lauren? It's like everything went to hell in a handbag over night."

When Blackstone returned, Lauren asked, "Need me to look him over?"

"Don't think so. He's dead."

∞

The storm had passed, but its ravages remained.

Maggie watched while someone covered Keith's body. *I really have fucked everything up. Keith is dead and it's my fault.* If she hadn't gotten involved with the Warwick mess, everyone would be safe now. *Why did I call dad and asked for his help?*

The two woman along with the detective in charge of the investigation stood in the hallway as the forensics squad went through their room.

Maggie snarled while Detective Blackstone questioned Lauren. The detective's tone and body language was borderline flirtatious. That was in sharp contrast to the question that edged with innuendo and accusation that she received. It was obvious to Maggie that the woman was confident in her attractiveness. Light brown hair that was in a ponytail and slipped through a baseball cap. She wore khakis, a blue shirt, and a black wool jacket with the bulge of her gun evident. Maggie had seen the arrogant and far too curious for her own good her type before. She knew it would be best to play things close to the vest, to choose her phrases very carefully. She had to find a way to ask what she needed to know without raising suspicions. *Best to just ask, get it over with, and see where it leads.* "Was it a professional hit?"

Detective Blackstone took a long hard look at Maggie. "No, I don't think so. They usually aim for the head. This was to the midsection. Why do you ask?"

Maggie lowered her head so the detective couldn't see her eyes. "I was just wondering."

The detective felt herself bristle at the woman's questions. *Just who does she think she is?* "Something tells me there's more to this story and I want to know what it is. Now you can either cooperate with me, or we can do this the hard way. It's your choice, Ms Sullivan."

Lauren watched the Detective Blackstone face off against her lover. She was confident that Maggie did not intend to answer the question. Lauren sensed that their exchange might become heated and there was a need to defuse things before the officer began asking questions neither of them wanted to answer. She inserted herself between the two women. "Detective Blackstone ... may I call you Marisa?"

"No. It wouldn't be appropriate."

"Okay then, Detective, Maggie has lost her good friend Keith and is rather upset. Considering what happened to my mother, I think her question was warranted, don't you?"

"Frankly, I don't see any reason to ask such a question unless there is some motivation behind it." Marisa's eyes narrowed as she watched both women for any indication they were withholding information. "I think you two are hiding something and I intend to get to the bottom of it."

"Listen to me, *Marisa*." Maggie moved closer to the detective. "I don't really care *what* you think. You do realize *we* were the ones shot at. My friend is dead and…"

They all turned in response to the sound of someone shouting. A uniformed officer was pulling a disheveled, agitated man along with him. He was dressed in faded jeans, a t-shirt, a green windbreaker, and shoes covered in mud.

"Get your hands off of me. You don't have any right to do this to me, asshole. Who the fuck died and left you boss?"

Detective Blackstone herded the two women into the room to remove them from a potentially violent situation.

The patrol officer had the cuffed prisoner firmly under control as they entered the room. "Detective Blackstone, look what we found hiding outside in the bushes with this in his pocket." He held up a plastic bag that contained what looked like a forty-four magnum.

The detainee shot daggers at Lauren and Maggie and then turned on the detective. "Are you the one in charge? I demand to know why this oaf dragged me in here. I haven't done anything wrong. I have rights, you know."

The detective's voice was calm, reassuring. "Just settle down, sir, while I get to the bottom of this. First, I need your name."

"Richard? Is that you?" Lauren asked with disbelief.

"You know this man?" Blackstone asked.

"Yes. Richard Eberly. He's an associate of mine in the research lab. What on earth are you doing here, Richard?"

"I'm in charge here, Ms. Walker. I think you should let me question him," the detective said.

"You're a sharp woman, Marisa. Why don't you hold off for a minute I bet he'll talk to her. Let's see what he has to say."

Richard ended their face off by taking a step toward his colleague. "Lauren, are you okay? I came here to be with you … to tell you how I feel about you. No one in Warwick would tell me where to find you. I had to sit in that damn café for days, hoping you would pass by. Lucky for me, your mother was shot and there you were." The man was sweating profusely and the gibberish he was spouting became louder with his rising passion. "Do you have any idea how I felt when I saw you hug that woman before you got into the helicopter? I was disgusted, Lauren."

Blackstone knew that as much as she would like to let him continue babbling, she did not want to risk the case against him by not reading him his rights. "Sir, I suggest you stop talking. It is my duty to inform you that anything you say can be used as evidence against you in a court of law."

"Go ahead, bitch, use whatever you want and see if I care. Don't you be telling me what I can and cannot do. Do you have any idea what it's like to see the woman you love become a pervert?"

Lauren's voice remained steady. "Richard, why didn't you tell me?"

Richard's hands clenched tight while he shuffled back and forth. "Why? What was I supposed to do? Run after the helicopter. But I did come to the hospital and I watched you in the waiting room. I saw you collapse in that woman's arms and then later, you hugged and kissed her. That made me so sick to my stomach that I had to throw up." He shook his head.

Lauren held her ground as he moved closer to her.

"How could you do that, Lauren? I don't know what that bitch did to you, but that's not who you are. I've worked with you long enough to know that. Doesn't my love mean anything to you?"

Maggie watched in fascination as Detective Blackstone furiously took notes. Richard reeked of cologne, whiskey, and sex. His glazed eyes greedily fixed on Lauren.

Anger and pity warred within Lauren. Pity won. "Richard, you never told me that you loved me. Let's go sit down." She took his hand, led him to a chair, and motioned for him to sit down. "Why are you here?"

"I came to Warrick to tell you how I feel about you. After what I saw, I came here to save you from that *dyke*. She's brainwashed you. I called here and warned this *dyke* that she would pay for what she was doing to you. I need to rescue you from her perversion. I even seduced the night clerk so I could get a duplicate key to your room, but that asshole across the hall got in my way. He tried to manhandle me until I showed him my gun." Richard began laughing the shrill laugh of the unhinged. "Big tough guy. Ha. I showed him all right. You should have seen his face when I shot him."

Lauren maintained her calm even though her heart was pounding. "Then what happened? Did you shoot into this room, Richard?"

He stood and took a few steps toward the shattered window. "I had to get out of the hotel in case someone had heard the shot across the hall. You should close your curtains completely, Lauren, especially if you are going to be doing disgusting things. When I saw the two of you naked I knew what was coming … it was more than I could take. That

116

bitch needed to be killed so I could save you from her." Richard stood. "After the window broke, I came in and shot again, but by that time she had dragged you into the bathroom. It was clear she was holding you against your will. I was about to kick open the bathroom door when the damn police showed up with all their stupid sirens blaring, so I had to hide outside until I had another chance to save you. This idiot grabbed me and brought me in here. I'm glad because now they can be witnesses to what she has done to you."

At that moment, the deranged man lunged at Maggie. Although handcuffed, he grabbed her around the neck. "It's time for you to die, bitch."

"Richard, no!" Lauren tried to pry his hands away.

"You need to be saved, Lauren, and I'm the one to do that. I love you." His voice cracked with emotion and he squeezed harder.

Detective Blackstone hit Richard with a taser gun and he immediately released his hold on the woman's neck.

Maggie fell to the carpet, holding her throat and gasping for air.

In doctor mode, Lauren knelt on the floor next to Maggie. "Move your hands and let me check your neck." Gently, she palpated the affected area. "Try to slow your breathing." She nodded with approval as Maggie took slower, deeper breaths. "I think you'll be okay."

"What kind of idiot handcuffs a man in the front?"

The detective glared at the officer that captured Richard.

Maggie looked directly at Lauren. "You never told me you had a jealous lover."

Lauren dropped to the floor with choked laughter. "You can joke at a time like this? I think he must have cut off the oxygen long enough for brain damage." She rested her forehead against Maggie's and gently kissed her, then whispered, "I'm sorry Keith had to die because of that idiot's infatuation with me."

Maggie blinked her eyes and smiled. "We aren't to blame."

Detective Blackwell cleared her throat. "Sorry I was so rough on you. I was only doing my job." She turned to the officer who waiting beside her. "Yes, what is it, Jenkins?" The man whispered something and she turned to the open doorway. There were two men there—Steven Walker, and another man she had never seen before.

Maggie didn't need to turn. She knew her father was near.

The detective sized up the newcomers. Walker oozed class and money and she knew he wasn't a man to mess with. The other man was clearly the more dangerous of the two. His whole demeanor bespoke power. He was a tall man who was about six two, with black wavy hair and chiseled good looks. Marisa was certain he was a formidable opponent.

"Mr. Walker, I'm Marisa Blackstone, the detective in charge. We have apprehended the man we believe is responsible." Her eyes focused on the other man. "And you are?"

"Patrick, Margaret's father."

"Well, Mr. Sullivan, this is a crime scene and I must ask you to leave." Deep blue eyes bored into her as the man reached in his pocket and produced a badge and ID. Seeing the insignia, she knew instantly that her assessment of power and danger was accurate. The man terrified her, but she wasn't going to allow him to know that. "That's all well and good, but this is my case and you need to leave."

Patrick lifted an eyebrow daring the detective to stop him before he walked to the two women on the floor. After kneeling down, he softly caressed Maggie's hair. "Are you okay, sweetheart?"

Maggie began to quiver as tears cascaded down her cheeks. Now that the cavalry had arrived, she no longer had to pretend to have nerves of steel.

Patrick scooped her up in his arms and carried her to the bed. He sat next to his daughter while he continued to soothe her with soft words.

"God, how did this get so out of control? I'm so sorry I couldn't keep Keith safe. Can you ever forgive me?"

"Darling, there is nothing to forgive. Keith was well acquainted with the dangers."

All eyes in the room were riveted on the display of affection.

Detective Blackwell marveled at seeing a man with such power showing such tenderness.

Lauren was intrigued by the man sitting next to her lover. She could see where Maggie got some of her beauty and wondered what her mother looked like. Lauren felt an arm go around her shoulders.

"How are you, honey?"

"Oh, Daddy." Lauren turned into her father's arms and her emotions overflowed in a wave of sobs.

"I saw your mother and she wants to see you."

Lauren tried to smile. "That's great news, Daddy. Maybe if we'd gone to see her when you called us, this wouldn't have happened. I never knew Richard loved me, certainly not that he was capable of murder." Lauren worried about Maggie. *I wonder if she blames me for Keith's death. Oh, Maggie, please, please don't hate me.*

Maggie's heart broke at the sight of Lauren's tears. She held out her hand. "Lauren, please come over here and meet my father."

Taking her father's hand, Lauren made her way over to the bed with her focus completely on Maggie. To know they were both safe, she needed to touch her. Richard could have killed Maggie and that would have destroyed her. "Hey, beautiful, I'm worried about you. Those are some nasty bruises on your neck." She touched them gently; the need to connect was overwhelming. "How does your throat feel now?"

Maggie placed her hand over Lauren's and smiled weakly. "It's a little sore, that's all. Lauren, this is my father. Dad, this is Lauren Walker and her father Steve."

The foreboding man turned to them, softened, and then offered his hand first to Steve, then Lauren. His voice was soft as he said, "I'm glad to meet you. My daughter speaks highly of you both."

After several minutes of exchanging pleasantries, Patrick went into take charge mode. "I'll find another room for you two so you can get showers and put on clean clothes. I assume you want to go to the hospital to see your mother, Lauren."

"Yes. I'd like to go over right now if it's okay with you, Maggie."

Maggie nodded.

Steven Walker cleared his throat to get their attention. "I'll clear things with the detective while you do that. You two ladies pack up whatever you have. By the time you're finished, we should be ready to move you into another room." Steven was sure the detective would see things his way...most people could be convinced, one way, or another. He turned to shake hands with Maggie's father. "Patrick, I'll meet you in the lobby later and we can discuss further plans."

Lauren and Maggie shared a quizzical look before collecting their belongings.

∞

It was only one block to the hospital and Lauren and Maggie chose to walk the short distance. At the insistence of Maggie's father, a stretch limo shadowed their movements.

"Is that really necessary?' Lauren asked.

"Until we find out if there is a hit out on us, yes it is."

"Maggie?"

"Yes."

"What happened earlier...I mean when Richard was shooting at us."

"I remember."

"I want you to know it made me realize just how important you are to me. I understand that there are certain aspects to your past that I might find unsettling but I don't want to lose you or what we have."

Maggie stopped. When she saw Lauren turn around, she opened her arms.

Lauren was in Maggie's arms instantly. "I was so scared."

"I was too, babe. I promise you I will do everything possible to keep you safe. And when we are sure your mom is out of danger, I will tell you everything about my past." She squeezed Lauren closer. "That is a promise."

Lauren lingered in Maggie's arms comforted by the love she felt from Maggie.

"Let's go see how she's doing and then find something to eat."

"Sounds good to me." Lauren grabbed Maggie's hand and they continued to the hospital.

∞

As they entered the hospital, Naomi, the pretty nurse from the night before, greeted Maggie. "You're looking much better today. Is there anything I can do for you?" She gave Maggie her most fetching smile and then a wink.

Lauren looked at the nurse with mild amusement. *Wonder what this is all about? I'll just play along and see what happens.*

Maggie managed a nervous smile. "Ah, ah…yes, I do clean up pretty good." Maggie put her arm around her shoulders. "Nice to see you again. We need to go now."

Smiling, the nurse said, "Dr. Walker, you have the most wonderful sister," before walking away.

"Sister? You told her I was your *sister*!" Lauren headed for the stairs seemingly to contain her anger.

"Lauren…Lori? Wait, you don't understand. Please wait." Maggie was practically running after her lover, only to have the door to the stairwell slam in her face. Undeterred, she hurried after Lauren. "Will you please wait for me? Come on. You have it all wrong. I never said that."

Lauren stopped and turned. "I can't believe you. How many nurses have you seduced since last night?" To Lauren the look on Maggie's face was priceless. It was a mixture of total disbelief and someone caught with their hand in the cookie jar.

"I...I can explain if you will just calm down and let me talk with you. I don't know her at all. I never told Naomi that I was your sister, I said ..."

Lauren wanted Maggie to squirm some more, all the while finding it difficult to control her amusement. "You don't know her, but you know her name?"

"Don't you remember ... I told you last night that the only way I got in here was to say I'm family? Baby, I don't want anyone but you. You are my sun and moon and stars and ... and my life." *God, how corny I sound.*

"Yeah, right, that's exactly how it appears to me. Did you give her your number and tell her to meet up with you later?" It was getting harder and harder for Lauren to keep it together.

Maggie's face fell and tears began to well in her eyes. "Lauren, you're the only one I want. Only you. Why can't you believe that? I haven't betrayed you. I would never do that. Please believe me."

Lauren moved closer, took Maggie's beautiful face in her hands, and gently kissed the tears away.

Maggie had not been expecting the tenderness, and her forehead creased into a questioning look.

Unable to contain herself any longer, Lauren chuckled. "If you could have seen the look on your face when she said the word *sister*... I thought you would never close your mouth." She sobered quickly. "I'm so sorry, I didn't mean to make you cry. I was playing with you."

"Playing? You were playing with me. I'll show you playing, baby." With her arms encircling Lauren's waist, Maggie pulled her extremely close then moved in on her lips, scarcely touching them. Every time Lauren tried to capture a kiss, Maggie would move just enough to be out of reach. "How do you like it, baby, hmmm?"

"Please, just kiss me."

"All in good time, love, all in good time." Her lips kept tantalizing until they finally softly touched Lauren's eagerly waiting lips.

After placing her right leg on the stair above, Maggie gently lifted Lauren to straddle on her thigh. Slowly she began to move back and forth, as she greedily kissed the luscious mouth. Boldly her tongue explored, reveling in the anticipation of what was to come.

Lauren's fingers tangled in her lover's dark hair and pulled her closer. Her hips began to grind against Maggie's thigh as she moved in time with the gyrating leg. Her moans were becoming deeper, more insistent.

A door slammed many floors above, followed by the sound of footsteps descending the stairs. Lauren shivered with desire as she whispered huskily, "Someone's coming."

"The only person I care about coming is you." Maggie captured Lauren's lips as her leg sped up its motion.

Lauren wanted and needed release—she couldn't stop. As the steps grew louder, Maggie increased the tempo. Soon her breathing became ragged as she pressed Lauren's center harder, sending her into the momentary oblivion of fulfillment. The louder the steps, the more passion until suddenly the sound stopped.

They heard the stepping sound increase before someone say *excuse me* as they went by them.

The two lovers were so lost in each other that they were oblivious to their surroundings. As Lauren erupted in wave after wave of satisfaction, she buried her head against Maggie's shoulder. She screamed in pleasure and fulfillment, and then began to kiss her lover feverishly. Deeper and deeper the kisses became until Lauren once again felt her body shudder in bliss.

She unbuttoned Maggie's jeans and lowered the zipper half way. Lauren's fingers slid slowly downwards. The nimble digits stroked the saturated center, applying alternately hard and gentle pressure, bringing Maggie to the brink only to back off at the last possible moment.

Maggie's legs were beginning to quiver. She didn't know how much longer she could hold Lauren there. "Oh, God, baby, please, I need to come. I need you now."

"Mmm … then you'll have me now." Lauren's fingers plunged deep inside as she felt the spasms begin to intensify.

Just as Maggie thought she could go no higher, Lauren began to massage her clit until all the nerve endings were on fire, wanting and needing release. And release they did, repeatedly, in an extended flow of passion. Maggie slowly lowered her beautiful lover to the step and they held each other, lost in the expression of their love. Small after tremors shot through their bodies as they whispered declarations of love. Ever so gradually, their heart rates and breathing began to return to normal. They adjusted their clothing, gazed into each other's eyes, and smiled their complete surrender.

"Guess we had better find our fathers and check on your mother. Think they're wondering what happened to us?"

Lauren couldn't help teasing. "They probably think we're off somewhere making love." She grinned. "And they'd be right."

Maggie laughed and pulled Lauren closer. "You, are the only one for me. Now and forever." She sealed her vow with a lingering kiss. "Let's go, before we're here all day." She winked at her lover as she took her hand and led her down the stairs to the door.

Chapter Nine

As days passed, Lauren and her father took turns keeping constant watched over Victoria. The many long hours of sitting by the bedside afforded Lauren the opportunity to reflect on the previous fifteen or so years, when the two of them had been at odds. *It's strange how I was barely civil to her, then this occurred and I realize how much I love her. I can't imagine ever being cold or harsh to her again.*

Her father had gone to get them coffee and Lauren stood looking through the glass window at her mother who, despite all she'd been through, was still stunningly beautiful. Hook ups from all modern technology had to offer monitored her vital functions. The doctors had brought her back from the drug induced coma, and she was becoming more aware of her surroundings. Doctor Green beckoned Lauren into the room. Butterflies danced in her stomach as she entered the ICU unit and sat down by her mother's side.

"Hey there, sleepyhead, how are you feeling?"

Victoria's face lit up in a bright smile. "Hi, pumpkin. It's good to see you. You look tired. Are you okay?"

Lauren's heart did a somersault when she heard the long retired pet name. "I'm fine, but you're right, I am tired." Too weary to do much more, she managed a small smile. "Dad should be back in a few minutes. He just went down to the nurse's station for coffee."

Her mother raised a trembling hand to Lauren's head and gently guided it down to her shoulder and began speaking the words she had used when her daughter was young. "Rest, I will be here watching over you." Then she stroked the brown hair as she had done so many years earlier when the child Lauren was nestled in her arms.

Mother and daughter locked in a moment neither would forget. Lauren closed her eyes breathed in, beyond the hospital smells, to that essence which was undeniably her mother. So overwhelmed by the deep feelings reemerging for her mother, Lauren began to cry.

"Why the tears, Lori?"

Her emotions spilled forth. "I love you so much. I'm so sorry for all those lost years."

Victoria continued to lovingly stroking Lori's hair. "We both have regrets. Shall we let them go and begin again?"

"I'd like that." Then Lauren closed her eyes and fell into a light sleep, safe in her mother's arms.

∞

Maggie and her father were having a quiet lunch in a small diner near the hospital.

"Dad, is the danger over now?"

His eyes looked off in the distance lost for a moment in a memory. "I have taken care of the mayor's associates."

Over the past few days, she had observed Steven Walker and her father huddled in intense conversations. "You've stayed here far too long. There's something else going on, isn't there?"

Patrick studied his daughter, gauging her possible reaction to his latest news. "Lester has resurfaced."

Maggie went still as a shot of fear went up her spine. "He thinks I'm dead, doesn't he?" She already knew the answer from the look on her father's face.

"We had a rogue agent, and before we could neutralize him, he told Lester you were still alive."

"I see." Her thoughts went immediately to Lauren and keeping her safe.

"He doesn't know your new identity or look, and he never will. I'm the only one that knows that."

Maggie's thoughts went to her mother and sisters, and how over the last several years the only contact they'd had was through secure phone connections. *Now what will happen?* "You know, when I first came here, I went down the river in a canoe without any preparation. I was trying to see if I still had what it takes to be in the field." Her eyes took on a distant look. "I almost drowned, but the survival instincts were still intact so I made it to the shore." A smile flitted over her lips. "That's where I first saw Lauren." Her voice was soft, reflective. "She's very special to me and I will never give her up. I am in love with her so please don't ask that of me."

Patrick's heart went out to his daughter. She had always been his favorite, a fighter, and a rebel filled with a passion for everything she did. At one time, her skills honed to perfection, making her his best operative. Ever since Lester's men had tried to beat the life out of her, her edge was gone. Patrick knew it, and so did Maggie. He had tried to keep her active, but the days of her usefulness were at an end. "I think it's time for you to settle down in one place. What would you think about a town like Warwick?"

Maggie smiled wryly. "I like Warwick very much. In fact, I was thinking the same thing. I am so tired of the deceit. I want my life back."

Now for the hard part. "Sweetheart, you know you must always be Margaret Sullivan. That's your life now. Otherwise, you and everyone you love will be in danger." Seeing the crestfallen look, he added, "You know that, don't you?"

She knew it, had always known it would come to that, but now that the time had come, it seemed so final. "Yes. I was hoping there would be a way for me to go back, but I know there isn't."

"Maybe this will help some." He handed her a packet of photos.

"What's this?" She pulled the pictures out of the package and began to look at them. One by one, she flipped through them, vaguely recognizing the venue but unable to place it. "I've seen this property before, but I can't quite recall where. Care to enlighten me?"

"It's located just north of Warwick on about ten acres."

"The Shelby place," she said, finally recognizing the house in the photos.

"Yes. At one time people called it *Gyrfalcon*? Rather appropriate, don't you think? You now own it? The view is three hundred and sixty degrees, so you'll have spectacular sunrises and sunsets. There are external and internal alarm systems, and I have arranged for additional protection."

To Maggie, there was no other word for the property but stunning. She flipped through the pictures again, impressed by the awesome home, and grounds. "For me? Why? I don't want to be a prisoner."

"Simple. I want to continue to keep you safe. It's obvious to me that you and Lauren are on the road to some sort of commitment. When I found out that the property was once called by your code name, I knew it was the right place for you." His eyes held hers captive. "I don't know what I would do if something happened to you, sweetheart. Someone in my position shouldn't have an Achilles heel, but you're mine. You always have been."

Maggie had never seen her father so vulnerable. *Maybe it's time for him to step down too.* "Any chance we could be a normal family and just all settle down together?"

His smile was fond. "My life has taken too many twists and turns of his life for that to happen. Let's get back to the hospital. I need to say my goodbyes before I leave tonight.

∞

Later that evening at a local restaurant, Maggie saw the far off look in her companion's eyes. "Lauren?"

"Hmm?"

"What are you thinking about?"

"Are you sure you want to know?"

"That bad, huh?" Maggie winked. "Yes. I want to know."

"I was wondering what size diamond you're going to buy me." A smirk crossed Lauren's face. "I already know the one I'm giving you."

Maggie's heart was filled with a warm fuzzy *I am home* feeling. "You want a diamond, do you? Then I'll design one just for you. Will you tell me about the one you have for me?"

"You'll see it later. Do you have any idea how much I love you? More than I ever thought possible." Lauren's heart was also filled with the same warm fuzzy *I am home* feeling.

"I have something to show you." Maggie placed the packet of pictures on the table and shoved them in Lauren's direction.

Her forehead creasing, she picked them up. "It's the Shelby place. I've always loved that place; it's so beautiful up there. Why do you have these?"

Smiling, Maggie picked up the picture showing the view from the house. "There is a bird called the Gyrfalcon. It is the biggest and most magnificent of all falcons. In medieval times, the aristocracy prized the bird for their hunting prowess. When first developed the land fifty years ago the owner saw a rare occurrence when a Gyrfalcon landed on his house. He took that as a sign and named his property after the bird."

Lauren's curiosity was piqued. "I never knew it by anything other than the Shelby place. What does this have to do with us?"

"If you like … it will be our new home." Maggie held her breath.

A smile of utter delight came over Lauren's face. "Really, do you mean it? Oh, Maggie, this is fabulous. I love that house!" Without thinking, she bent in Maggie's direction and gave her a hug followed by a passionate kiss.

For a moment, the entire restaurant was quiet, as the other patrons stared with their mouths agape. Finally, one man coughed loudly to get their attention. Lauren looked up, saw everyone staring, and her face instantly flushed a bright red. She returned to an upright position and looked at her plate. Then, remembering her words to her mother, she looked up and smiled brightly at everyone in the room. *This is my love, and I'm proud of her, of us.*

Amused by the incident, Maggie smiled. "I'm proud of you, Lauren. It won't get any easier, but the first time is always the hardest. I love you, and if I thought these people were worth it, I'd give them another show." She chuckled before she took her lover's hand and gently kissed it.

They continued to eat and talk about the house, making plans for decorating and moving in. After a few moments of eating in silence, Lauren set down her fork and stared at her lover. "Maggie, if I wanted to find my sister, how would I go about it? We don't know where she is or anything about her."

"Love, remember when we were having that discussion about my past?"

Lauren nodded.

"Unfortunately, circumstances prevented me from telling you everything. I, or rather my father, has already found your sister. I have a file on her, if you want to look at it."

"You do? Yes, I want to see it and know everything. Do you remember any of what you read?"

"She is the head of a small but influential, pharmaceutical company in Houston. There is a picture in the file. She is tall and very beautiful, with long black hair and blue eyes. She reminds me of your mother. I'll let you read the rest. It's rather interesting the turn her life has taken."

Lauren smiled softly. *A sister... How wonderful.*

Chapter Ten

Going into the convalescent's room, Dr. Green nodded at Steven and Lauren and then smiled at his patient. "How are you feeling, Vicky?"

Vicky liked this doctor. Throughout her period of convalescence, he had been straightforward, never mincing words about her prognosis. "Tired and sore would about sum it up, Phil."

"That's to be expected." He inspected the incision sites and then looked at her chart. "I am concerned with the output of your kidneys, Vicky. Your blood pressure is high, and tests indicate problems. I'm going to order medication that will help, but I want you to know there is a good possibility of renal failure." The look on his face underscored how serious that could be.

Steven taken back by the frankness of the discussion, asked, "What caused this, Doctor?"

"Could be a number of things related to the loss of blood followed by the surgery. She is lucky to be alive. Why don't we see what happens in the next twenty-four hours. She is still putting out some fluids, which is encouraging, but there is a strong possibility that won't last much longer. We need to prepare for what might come."

"If she needs a transplant I would like to be tested as a donor." All eyes turned to Lauren.

"I can arrange that. If it comes to that, we will have to move your mother to another hospital. They don't do living transplants here."

There was no hesitation whatsoever for Lauren. Her mother was in need of a kidney and she was prepared to do whatever was necessary. "No problem," Lauren replied. "How soon can we start the testing?"

"I'll arrange it for later on today. You do know there's a possibility you won't be a match. Of course, with a blood relative, especially a child, the probability of matching is greatly increased. Check with me in thirty minutes for the times. Vicky, you take care. I'll be back this evening to see you before I leave for the night."

As the doctor left, Victoria and Steven made eye contact, conveying unspoken words.

"Lori, is Maggie still here? I would like to see her and thank her for all she has done." Vicky's eyes went once again to her husband and he nodded, answering the unspoken request.

"Why don't my two best girls have some time together, and I'll see if I can find Maggie." He smiled and kissed his wife before going out the door.

∞

Entering Victoria's room, Maggie heard the two Walkers laughing. "Is this a private party, or can anyone join?"

Lauren's eyes lit up as she walked over and gave Maggie a hug and kiss. "You, my dear, are always welcome. Mother and I were just reminiscing about the day I decided to sit out on the roof when I was four. Did your dad get off okay?"

"Yes, he did. Vicky, it's good to see you looking so well." She walked over to the bed and bent down to place a kiss on the woman's cheek.

"Thank you for everything. I understand your father was very helpful, as well. When you speak with him, will you convey my thanks?" The fatigue and strain were visible on her face, but she needed to talk with Maggie and Lauren and it had to be now. "There's something we need to talk about."

Lauren knew by the look on her mother's face that it was serious. She didn't know if either of them was up to such a talk. "Mom, why don't we do this later? You look like you could use a nap."

"No, it has to be now. Lori, I need you to help me understand."

Yep, this is serious. "Okay."

Victoria took a deep breath and exhaled slowly. "First, I want you both to know that I can't thank you enough for what you've done for me over these last few weeks. I regard Maggie as a kind and decent woman; I like her. That being said, I am not going to pretend that I understand why you two find it necessary to be lovers. Can't you just be friends? Don't you know what your lives are going to be like? Sex with another woman ... I just don't get it."

Lauren looked out the window while she gathered her thoughts. Her mother was a gifted jurist and she wouldn't ask any question to which she did not already know the answer. She had some other purpose, but Lauren didn't know what it could be. She finally spoke, all the while looking at Maggie. "Mom, it isn't about sex, it's about how I relate to Maggie. When I look at her, my heart fills with so much joy and happiness that sometimes I think it will explode. I have never felt so loved. With her, I can be me. No pretenses, no games, just me—Lori. I know that I can tell her my deepest, darkest thoughts, and she will understand and be accepting. She makes me feel totally loved and so safe. There is no place I would rather be than by her side. She takes my breath away. It is corny to say but she completes me. I've

136

spent all my life chasing after something. Almost from the moment I saw her, I knew my search was over. Yes, we have sex—and I had no idea making love could be so all consuming and fulfilling—but that is only a part of the whole." She looked lovingly towards Maggie.

"Do I know what our life together will be like? Probably not completely; but when it comes right down to it, I don't care what others think or say. Knowing what I do now, I could not live my life without her. The love I feel for her is my passion and always will be." She walked over to Maggie and placed her hand over her lover's heart. "This heart beats for me."

For Maggie, there was no one else in the room, only Lauren. After placing her hand over Lauren's, she smiled. "Yes, it beats for you and you alone." She lifted the hand to her lips and gently kissed the fingers. "Lauren, I was lost and searching. You saved me from a life of aimless wandering. When I was being pulled under by the current and had to make the decision to fight it or just let it take me, from somewhere in the universe your heart and soul spoke to my mind and said, "I am so close; fight for me." And I did. Will you come and live with me, and be my partner throughout this life and whatever lies beyond?"

Tears of joy streamed down Lauren's cheeks as she held Maggie close. "Yes, my love, for all time and beyond."

Vicky knew what she suspected was true—they had an extraordinary love. "Thank you both for your honesty. I just needed to be certain" She wiped a tear from her eye. "This whole ordeal has made me reevaluate my life, and I would like to see if I can mend some old wounds. Lori and I have done that, but there is one other to whom I have done a great disservice, and I need your help in rectifying that." Her eyes searched each woman, hoping they would give her that chance.

Arm in arm, Lauren and Maggie looked at Vicky. "Anything."

"I want to find my other daughter. It seems so strange to say that aloud after all these years of speaking it only to myself. I want to try to make things right between us if that is at all possible. Will you help me?" Tears coursed down her cheeks. She needed to come to terms with the child she had abandoned forty-one years earlier. She knew it would be next to impossible to find her daughter but if there was any possibility, she needed to seize it. "I betrayed her, abandoned her, something that is not easily forgiven. But I want to try."

Maggie looked deep into Vicky's eyes and saw nothing but sincerity. "Consider it done." Maggie's mind drifted back to a previous conversation with one Harriet Aristides. *Damn I hope this time she is more receptive to my call. I think it will be a good move to speak with the uncle first. Maybe he can persuade her to hear me out. After dad gave me the information about Vicky's first daughter, I was just trying to feel her out about her feelings about her mother. Now that Lauren is in my life it is paramount that I succeed in reuniting them all.* She silently laughed. *I guess this time it would be a good move to leave my name.*

Lauren reached out for Maggie's hand. "We must somehow convince her to meet with mother."

"Convincing her might call for some fancy footwork, but you can work miracles so we are already a step ahead."

"Thank you, both." With that, Vicky closed her eyes and, as she fell into a deep healing sleep, her thoughts were full with the possibility of new beginnings with her daughter Harriet. She knew she was gravely ill, and if trying to reconcile with her firstborn were the last thing that she did in her life, it would be worth any heartache she might feel if Harriet rejected her attempts. And, it would be an additional blessing if Lauren connected with her sister, who was blameless in all this. There could be no better ending to her life.

Book Two

A Single Tear

Chapter One

The woman at the highly polished oak desk virtually threw the phone across the surface as she ended the call that had taken her completely off balance. A nameless person had the audacity to call her private home number, how they had achieved that would have her pondering the matter at length later, for now she was seething. Why would anyone think it a marvelous joke to inform her that she had a sister? Who cared if she had a sister anyway? *Certainly not me.* A mother who hadn't bothered with her for the best part of forty years was something she preferred to leave dead and buried. Except, even for one as focused as she, there could be no trap door that miraculously spirited away the fact that the woman existed. As she contemplated the unknown source of the information, she laughed cynically. *It has to be a hoax.* The supposed sister named Lauren was in fact a figment of someone's sick, fertile imagination. She had no doubt that it was all a ploy by an opposition that would stop at nothing to undermine her determination in steering her company toward new and exciting prospects that had recently appeared on the horizon. Her thoughts discarded the phone call completely as she began to travel down a path that would until the day she died be painful, how could it not be?

∞

They say that memory becomes softened, blurs over time. Harriet Aristides was sure that wasn't true and never would be. Five years later, her pain was as

143

acute as on that fateful day when twisted metal and broken bodies robbed her of her dreams, and her life.

In front of the small shelf in her living room, she glanced at the few souvenirs she allowed to remain, reminders of what had been. An overwhelming sadness once again gripped her heart as she gazed first at the family photos of her Uncle Harry, and then of Abby's parents and kid sister. *How can life be so cruel?* A small smile quivered around her lips as she looked at the picture of her uncle, who had welcomed her as his own. Her own parents were…what exactly? Explorers of the world—Don Quixote's in search of life's true meaning. All she knew was that the pregnancy and the burden of a child were unplanned and not welcome in their lives. Her punishment for being born was an unceremonious dumping into the lap of her namesake at six weeks of age while her mother and father disappeared to God knew where on a search for their inner selves, or whatever they called it back in the Sixties. Harriet never saw them again. She was better off without them, or so she told herself when birthdays and holidays rolled around. Truth was, it was easier to reject them than to accept the fact that she was not wanted. Her uncle had tried to convince her that her parents were not as black as she had painted them. When he finally told her that her father was dead and had died years ago, he had made things worse and not better. Her mother had apparently simply forgotten about her and married again, and, if her uncle was to be believed, had started another family. Had she abandoned the children of her second marriage—seemingly not. Abby's parents were also explorers, but of a different breed. As scientists working for Global Research Pharmaceuticals, the same as Harriet, they lived in the most remote areas of the world. Their explorations involved searching for cures for horrific diseases. *God, how I wish I had met them,* she thought as she lovingly ran a tapered finger across their photo.

The bittersweet memory of Abby bursting into her office and announcing she needed to contact her parents brought a tender smile to Harriet's face. The blonde dynamo, breezing confidently into the CEO's inner sanctum where only the brave or foolish ventured, had entered the wrong office. Harriet sat there, totally rocked by the presence of the young woman, and then did exactly what Abigail Martin had requested. In no time, personnel set about the task of locating David and Eden Martin. The staff thought it was an odd request, coming from Harriet Aristides, but no one ever questioned her orders.

Abby was never out of her life from that moment until her world shattered.

She stroked a gentle finger over the picture of the two of them smiling for the camera while attempting to shake the reminiscences from her mind. It was the best one ever taken of them together. They had been ecstatically happy that day—the day Abby announced that she was pregnant. There wasn't going to be any unwanted baby for them. They both wanted the glorious gift.

The next picture was of Abby flanked by Sam Parry, their baby's biological father, and his partner Jack Washington. Abby had been about six months pregnant at the time. It was difficult to tell who was happier—Abby, who looked radiant, or the men who simply adored the bubbly warm-hearted woman. She had captured their hearts too.

Harriet picked up the miniature porcelain dog, a West Highland Terrier with a grin on its face. Abby had given it to her on her birthday...the day before the accident. Abby announced confidently that when their baby was walking, they would have a Westie, and unlike them, their baby would have the luxury of growing up with a pet. Harriet laughed softly recalling the name they gave their future pet. Charlie.

All those dreams had been shattered the day Sam agreed to take Abby for a check-up two weeks before the due date. An emergency meeting concerning a looming crisis in Puerto Rico prevented Harriet from accompanying her to the appointment. At the time, the crisis was paramount, nothing else had been more important. *Nothing else was important.* The words haunted her. *Damn! How could I have been so preoccupied?*

The solemn woman put the delicate piece back on the shelf and walked away, trying to distance her mind from the memories. *God, time is flying by and I really don't care. The sooner my life ends, the better.*

The memories continued to flow unchecked...

Abby insisted that it was a routine check up and Harry should go to the meeting. After all, the baby wasn't due for two weeks and Sam could call her if there were a problem. The pregnancy for Abby had been a breeze.

"Why will this time be any different?" Abby reasoned.

Harriet pouted.

Abby handed her the brown briefcase and said, "Go, make money. We need it for the baby."

That was not strictly true. Harriet's uncle was reasonably well off and had organized a trust fund, which she hadn't touched. Besides, she was vice-president of new acquisitions and a rising star in the company. Their baby would want for nothing. The meeting had been both important and profitable. After she single handedly solved the problem in South America, the board ended the meeting by announcing she would be the new president of acquisitions. In addition, if she consented, she would take over the business in the not too distant future. *Oh yeah, I wanted it.* Everything was going so well. Abby was going to be so happy.

Harriet was conversing casually with a board member when her secretary Sally approached. She rested a warm hand on Harriet's arm and began guiding her away from the others into an adjoining empty office. Harriet glared at the woman. No one ever touched her, much less forced her to go anywhere. However, when she saw the red, swollen eyes and the distress in them, she allowed the contact.

Once they were out of earshot Sally spoke in a quivering voice. "Ms. Aristides, I have a message from a Mr. Washington."

"Talk to me, Sally. Is there a problem? Has something happened?" asked Harry, a feeling of dread washing through her. The woman burst into tears as Harriet gently sat her down in a chair in the empty office.

"I'm so very sorry, Ms. Aristides."

Harriet knelt down beside the distraught woman looking her straight in the eye. Everything seemed surreal as she went through motions that were foreign to her. "What's the problem?"

Sally gave her an anguished glance. How do you tell a person this kind of news? How? "It's Ms. Martin. She…she…" Sally broke into sobs and the tears flowed freely.

Harriet stood up, her body stiff, rigid as a board, unable to shake the sinking feeling inside. Her mind envisioned various scenarios. Is it the baby? Is something wrong with the baby? Did she lose the baby? "Abby? Sally, what about Abby? Is it the baby?" Harriet asked, her stomach somersaulting at the thought. We so wanted the baby, especially with today's news.

Sally gazed up at her boss with tear-drenched eyes. "Dead," she managed to say, still sobbing.

Harriet had learnt early in life to accept that life was unpredictable and could change in an instant. It was paramount to not let others see the effect the change caused or they would assume they had the upper hand. Drawing upon years of habit, she schooled her features although her emotions were churning. "What exactly did Jack Washington say, Sally?" Harriet asked forcibly. Her mind seemed unable to take in that it was Jack, not Sam, who had called.

Sally, physically shaken by her boss's glare, mumbled a few inaudible sentences.

"Tell me, Sally? For God's sake, who is dead? Is it the baby?"

This time her secretary responded coherently and clearly. "Yes, the baby is dead."

Harriet turned away. She'd known the answer before she asked. Then, she stood as rigid as a statue as the next, horrible words destroyed her life and her dreams for the future forever!

"There was an accident, a car accident. Abby, the baby and Sam are all dead."

Was that an echo? The words rang around the room, echoing in Harriet's head as she tried to digest their meaning. "Abby's dead?" Harriet whispered, her face ashen, her body unmoving.

"Yes. I'm so sorry, Harriet."

"Then I'm dead too."

The words dropped into the silent room like the tolling of a death knell.

Chapter Two

Harriet never shed a single tear for her lover, their unborn child or their friend. Inside, she'd died with Abby, who had left her alone and lost. Everything changed that day: her job, her life, and her reason for living. She existed—nothing more.

Five years later, she was still there, a shell going through the motions of life, the flame inside no longer burning. She concentrated full time on her profession, learning all aspects of the job, locally and globally. After three years of intense training, she had succeeded the retiring president. Success, though sweet, never eased the sadness and loneliness in her life. Only Abby could have done that, and she was gone.

With a shake of her head, Harriet picked up the list of attendees for the annual luncheon honoring the company's unsung heroes—the scientists who lived in precarious conditions to provide the research that would be the basis for making a fortune. Quickly scanning the names, she found only a few that she knew well. As she had expected, the names of David and Eden Martin were not on the list; she knew exactly where they were. Half of her wanted to meet them, however the other half of her was glad that they couldn't be there. *It would be too difficult to meet them, especially now.* Sighing, she put the paper in her briefcase and closed the flap. Right after the accident, she'd kept track of Abby's family, but over the years she'd simply lost herself in work. It was her way of combating the pain and loss she felt each day when she woke up alone.

Another day, another dull day. Harriet picked up her keys and briefcase and left the apartment behind, along with her memories.

∞

For seven years Sally Smith had worked with the boss she liked, as well as respected, benefiting from every promotion Harriet "Harry" Aristides received. Being personal assistant to the president of the company was difficult at times, but it was also rewarding. The money was wonderful, and Sally was certain her benefits package rivaled that of the most senior executives.

At one time, she wasn't sure she could handle the demonic workload her boss had taken on when personal tragedy had devastated her. Over time, she could see a glimmer of the old Harry coming out now and again; that quirky humor she had been famous for and the smile that could melt the hardest of hearts now appeared a little more frequently. A year ago, when her second in command, John Fredericks, celebrated the birth of his first child, the old Harry shone through. With a dazzling smile, she personally made the speech and raised the champagne glass to celebrate the event.

"Good morning, Harry. How are you today?" Sally smiled warmly.

Harriet towered almost six feet tall, with shoulder length black hair and an angular face that was a pleasure to see. Her pale blue eyes softened her features a little, giving them a comforting, rather than harsh appearance. Her usually stern demeanor lightened occasionally when she smiled. She was one of those people who never had a hair out of place and was impeccably dressed all of the time, which some found intimidating.

"I'm very well, thank you, Sally, and yourself?" Harriet collected the mail from her in tray.

"I'm great. It's going to be an interesting day, I think." Sally smiled as her boss spun around to stare at her curiously.

"Interesting…how?" Harriet asked directly.

"Because of all the scientists arriving en masse today. Haven't we around thirty showing up?" Sally chuckled at the perplexed expression on her boss's face.

"Yes. Do we have everything arranged?"

Sally wondered how the guests interacted with her boss, who wasn't exactly the most sociable host in town. *Of course, if past functions are any indication, Harry will rise to the occasion and pull it off without a hitch.* "All done, only need the guests."

"Excellent, you know I dislike surprises." Harriet turned her attention to the mail in her hand, noting an envelope from South America marked "Private". *Interesting.* She walked into her office and closed the door.

Sally considered the comment. *No, you certainly don't, do you? Not since*—her boss's partner had been a very special woman and their love for each other evident—*the anniversary of Abby's death is in three days. That means Harry's birthday is tomorrow.* Harry always took the anniversary day as a holiday. If she didn't have a single other holiday in the year, that one was the one she took without fail. *I wonder what she does on that day.*

The door to Harriet's office opened abruptly. "Find Seth Roland. Oh… and I need the best

152

synthetics expert we have on staff in my office in ten minutes." The door shut as quickly as it had opened.

∞

Seth Roland, senior project engineer for South America, rarely set foot in the executive office. He'd worked for the company for twenty years and was perfectly happy doing the type of work he did. If anyone needed staff allocated, area calculated, or equipment for special projects, Seth was the man. His boss, Tad Grayson, was an ambitious high flyer, something Seth was pleased to leave to him. Since Tad was in China, he suspected that was why he'd been summoned to Harry's office. *Well, I'll find out what they wanted me for soon enough.*

Entering the elevator, he smiled at a pretty blonde who couldn't be more than five foot three or four; she was such a tiny thing. He grinned at her as she looked at him quizzically, her finger hovering over the floor level panel.

"Top floor, please." When she didn't move to press any button, he glanced her way. *That floor is lit up already.* "I guess we're going to the same place."

Nichola Ralston had been astonished when her superior told her to report to the president's office and to go immediately. "Yes. I've never been there before, what about you?" she asked the man shyly.

Seth heard the nervous tone in the young woman's voice. She looked like a child on her way to the principal's office. "It's been a while. Where do you work?"

"I'm from the research lab. Never thought I'd be called up to the executive suites. It's rather extraordinary."

"I know what you mean. I've been there before, but it still feels strange." Seth cleared his throat, trying not to let his own nervousness show in his voice. "Who are you going to meet?" he asked casually.

"The president," Nichola announced. She choked back a nervous laugh at the surprised look on the man's face.

"So am I." Before they could discuss it further, the elevator stopped and the doors opened on the plush carpeted area, which housed the senior executives of the company.

∞

Sally saw the pensive looks on the two people entering Harriet Aristides' private conference room. Harry spent many hours of her day in this room and she insisted it feel comfortable. Usually the short and to the point meetings were held right in her office. If Harry was seeing them in the conference room, it meant the meeting was going to be longer than ten minutes. *This must be something big.* Sally smiled at them to set them at ease. "Hi, Seth, Ms. Ralston, Ms. Aristides will be along shortly. Please have a seat." She gestured toward the table. When they had complied, she asked, "Would either of you care for a drink while you're waiting?"

"Thanks. I'll have a coffee, black." Seth accepted gratefully. *At least it will keep my hands busy while I wait for whatever's about to happen.*

Sally nodded and turned to the young woman. *She looks petrified. Well, Harry does have a reputation when things don't go well, but who doesn't?* "And for you, Ms.Ralston?" she asked with a reassuring smile.

Nichola was too nervous to drink anything for fear it might choke her, but she also didn't want to refuse the offer. "I'll have...ahem...a coffee, too; I take mine white. Thank you."

"I'll be back shortly with your drinks." Sally bustled out of the room.

"Do you know why you're here?" Seth asked, noting the young blonde wringing her hands. *She's terrified for sure. No wonder. Hell, she can't be more than twenty if she's a day.*

Nichola's silver flecked green eyes gave him a wide eyed look and she shook her head. "No. My boss said that the president wanted the best synthetic expert on the staff and told me to get up here fast." The young woman's face took on a sheepish expression as she humbly dismissed her talents.

"Synthetics, huh? Interesting. I'm a project engineer for the South Americas; I allocate staff and resources...that kind of thing," Seth volunteered. As they both fell silent, he looked around the room. The large table, which sat center stage, had eight chairs flanking it and a flat screen computer console at each end. The décor was done in pastel shades, which made it feel airy and light, not at all imposing, and special edition prints adorned each wall. Seth gazed at the print immediately opposite him. The vivid still life was of a vase of flowers on a rustic table, next to a window that overlooked a summer field filled with yellow flowers. It was quite a restful picture. *Wonder who has the original, if this is just a print as the plaque there in the corner indicates.*

The door opened and Harriet Aristides walked into the room. Instead of sitting at the head of the table, she sat opposite the two of them.

"Thank you for arriving promptly, Mr. Roland and Ms...?" Harriet's gaze flicked to the young woman.

"Ralston. My name is Nichola Ralston," she rushed out, turning a delicate pink.

"Ms. Ralston." Harriet nodded, then fingered the document cases she'd brought with her before opening one with deft precision and selecting a report. Her slim fingers quickly turned over the paper as she gave them each a look that seemed to evaluate them down to their toes.

Sally returned at that moment, and placed a tray with steaming mugs of coffee next to the visitors. "Ms. Aristides, will you need anything else?"

Smilingly slightly, Harry looked at her PA. "Call me when it's half an hour before I'm needed at the luncheon."

"Of course."

"Now, shall we get down to business? I think you will both find this most interesting. Please look over this report." As she passed documents across the table, Harry watched them through half closed eyelids, a practice she'd mastered over the years. *That often duped Abby into thinking I wasn't paying attention. There was that time... Yes, well that has to be for another day.* She shook away the old memory and focused on the matter at hand.

She gave them a few minutes to review the document before speaking again. "As you can see from the data, our scientists who are in the Brazilian interior, claim to have achieved a breakthrough in their research. From all indications, it has the

156

potential to be more powerful than any drug the current market leaders have." Harriet stood up and walked over to the window before she continued. "As we presently have nothing in that line, this is a development of major importance for the company. I want a team on an immediate charter to rendezvous with our agent in South America. They will then be taken into the interior to meet the scientists who are responsible for this opportunity."

As her colleagues digest what she had said, Harriet's mind drifted slightly. She considered all the scientists she was about to meet at the luncheon and each of their contributions to the company. *If this discovery has even half the potential indicated, the scientists responsible will be overnight millionaires, possibly even billionaires by the time the drug gets to the marketplace.*

"Seth, allocate me the best possible team and equipment; spare no expense. They'll all be on bonus." Harry gave the man a long glance. She knew he excelled at his job and would put together the right team. None of the teams he sent to South America ever came back empty handed, or ready to cut each other's throats. Teams having to work in primitive spots for months if not a year or more at a time made his judgment in the selection process crucial.

Nichola resumed twisting her hands under the table and closed her eyes briefly as she wondered what her role would be. She was a lab scientist, having no desire for field experience, unlike others she'd known. Although she had good reasons, few took the time to understand her reluctance to leave the lab.

"Ms. Ralston, I want you to go along with the team. Talk with the scientists and undertake the initial rudimentary synthesizing to validate their findings…"

A strangled shout of "No!" came from the young woman.

Harry pierced the girl with a sharp glance. She would have to check out the viability of the lab manager and her decision to send this woman to her office. "Did I hear you say no?"

Trapped by the blue eyes, Nichola swallowed hard. "I…that is I…I'm a lab scientist, I've never been out in the field before."

"Neither have I, but I'm going as well," Harry said dismissively.

Seth Roland couldn't believe his ears. *Is she really going to rough it in the field for a week or two? The set ups are invariably remote, miles into the interior. How will she deal with that?* "I didn't know that," he said quietly. *Damn, this is going to make a big difference in the choice of personnel, not to mention the equipment.*

"You couldn't know. I just made up my mind. I'll only be there for a short while and not as a member of the main team. In fact, I will only stay as long as it takes Ms. Ralston to do the preliminaries and then we will travel back together. Ms. Ralston, how does that sound to you?" The shocked expression on the younger woman's face amused Harry. *She's probably no more shocked than Sally is going to be when she finds out. Anyway, it will give John a chance to do something more substantial than just my bidding.*

"I can't go," Nichola whispered despondently.

Harry was surprised at the confession. *What's wrong with her? Doesn't she know what's at stake here...that careers are advanced or ended with this type of opportunity?* "You can't, or won't?"

Nichola gave Harry a strained look and then hung her head, unable to maintain eye contact with the older woman. She could tell her boss was not happy.

"Since you refuse to answer, I will take it is as won't," Harry said, annoyed.

Nicola eyes darted around the room, refusing to make contact with the woman who was clearly irritated with her refusal. Harriet Aristides stood there, towering over her, anger glittering behind the sharp intelligent eyes. *How can I explain...how can I make Harriet Aristides understand?*

Harry walked over to the door and wrenched it open in frustration, stomping out to see her PA.

Seth's gaze followed her departure, then swung back to the young blonde. *Of course, she could be so brilliant at her work that refusing the president of the company doesn't matter, but I doubt it.* No one, no matter how good they were, ever refused a direct request from Harriet Aristides. Knowing that the young chemist's career was essentially finished if she didn't make the trip, Seth asked gently, "Why can't you go?"

"It's complicated; I'd rather not say," announced Nichola tremulously as she dashed away a stray tear in annoyance. She knew she excelled at her work, while deliberately keeping a low profile with no problems. The stability of the hours and the wonderful working conditions were a joy to her. Over the last three years, she'd been decorating her home, albeit an apartment, and it was just beginning to take shape. *This surely can't be happening to me.*

"Okay, but she's not happy." Seth waved in the direction of the door.

"I know." Nichola took a deep breath. "Do you think she'll fire me?"

"I'm not sure. She might be annoyed, but she's no fool either. If you're good, she'll want your know how here, not with a competitor." Seth smiled at her as Harry came back in the room.

Harriet was not just annoyed, she was furious. This *teenager* had put a spoke in her wheel and derailed the project for the moment. Harry had put a call in to Diane Leyman, Nichola's boss, and she had been adamant that the young woman in the conference room was the person for the job. There were others in her lab but none were as instinctively gifted as Nichola Ralston. The only one who might be of the same caliber was in China on the new project there. Harry sighed deeply and whispered, "Shit!" It would take the best part of a week to extract the other scientist and she didn't have a week to waste. Taking a less than expert synthesis with her was unacceptable, but she did not intend to give the impression that she was off track.

Her voice was cold, business like. "Ms. Ralston, you may go. Thank you for your time. Seth, get me the initial proposal for the trip by the end of the day."

Seth quickly moved out of the room. There was no time to waste if he was to find the right team, equipment and be ready for a six a.m. departure. The importance of this mission was not lost on him as it apparently had been on the timid young woman he'd left behind.

Nichola slowly made her way to the door only to turn and look at the bent head of the woman scanning papers. Her heart skipped a beat as she felt a rush of sorrow. *She looks so lonely.*

"Ms. Aristides, thank you for offering me the chance to go on the trip." After she'd said the words, Nichola realized how foolish they sounded. It was a job, nothing more.

Harry looked up and her pale blue eyes filled with slivers of ice, cool and unreachable, glinted at the young woman. She set her jaw, pursed her lips and replied, "Fine."

Nichola heard the finality of that one word as she closed the door behind her.

∞

"Nicky, it is such a wonderful opportunity. How could you turn it down?" Diane Leyman asked. She was not only puzzled, but also very annoyed at her employee's refusal. *Turning down a personal invitation from the president of the company gives the impression that the entire department is incompetent.*

"I told you when I came to work here, Diane, that I wanted to be a lab scientist only, not a field scientist!" Nichola liked her boss and was even friendly with her outside of work, but on this point, she remained adamant.

"It's not forever, Nicky, only a couple of weeks. Hell, if Ms. Aristides is going too, it won't be that much longer. You're the best we have in this field; who else can I send? Saul? He hasn't your expertise, and besides, he's still weak from that bout of flu…wouldn't last a day in that terrain. Christy? You know yourself she isn't in synthetics. Adam? He's in China and wouldn't arrive back in time. There's always me. I'm good, no doubt about that, but you're the brilliant one in this area." Sighing heavily, Diane gave Nichola a beleaguered look. "You tell me what I can do, Nicky. Right now, both our names are mud. This is a very important venture for the company. Tell me what to do." The exasperation and disappointment were evident in her voice.

"I've let you down, haven't I? You're right; there really isn't anyone else. But I don't know if I can do it. It's personal, Diane. I wish I could say more, but it would serve little purpose." Nicky sighed as she turned to the window and looked out, trying to collect her thoughts.

"Lots of activity out there. What's going on today?" Nicky asked and heard a faint snort from Diane.

"Well, it's the annual bash for the field scientists…a luncheon in grateful appreciation for their role in the company. Obviously not everyone can participate, but those that do enjoy it immensely. They say the pampering is one of the highlights of their year after some of the places they've been in." Diane chuckled as she pictured some of the faces, particularly Eric Lasser. He would invariably drink too much and try to kiss Harry, who would politely sidestep it, like she did every time. He was an excellent man, although ill health was forcing him to take fewer and fewer assignments.

"I didn't realize it had come around again so soon," Nicky whispered as she saw several people vacate the vehicles and walk towards the reception. Recognizing one of the visitors, she pulled back suddenly.

Diane looked at her quizzically, concerned for her friend who looked like she'd seen a ghost. "Is there a problem?"

Sometimes you have to do the right thing in spite of your fears. Nicky knew that such a moment had arrived; she had to step up and face the challenge. "No! I'll go, Diane. You can inform Ms. Aristides I've changed my mind," Nicky replied quickly.

Diane forgot about everything else as she beamed at her friend and dialed the executive offices. "Way to go, Nicky. I promise you won't regret it." Connected to Sally Smith, Diane explained that her chemist had changed her mind and agreed to the trip.

Chapter Three

Nicky sat alone in the virtually deserted, small dining area. Most people were either out for lunch or attending the festivities in the main dining hall. It was just as well, for at that moment she needed the solitude. *Okay, I'm going on a field trip. How bad can that be?* she groaned inwardly. She'd promised herself she wouldn't assume her parents' role. Her formative years had found her in many remote places with no roots or a place to call home. When she left that life for the university, she promised herself that she would have a home, family, and roots. Now here she was, agreeing to go on the very thing she'd come to hate. It was the ultimate irony.

I should have kept my promise to myself and refused to go. I should have explained to Diane about my life and my family. She would have understood. What possessed me to change my mind? Harriet Aristides! The lonely, despondent woman spoke to her heart. *How can I not go?*

"Hello, squirt." A man's deep voice boomed out, echoing off the walls.

Nicky didn't need to look up to know who possessed the voice. "Uncle Eric, how wonderful to see you." Nicky glanced up into twinkling brown eyes and a smile spread across her face. She had never been able to resist his bear like charm.

"Nicky, you look wonderful."

The giant of a man held out his arms and she rose from her seat and walked into them. He was about the nearest thing to family that she ever saw anymore. Nicky hugged him as she kissed his cheek. "Thanks, you don't look so bad yourself. I saw you arrive earlier. I thought you were in Europe."

"I was, now I'm here. Anyway, I made a promise to myself and I wanted to see if I could make it happen." Eric Lasser grinned at the small woman in his arms; she was a true product of her parents. He was certain she had both their intellects and had always been in the thick of things when she was growing up. *I wish I knew what happened to sour her love of the roaming life.* Her parents' hearts had been broken when she refused to work with them after graduate school. *Still the kid has her own life and from what I've heard, she's doing quite well.*

Nicky laughed and stood facing him. "You can't fool me. You enjoy the free drink and food, Uncle Eric."

"Ah, but I have an ulterior motive for being here too." Eric smiled at her wickedly. He released his hold on her, sitting opposite her after she sank back into her seat.

"Now what would that be, I wonder?" Nicky smiled warmly. Eric was a wonderful man with a great sense of humor. However, once the drink took hold of him, he tended to lapse into foolish tricks that often embarrassed him as well as others around him.

"Oh, you know me, Nicky: I have the need to try and achieve anything that is out of my reach." He chuckled and was about to say more when he spotted the familiar figures of Harriet Aristides and John Fredericks walking toward them.

"Speak of the devil himself, or should I say herself," Eric whispered conspiratorially, winking and nodding in the direction of the approaching couple.

Oh, shit. Nicky thought as she wondered if it would be prudent to leave the room before anything happened. "Ms. Aristides? You were talking about *Harry*?" Nicky asked quietly as the woman neared

165

their table. Nicky prayed she would go right on by; however, some wishes had a way of not coming true.

As the older woman stopped at the table, she gave the two occupants a cool level glance. "Mr. Lasser, I wondered why you hadn't arrived at the luncheon. Ms. Ralston, I have been informed you have changed your mind." Harry spoke quietly, watching the two of them carefully whilst waiting for an answer.

Eric Lasser rose from his chair and winked at Nicky as he held his hand out for Aristides. "I was about to join the festivities, but, as you know, Harry, I can't resist the charms of a pretty woman."

Eric's response astounded and fascinated Nicky that he used the boss' nickname with ease. The woman in question surprised her by smiling genuinely at him.

"Yes, you do have an eye for the ladies. That's true. Ms. Ralston may be my savior today too, in a very different way." Harriet Aristides gave him a brief grin and then turned her attention to the young chemist.

Nicky was concentrating so hard on watching Harry's expressions that she was shocked when the pale blue eyes captured hers in a quizzical, laughter filled gaze. "Yes, I changed my mind," Nicky finally stammered out. The piercing glance that earned her connected deep inside, sending waves of warmth through Nicky.

"Thank you for agreeing to participate in the trip," Harriet acknowledged. "Now I need to make a couple of calls and Eric, perhaps you will join my table when you finally do attend the luncheon. John here will see to it that you sit next to me. Now I must go, I'll catch up with you both later." Harry walked away from the two as she talked in a low tone to her second in command … others unable to hear the conversation.

Eric rested his chin in his hands, giving her a speculative gaze. "So, young Nicky, what have you agreed to that could possibly concern the big boss herself?"

"Oh, it's business, Eric, and secret. You know what it's like in this game. Anyway, how come you get to call the boss 'Harry' and she didn't blink an eye?" Nicky was intrigued.

Eric gave out such a loud bellow of laughter that the few people at the farthest end of the room looked in their direction. "She and I go back a few years, and we cared about the same person very much." Eric's smile faded from his face and a wistful look came across it. He saw a similar one mirrored in the eyes of the younger woman.

"Abby," Nicky said.

"You've never told her about you and Abby?" Eric asked quietly.

"No. It was never the right time, and now I don't think it would serve any useful purpose. You know, whenever I see Abby, it's a vivid picture of her laughing, joking, and enjoying life. When she left us to go to the States, nothing was ever the same for me again. Then, when she died, something died in me as well, changing my whole outlook on life. How could I tell the woman who loved her so deeply about that? I didn't see any need to cause her more pain."

"Perhaps, but it…" He was unable to continue as John Fredericks came back to the table.

"If you're ready to go to lunch, Mr. Lasser, I'll ensure you are seated alongside Ms. Aristides." The thin bespectacled man gave Nicky a brief, apologetic smile.

Nicky had always considered John Fredericks the epitome of the stuffed shirt executive, the caricatured accountant come to life. In actuality, he was probably all of those things and so much more. His benefit initiatives for the staff, both on the job and in their off hours, were extensive and compassionate. Some people even joined the company for the benefits alone.

"Well, Nicky, it seems I have to go. But how about we meet up tonight for supper?" Eric offered as he stood.

Nicky raised her eyebrows. She knew he wouldn't remember the date if he drank too much during this lunch...and there was an open bar. She would be dining alone.

Eric saw the look and grinned at her knowingly. "Okay, how about breakfast tomorrow? Six a.m. sharp." He blew her an exaggerated kiss.

Nicky couldn't help laughing at his sign of affection. "Okay, I'll meet you at Lady's, but you'd better make it five-thirty. I might have to cancel if plans change here."

"No problem, sprite." Whistling softly, he followed Fredericks.

Watching him depart, Nicky smiled with affection. Then she looked down at her watch and realized she'd overextended her lunch hour.

∞

A distinctly affable Diane met Nicky when she arrived back at the lab. "Why don't you take the rest of the day off, Nicky? Right now the details are somewhat sketchy, but you'll need to get everything you might need ready for the journey tomorrow."

"Do you have any idea what the departure time is?" Nicky moved toward her workstation and began putting her things away.

"Hmm, not really. All I really know is that you should take as little as possible. They promised to send me the list of the required gear later on this afternoon." Standing closer to her friend, she patted her hand. "Listen, as soon as I find out the final details, I'll come by your apartment and let you know the where and when." Bending slightly so she could see Nicky's face, she asked, "Are you okay?"

"Diane, do you think Ms. Aristides is still upset with me for saying no to begin with?"

Diane smiled and gave a small snort. "All I can tell you is that when I called her, she seemed truly glad you would be going. You came through for the company at short notice, Nicky; I don't think that will be forgotten." Smiling warmly she added, "You did good, kid."

Placing her personal technological gadgets into a small bag, she looked directly at her boss. "I'm relieved to hear that. It would have been difficult on the trip if she was still upset." Looking around the area, she shrugged her shoulders. "Guess I have everything, now I'd better go home and get my gear together." She nodded her head as she hesitated, her feet unwilling to move. "Okay then, I'll see you later on Diane." She was almost to the door when she heard Diane call out to her.

"Nicky."

"Yeah?" she responded, relieved that she could delay her departure a bit longer. "Is there something you need me to do here?" she asked hopefully.

Diane had to laugh at her obviously nervous colleague. "No, you're all done here." She walked over to her friend and hugged her. "You need to lighten up. Everything is going to be okay. It's just a field trip and nothing more." Stepping back a step she added, "Have a good time, my friend. Try to relax and enjoy yourself. Who knows, you might love it. Now get going and I'll see you before you go."

∞

As she entered the elevator and pressed the button for the garage, Nicky wondered how she would fill the next four hours. She certainly didn't need the time to pack, since taking as little as possible was second nature to her. Climbing into her car, she ticked off in her mind all the essentials that would be required for the short, unexpected, and unwanted trip. An image of Abby rose in her mind, side tracking her thoughts. She vividly recalled a time they had been happy together and, like clockwork, tears began to trickle down her cheeks. *All these years later and just the thought of her still brings tears to my eyes.* Once Abby had gone away, Nicky found it difficult to concentrate on what her family planned for her. Somehow, it all seemed somewhat irrelevant.

Her imminent journey back to the life she had left behind triggered a flood of memories. It had been twelve years since Abby had left her in that remote camp, fifty miles from nowhere. Abby announced that she'd had enough of the backwaters of mountain and forest ranges to last her a lifetime. She was twenty-one and wanted to experience the other world—the one with possessions, television, music, and most of all, people. It had broken Nicky's heart when no amount of pleading by her parents could persuade Abby to change her mind.

Abby's bid for independence led her to Houston, Texas, the location of the headquarters of Global Research Pharmaceuticals, the same company her parents worked for, and to one Harriet Aristides. It wasn't long after that meeting that Abby fell head over heels in love with Harry and vice versa. Not that it was a surprise, for Abby had been a beautiful woman with an amazingly gentle and compassionate nature. Natives they came across on their travels had called her *white angel*. Her effect on those she encountered was astounding. *Why did she have to die? What I wouldn't give to hear that sweet voice or see that brilliant smile once more.* Tears fell freely.

Abby's letter about her newfound relationship with Harry finally found its way to the jungle. She wrote of the love and happiness she had found, and it was then that Nicky knew Abby would never return. The heartbreak she felt was devastating; it brought a deep sadness and restlessness to her life. She was inconsolable. Eventually, she rebelled against the life she was leading and told her parents she would be going to America for schooling. As she predicted, they protested and tried to cajole her into staying. Although all their points were valid and it was true she would learn more from nature firsthand, she wouldn't change her mind. Ultimately, they realized Nicky would leave with or without their blessings and consented to her leaving. They fully expected that once she received her degree, she would return and work alongside them as they had always planned.

Her parents were both world renowned in the scientific community. Her father was a superbly gifted botanist known for his many discoveries in plant medicines. Her mother's scientific skills coupled with a methodical planner mentality would often unlock the hidden secrets in their research. Together they made a formidable team, discovering the bases for many new drugs to fight the world's illnesses.

Once she graduated, Nicky vowed never to return to the jungle. Her pubescent anger over Abby's new relationship kept her from immediately contacting her sister, but she had intended to call her when she had cooled down. Instead of speaking with her parents face to face, she took the coward's way out and informed them by mail of her determination to remain in the States. The letter took six months to reach them and by a cruel twist of fate coincided with the news of Abby's passing. Whether it was the loss of Abby or their mellowing, for once they didn't deter her, allowing her to choose her own path. With her degree in hand, and using her mother's maiden name, she applied for a job with the same company that employed her parents and had employed her sister. With her impeccable credentials, being hired was inevitable even without revealing her parentage. No way did she want any favors from the boss, particularly as the death of her sister would still be raw for both her and Harriet Aristides.

Several months after Abby's death, Nicky had come close to talking to Harriet Aristides…after all they both loved Abby and it was only logical that they should talk about her and their mutual loss. But Harry had gone abroad, and Nicky never again worked up the nerve to talk with her. Time heals, and so it was for her. However, it appeared that in Harry's case, that hadn't happened. *How terrible not to be able to let someone go! Now that we'll be spending some time together, I have a wonderful opportunity to lay my cards on the table about Abby, if I dare.* It was one of the reasons she'd changed her mind.

The honking of a car horn brought her entire focus back to the roadway; she was almost home. Negotiating the turn into the parking lot of her apartment building, she looked up at her balcony. It was flooded with color. The flowers and plants she grew were a way of remembering her roots. One day she might own a house with a decent sized yard and she could grow more than what she could fit in a five foot long box. She made a mental note to ask Diane if she would drop by during the week to take care of her plants.

Chapter Four

Never in seven years had John Fredericks ever known Harry to do anything on impulse. "This isn't like you, Harry. Why this discovery...now of all times?"

"This *discovery*, as you call it, John, may well hold the key to the future, and that I want to see firsthand. As to why I want to go now," she said arching an eyebrow, "now is as good a time as any for me to participate in a field trip. Call it a learning curve. Hell, it must be about the only thing I don't have a nodding acquaintance with in the company."

Also puzzled by Harry's out-of-character behavior, Sally listened for a clue. But her boss was an emotionally closed book. Therefore, her decision shouldn't have come as a surprise. Sally's heart ached for the lonely woman. Never in her life had she seen anyone so consumed with grief for a lost love. She'd had the privilege of witnessing firsthand a love that had left both women completely lost in each other. Sally had often found herself feeling jealous of the love so pure and deep. *Maybe mourning this long was called for.* "Want me to reschedule Guy Cole for next month?"

Harry looked away from her second in command to her PA. She knew John would be fine with Sally to back him up along with his own efficient PA, Jane. "No. John can handle it. Can't you?"

John cleared his throat before he choked on the words. "I don't think that's a good idea, Harry. He's trying his damnedest to take over the company and you know he has two of the four largest shareholders in his pocket already. Not to mention he's buying stock on the open market."

"You can handle it. Sally has the files and you just have to convince him that it isn't in his best interests. I have faith in you and in our personnel."

"You know if I fail and he convinces Shekia to go over to him, he could end up with controlling interest. I think you should meet with him yourself, Harry."

Harry pursed her lips as she considered the ramifications. Shekia Canning had always been loyal…to a point. Right now, the grapevine indicated she was financially embarrassed and that could be trouble. If presented with the right proposal, she might be willing to part with the shares her father had left her. It was up to them to see that that did not happen. "She *could* go over to him, you *could* fail, and he *could* end up with controlling interest. None of that is a certainty, and yes, all that could happen. Why not make it, she *didn't* go over to him, you *didn't* fail, and he *didn't* gain controlling interest."

John heaved a sigh and smiled at the woman who trusted him with the well-being of the company. He wouldn't fail the company, the employees, but most of all—her, *she* trusted him.

"*Didn't* is the order of the day then, Harry. Sally, you had better pass those files to my office as soon as possible, and tomorrow we can get together with Jane to work out a plan of attack."

Harriet Aristides chuckled softly. Her second sounded as if he was going to detail a battle plan— which it was. Guy Cole was no pushover; he had been a rather irritating thorn in their side for some time. "Excellent. I'll call you before I leave, John, and brief you with what needs attention in my absence." She turned back to her desk and contemplated the mountain of files.

"Okay, boss." Fredericks walked out the door leaving her and Sally alone.

Several seconds passed and neither woman spoke, then Harry looked at her PA with a wry smile. "Okay, go ahead, say it."

"Say what?" Sally knew exactly what Harry meant and sat down opposite the woman, watching her fingering the locket she wore around her neck.

"This is short notice...why are you going...have you lost your mind? You know those kinds of questions."

"It is short notice, but that's your prerogative. As to what has gotten into you...well...I figured you had that one covered."

"I know you, Sally," Harry said, arching an eyebrow. "We've worked together for several years now and you always have something to say." A small smile played around her lips. "Why change a lifetime habit now?"

"Oh, I don't know, you're changing, so why can't I?"

Both women made eye contact and Harry laughed at the absurdity of the conversation.

"I'm sorry I can't make your dinner party this Saturday."

"I knew it! There you have it, that's the reason you're going."

"Yep, that's it exactly. Any chance that you're having caterers this time?"

Sally gave her an affronted look. She thought Harry had enjoyed the barbecue last year, though she actually hadn't cooked. "What! You didn't like my cooking?" she teased.

"You didn't cook, Sally, and I loved the food. I merely thought you should give Ethan a break. I don't think he left the kitchen all the time I was there."

"He loves it...and, if I remember correctly, you left early."

"Yes, I did. Sorry. Next time I'll stay longer."

Sally's face filled with warmth and compassion for the lonely woman. Harry was brilliant, had money, a position others would kill for, but she didn't have the essential light that made life worth living. It had died along with Abby. Somewhere there had to be a reason for Harriet Aristides to light that flame in her heart again. "When you come back, how about dinner and I'll cook?"

"I wouldn't miss it, Sally. Thanks."

"Shall we go over which of these files you will take and which ones John needs to deal with?"

"Guess we'd better or I'll never get out of here tonight. I still need to pack. Sally, will you please check on how the arrangements for tomorrow are going? We need to inform the other members of our team as soon as we have the particulars."

"I'll get right on it and make sure the information is distributed, and then I'll come back and help with the files. Anything else you need?"

The question went unanswered as Harriet became absorbed in the pile of files. Smiling and shaking her head, Sally quietly left the office, all the while wondering what was really going on with her boss. *Oh, Harriet, what are you up to now? The field is no place for you! Do you have any idea what you're getting yourself into or what's ahead of you?*

Chapter Five

The airport bustled with life as Nicky transported her few necessities to the gate. Since it was a private flight, only those going in the field with her would be there. Of course, that meant the boss, too. She shuddered at the prospect of being in close company with Ms. Aristides. *How odd for Harry to go!* When Diane brought the itinerary, she said the company was buzzing with the news of Harry going on the trip herself. Speculation was high that it was a spectacular discovery for otherwise she wouldn't bother. *I just want to go, do my job, and then come home.*

Once airborne, they would apprise each participant of all pertinent information regarding the mission and the extent of his or her involvement. The entire scenario reminded Nicky of a mystery movie and it made her smile.

Arriving at the gate, Nicky panicked when she saw only Harry standing there, looking at her watch. *Shit, I must be late. What a great start this is.* She handed the attendant her documents while nervously glancing in the direction of her boss. Then, taking her papers in hand, her feet reluctantly took her in the direction of Harriet Aristides. She took a deep breath, ready to face the fury of her boss for being late. "Ms. Aristides, I'm sorry I'm late. I was told the time was—"

Harry smiled inwardly as she held up her hand to stop the nervous words pouring out of the pint-sized woman. Hard as she tried, she couldn't help herself from warming to Nicky.

"No…no, Ms. Ralston, you're not late. I like to see that everyone is onboard, that's all. Why not take a seat and settle yourself for the flight."

"Thank God. I wouldn't want to get on the wrong side of you. I did enough of that yesterday," Nicky replied without thinking as she passed the much taller woman.

"Really? Have I got a wrong side?" Harry's eyes scanned the single bag the small woman was carrying, assuming she had stowed away her other baggage.

I cannot believe I said that! What an idiot she must think I am. The faster I get on that plane the better! Nicky turned and gave her boss a shy smile, "Haven't we all?" The scrutiny of the piercing eyes was more than she could handle. Had she paused for one moment she would have seen the laughter brimming out of the blue eyes.

Nicky was not prepared for what she saw when she entered the plane. Her eyes widened as she took in the plush appointments of the interior. *Wow, bet this is more comfortable than my apartment. This is fantastic.* She had heard about the charter plane, but nothing compared with seeing the actual thing. *It's more like a conference room than an aircraft.* The surroundings enthralled her and Nicky was even more surprised when a bear hug engulfed her. *That can only be...*"Uncle Eric!"

"Why, Nicky, you got my message to have breakfast here instead of our usual retreat."

"Uncle Eric, how...why...what...My God, I didn't know you'd be here."

Eric Lasser emitted a huge belly laugh that had others around him turning to laugh at the man and the surprised woman who was like a midget in his grasp. "Oh, I wouldn't miss this one for the world, darlin'. Once we get airborne and you read the game plan, I think you'll be glad you came on this little excursion. Now come on, I'll introduce you to the others."

Everything was happening so fast Nicky wasn't sure whether she was dreaming. The whirl of emotions and fear that had overcome her earlier quieted significantly from knowing that Eric was on the team. *So many new faces and names how can I ever remember them all?* Taking a deep breath, she followed him as he introduced her to what would soon be her colleagues in the field.

Neil Jenson was a middle-aged biologist who reminded her of a blending of the professor on *Gilligan's Island* and one of her lab assistants in grad school. Then there was Rita Lawrence, a medical doctor who specialized in rare diseases. She was about five-seven with short, dark hair and a trim body. Nicky judged her to be in her mid thirties. Finally, there was Evan Tremayne, who was probably in his late twenties and the engineer of the group. He was the typical engineer type…kind of goofy-looking in a cute way. His sandy-colored, thick curly hair seemed to have a mind of its own, spiking in every which direction. She half expected to see white tape around the bridge of his glasses and laughed inwardly when there was none. They all seemed friendly enough and eagerly welcomed her as part of the group. Nicky wondered if that was because of her or Eric.

They stood talking and laughing when, to everyone's surprise, Harriet Aristides appeared. With her was a clean-cut executive type.

"Excuse me. Let me introduce Peter St. Clare. Peter will be in charge of the team. He reports directly to me and only me. Therefore, I expect him to be afforded the same respect you would give me." With that, she turned and headed toward the cockpit.

"Ladies and gentlemen," Peter said, "I am looking forward to meeting everyone. I'm sure that over the coming months we will all get along well. Each of you has an expertise in a specific area and that is why we chose you. Once we are airborne and I pass out the reports and task lists, it will become clear to you what is at stake here. Please make note of any questions you might have for an informal meeting I will conduct to discuss the details. What we are about to embark on is of great significance, not only for our company, but for the world's population, as well. Now if you will please take your seats for takeoff, I will pass out the particulars shortly."

Eric grinned at Nicky, motioning her to take a seat by the window. "I know you from old, Nicky. Only the window seat will do, right?"

Nicky smiled and nodded as she took one of the seats next to a window and strapped in. *One thing's for certain, there's no going back now. I'm committed to this for as long as Harriet Aristides is.* She watched as Harry settled in a seat in the front corner of the aircraft, seemingly not wanting to associate with anyone. Surreptitiously looking at the lonely woman, Nicky was feeling sorry for her until something else caught her eye. The strain on Harry's face was evident as her knuckles turned white when she gripped the armrests. *No wonder she wanted to sit by herself...she doesn't care for takeoff and isn't about to let anyone see her weakness. Hmm, she's human after all!*

Chapter Six

The hot, humid air of the South American country blasted them as they disembarked from the airplane. The air seemed to drip with moisture and they wondered if they could survive under such conditions for several months. All except for Nicky. It was like coming home for her.

Harriet mopped her brow of the sweat that seemed to become more copious the more she wiped it away. *What have I gotten myself into here?* She shook her head as she surveyed the small, dingy airport café where they had been waiting for over an hour. The guide who was supposed to take them to the team headquarters in the interior was late and it irritated Harry to no end. She hated waiting and this guide, Sebastian Roja, was trying her patience to the maximum.

Her gaze traveled to the others in the party who were sitting together drinking bottled water or other beverages. For some, it would be the last night they would spend in any type of civilization for months, and she fleetingly wondered how they would spend their evening. She really didn't care what they did, as long as in the morning they were fit to travel and do their jobs.

Her eyes settled on the youngest member of the party—Evan Tremayne, who at twenty-four, looked more like a sports jock than an engineer. His rumpled appearance belied the muscular body. *Bet he was involved in some sort of athletics in college*. She had looked over his résumé, but only the last couple of years; that was all that mattered to her.

The surprise had been Nichola Ralston, who she originally figured to be twenty-two and fresh out of college. Harry was shocked when she read the personnel file and found that the small blonde was almost twenty-seven, with a graduate degree and very impressive credentials. To career oriented Harry, it seemed strange that the chemist hadn't wanted a field trip. That should have been the icing on the cake. *Hmmm, something just doesn't track. Why did she say no, and what the hell is she doing here now?*

Eric Lasser had been the coup for her. His knowledge of the resources of their target location was superior to that of any of the other team members. Many years in the field had left him less than one hundred percent fit, but once she'd told him the people who had submitted the initial reports, he'd agreed to go. Smiling to herself, she recalled how he'd almost begged her to be included when they were at the luncheon, even without having heard all of the particulars.

Sally never asked her why she was going and even if she had, Harry wasn't sure she would have told her the truth. The team that had sent in the report had been Abby's parents, and once she verified, she couldn't help herself. She had to go. She'd never met them when Abby was alive. Sadly, torrential downpours had made it impossible for them to attend Abby's funeral. Now she had a chance to speak with the parents of her lover and she couldn't pass up the opportunity. It called to her as nothing else had in years; she was helpless to do anything else. Her emotions were taking her on a roller-coaster ride as fear and curiosity vied for supremacy inside her gut.

Perhaps there, in those unwelcoming surroundings, she would finally be able to come to terms with Abby's death. She hoped that once she met Abby's parents, the reality of her partner's death might begin to sink in. *Oh, how I wish it were so different, so very, very different.* She recalled how they had made plans to visit this very place after the baby was born, to introduce the grandparents to the new addition to the family. Now, she came alone, looking for solace and the one last link to her love.

Harry closed her eyes to the pain before reopening them and looking at her watch. It was past midnight. It was her birthday. There, in a rundown airport with people she didn't know or really care about, she sat alone. She wondered how many more lonely birthdays she would have to endure before the end came. The fact that she was about to set out on an expedition she really wasn't that comfortable with was unsettling to her. Of course, none of her employees would ever be privy to that fact. She would go forward with her boss persona intact. Her eyes drifted over to Nichola Ralston and a warm smile crept over her face. *Maybe not everyone is a stranger.*

∞

As Harriett waited in the hotel lobby with the others for their guide she looked through a grimy window and thought, *I must have been out of my mind to come on this trip.* A male voice with a pronounced accent startled her, "Ms. Aristides?"

Looking up into the gray eyes of a tall man with a swarthy complexion who looked like a Latino Mel Gibson. *Whoever he is, he's nice to look at.* "Yes. And you are?"

"Sebastian Roja, at your service." He made a short bow and held out a large hand to her.

"Mr. Roja, you're late."

The man gave her a long, concentrated glance and then a wry smile. "Sorry. I got snarled up in traffic."

With a cool expression hiding her inner feelings she thought, *at this time of night-yeah sure!* "I see. Well, you'd better show us to our hotel so we can all get a shower, change, and find something to eat."

"At your service, boss, I know just the place to eat."

His wink and the condescending way in which he *said* boss made Harry grind her teeth.

"My people are over there. Make sure they are taken care of first; they are your priority."

Harry watched as he nodded then walked over to the other six travelers, who gave him a roar of welcome. Sighing heavily, she looked at her suitcase and her hand luggage feeling the heat becoming more oppressive, if that was even possible. *How I hate this type of tropical climate.*

As she lifted her suitcase, briefcase, and other items of small baggage, she looked over at the others and saw that most of them had only two pieces. Nichola Ralston had just the large hand baggage she'd brought with her to the gate. *Either she doesn't know how to pack, or she knows something we don't. I guess we'll find out before too long.*

Once they left the building, the humidity added to the already oppressive conditions. Pulling at her blouse, she thanked God for natural materials. *I'd look like I was covered head to toe in perspiration instead of just feel it.* Harry then noticed Roja talking to Nichola Ralston in what could only be termed a flirtatious manner. If body language was anything to go on, the young scientist didn't welcome his advances. She'd started to move in that direction to

185

intervene when Eric came to the rescue first. *Oh well, that saved me from getting involved personally. I'm not here to be one of the gang.*

Harry couldn't believe the vehicle the guide had for them. It was worse than a clunker and she wondered if it would make it to the hotel, much less to the starting point for their trek into the jungle. As they all climbed inside, Harry found herself sitting next to Dr. Lawrence. She quickly recalled the contents of Lawrence's file and other than being an expert in her field, there wasn't much else of note. Not that anything else mattered. Harry only required the woman do her job well. She wasn't particularly interested in knowing anything more about the doctor, or any of the other participants. Giving the woman next to her a cautious smile, she closed her eyes and settled her head against the backrest of the seat. Soon her thoughts were going over the conversation she'd had with Jack Washington the night before...

"I can't make it, Jack."

"You can't make it? Damn, Harriet, that's a first. Don't tell me you've finally taken my advice and moved on."

"Jack, be serious."

"I was, Harriet. I was." The man shook his head. How he wished his friend would move on. She had been stuck in an emotional time warp since Abby died, and he knew that wouldn't have been what Abby wanted. Time was a great healer, but not for Harriet. She just seemed to be the one it left behind. "Okay, why can't you make it?"

"I have a field trip. It's important."

"Jesus, it must be! Give, Harriet. What's so important about this venture?"

"Abby's parents."

Jack pondered that for a few seconds before replying. "I love you, babe. You know that, don't you?"

Harry had to laugh. He was the only one who had ever called her "babe" and remained unscathed. "Yes, I know, and I love you, you reprobate."

"Reprobate, really! How can you say that?" He chuckled, knowing that it was true to a degree. Since Sam's death, he'd gone from one relationship to another. He might reprimand Harriet about getting on with her life, but he wasn't doing so well either.

"You work it out. Will you light that candle for me, Jack? You know how important it is to me."

The words, so solemn, caused him to catch his breath. Each in their own way missed their partner. The anniversary of their deaths was the one day of the year when they got together and remembered them as if they were still there.

"I'll light three, one each for Abby and the baby, and one for you, Harriet."

"I'm not dead, Jack!"

"Aren't you? In those things that matter in life, Harriet, aren't we both? Maybe God will take pity on us one day and let us love again."

As his words echoed in her head, her mind questioned, why would I want to love again?

Everyone sighed in relief as they arrived at the hotel. All were looking forward to a shower and cooler clothes and best of all—sleep. Entering the lobby, another collective sigh could be heard as they realized it was not a five-star hotel...one star would be stretching the point. Just the same, it was better than the tents they would be in the next night. They

187

made plans to meet back in the lobby later in the day for one last civilized dinner.

Several hours later Nicky and Eric were the last to arrive in the lobby. As the others were scrambling for places on the bus, it gave them a few moments alone to speak to each other privately. Eric had watched as she read the details of the project on the aircraft. He'd seen the indecision on her face. And he thought the time had come for her to tell Harriet everything. "Nicky, have you considered telling her?"

"I wouldn't know how to, Uncle Eric. Too much time has passed. What will she think of me if I tell her now? It is just too complicated."

"It's easy, kid, really. You just go up to her and say, 'Hey, boss, we loved the same person and this is the story'." Sebastian Roja interrupted stopping him from adding more.

"Ms. Ralston, Mr. Lasser, we have the table booked at the restaurant I mentioned. A good friend of mine owns it and he will treat you right. Trust me."

Eric had seen his kind before—smarmy and out for a fast buck. No doubt, he would be on the lookout to take the company for everything he could get. He was probably getting a kickback from the restaurant as well as the hotel. Moreover, Eric wasn't happy about how this South American looked at Nicky, undressing her with his eyes. *Bet it doesn't take him long to make a move on her.*

"I'm sure it's a very nice restaurant, Mr. Roja."

"Please, please, not Mr. Roja. You make me feel like an ancient monument. Sebastian or Seb would be much better." He leered at Nicky's breasts. "Very friendly, wouldn't you say, Ms. Ralston?" His dancing eyes waiting for her to extend the same courtesy with the names.

She really didn't want to get too friendly with Roja, he wasn't her type at all. He was, in fact, very far from what she preferred. Nevertheless, she accepted the inevitable. "Sure, okay, aahhh my name is Nichola."

"Ah, a beautiful name for a beautiful lady. Come, please. I have the bus ready. The others are all aboard."

He linked his arm with Nicky's and Eric had to force a smile, stopping himself from making a comment about Roja's trite response. As they climbed aboard the bus, Nicky stopped so suddenly that Eric cannoned into her, muffling an oath as he stubbed his toe on one of the seat's iron legs. "What's the matter, Nicky? Forget something?"

Nicky glanced around the small confines of the bus and turned questioning eyes to Roja. "Where is Ms. Aristides? Didn't she want to come for a meal too?"

Evan Tremayne laughed from his spot at the back of the bus, "Hey, Nicky, she's the boss, remember? Why would she want to consort with us? Don't you think she'll get enough of our company from tomorrow on?"

Nicky shook her head at Evan's comment. He certainly wasn't the geeky engineer her first impression said he was.

"Evan, you've made some mighty big assumptions about the boss there. I'll have you know she's no snob, Eric said. "She might be in charge of the company, but she's a down-to-earth kind of woman and I wouldn't want you to get into deep water if she heard you saying that kind of thing."

"To be honest, Nichola, I did not ask. I...I thought she might be too busy, you know? She might want some peace and quiet before setting off into the interior. You want me to ask?" Roja didn't seem overly eager to go and ask the question. His mind was on the fact that delaying their arrival at the restaurant, and that meant a loss of money.

"No, I'm sure it's as you said, she might want to be alone." Nicky's words fell heavily in the now silent interior of the bus.

Eric shrugged. Admittedly, no one had seen or heard from the boss since they arrived at the hotel earlier. But that didn't mean she wanted to be alone; maybe she had lost track of time. "I'll see if she wants to attend. Either way, I'll take a taxi to the restaurant. You all get on your way and I'll be there before you have time to miss me. Be good, squirt." He winked at Nicky as he retraced his steps and watched from the curb as the vehicle moved away.

"Now, to see if Harry really does want to be alone," Eric said to no one in particular.

∞

There was no answer when Eric knocked on the door to Harry's room. *Wonder if Harry is even in there.* He placed his ear close to the door, he didn't hear any movement, but decided to give it another try. Then he heard footsteps on the other side of the door and waited for it to open.

Eric was surprised at Harry's casual appearance. She was dressed in a denim shirt with three buttons undone that revealed lightly tanned skin. Her jeans fit tightly, revealing sexy curves to great effect.

"Eric? Is there a problem?"

She was wearing glasses, something he hadn't seen before. They were small and neat, giving her what he would describe as a cool, studious appearance. "No problem, Harry, just wondered if you wanted to have dinner at the restaurant Roja has arranged for the group this evening." He saw her lips curve into a small smile as her blue eyes warmed slightly.

The notion of enjoying a decent meal in the company of others was quite agreeable; it was her birthday, after all. Anyway, she needed a break from writing reports and she could do that when she came back. Then she could e-mail them to Sally before they left for the interior. "How long have I before you leave?"

"Well...the others have left. Uh, I came back to see if you wanted to join us. It appears Mr. Roja didn't think to ask you."

Harriet's eyebrows rose. "I see."

The few words sounded despondent and Eric felt sorry for her. He knew she had never recovered from Abby's death, made even more tragic by the baby's death as well. He fleetingly saw the loneliness that was often mistaken for aloofness as he smiled encouragingly at her.

"What about the others, did they think I wouldn't want to eat with them too?"

"Of course not, Harry. In fact, young Nicky was the first to ask where you were as we boarded the bus. She missed you immediately." Eric grinned as he saw the surprise reflected in the expressive blue eyes.

"Really? I'm surprised." *To say the least.* Harry had the distinct impression that she intimidated the young woman. She would have thought the blonde would have welcomed having one last evening without being thrown into her company. They would be together for the rest of the trip and Harry didn't

191

believe Ms. Ralston was looking forward to that at all. *Guess I need to rethink that idea,* she thought as unexpected warm feelings for Nicky bubbled up.

"She's a very surprising young woman once you get to know her."

"I'm sure you're right, Eric. Well, if you want to call a taxi, I'll meet you in the lobby in just a few minutes. I need to change…"

"No, Harry, what you're wearing is perfect. I heard the place has air conditioning, thank goodness, so it won't be a sauna as we eat. If we go now, we'll only be about fifteen minutes behind the others."

"Okay. Step inside. I need to close down a couple of things on my computer."

She walked to her laptop, quickly typed for a few moments, and then shut it down. As she was doing so, Eric sat on the sofa in the large room and looked around the place. It was similar to his in decoration except it was twice the size of his room. *Guess there are perks to being the boss.* He grinned as he watched her switch off the computer and go into the bathroom.

On the coffee table, he saw a couple of magazines and, surprisingly, several birthday cards. Picking up one from someone named Jack, he read the witty verse. He heard her moving around in the bathroom and with a guilty glance in her direction, picked up the other three from Sally, John, and Uncle Harry. Once he saw the private message written by her uncle, he knew he had been wrong to look at them. He was so engrossed in his find that he failed to hear Harry approach.

"You find looking at my birthday cards interesting, Eric?" She wasn't pleased at the intrusion into her private mail, but she should have expected it from this brash man.

"I'm real sorry, Harry. Is it today?"

"Yes, it is, and don't ask because I won't tell."

"Oh, that's not fair, Harry. How did you know I was going to ask you anything anyway?"

Harry had to applaud his audacity. "I have known you for several years now, Eric, and you wouldn't hesitate to ask how old I am."

"Well, gee, Harry, is it a secret?"

"A secret...no. It's in the company records if you want to check them out."

"Oh, come on, Harry, make an old man happy and tell me?"

They eyed each other for several seconds. Harry shook her head then smiled. This man had been close to Abby. She'd said he was a surrogate uncle and a great friend of her parents. Until Abby's death, Harry could count on one hand the number of times they had seen Eric. Three years ago, his own health began to let him down and he turned up at the yearly shindigs if he was in town. "I'm forty," she said, chuckling as she saw his eyes blink in what she hoped was disbelief.

He was astonished. *Thirty-five maybe, but forty never!* "I don't believe it one bit. How can you be forty?"

"Well, that's what it says on my birth certificate, so I guess it's true. Unless you know something I don't?" Her eyes twinkled with laughter at his expression. He was genuinely surprised.

"Then it is even more important that we get ourselves to that darned restaurant. We have something to celebrate." He stood up and winked at her as she shrugged at his exuberance.

"Okay, how can I refuse?" She picked up her purse, followed him out of the room, locking the door behind her as he pressed the button for the elevator.

When they arrived at the restaurant, the others warmly greeted Eric and Harry. Eric sat next to Nicky while Harry sat across from them. After everyone's meal arrived, Eric stood up to make a toast. "Ladies and gentlemen, may I have your attention, please. I would like to make a toast, if you don't mind."

Harry laughed for she knew exactly what he was going to say. "Eric, if you plan to say what I think, in the interest of job security, I would suggest you might want to reconsider."

"Not a chance, Ms. Aristides. Please raise your glasses in honor of our esteemed leader's birthday. Happy birthday, Harry."

"Happy birthday," went around the table.

The night continued with everyone wringing every bit of pleasure from their last night of comfort, before heading into the jungle that awaited them. Harry kept quiet listening to the others, only occasionally adding a casual comment. Overall, everyone had a good time laughing, drinking, and enjoying the company.

Chapter Seven

After the ride from the airport, Harry decided that they needed a different vehicle for the trek into the interior. Since Roja couldn't come up with a large enough vehicle for them all to ride in, they now traveled in two rather than one. In the second one, Rita, Neil, Nicky sat holding onto straps to keep from landing on the floor.

"Anyone would think she's a totally different person," Rita Lawrence sniped to Neil Jenson and Nicky as they jostled over the rough terrain.

"What do you mean, Rita?" Neil asked. He hadn't particularly noticed any change in their boss.

Nicky waited for the reply. Harry had been rather quiet, that much was true, but she hadn't been obnoxious in any way. Unless she had missed something, Rita's comment was completely unwarranted.

"I said *good morning* to her at breakfast and even sat at her table so she wouldn't be alone, and all I got was a closed expression barely acknowledging me."

Neil laughed, even as he felt himself bounce out of his seat as they went over another large pothole. *The driver must be a masochist or something; he seems to hit every bump in the road.* "Maybe she had a hangover. She drank a few glasses of wine last night and who could blame her, it was her birthday." Neil attempted to change the subject and squelch Rita's obvious, escalating irritation.

Rita ignored the comment. "She could have at least said good morning."

"Maybe she has things on her mind that we don't know about," Nicky replied quietly.

"Oh, you would say that. Are you hoping she's going to notice you?" Rita spat out in what sounded like jealousy.

Nicky glanced at the doctor in surprise. "What do you mean?"

"Come on, everyone knows she's gay and she's available. A pretty thing like you might try to turn her head."

Outraged, Nicky retorted, "Don't be ridiculous, Rita. I have no such notion. She's the boss, that's all, and I respect her."

"Hey, ladies, cut the bitching," Neil interjected. "We're stopping…thank God." They had been on the poor excuse for a road for over three hours.

"Are we there?" Rita demanded, but the man driving the vehicle merely turned to them with a grin, his English barely intelligible.

The vehicle in front of them had stopped. Harry, Eric, Evan, and Peter were climbing out of the car while Roja removed their belongings. Peter rushed over enthusiastically. His initial stuffed shirt appearance on the aircraft was now at complete odds with his serviceable trousers, shirt, and jacket, obviously chosen with regard to the terrain and the climate.

"This is the end of this leg of the journey. From here on, we're on foot; I hope no one is wearing new boots. Everyone gather up your gear and meet us over there." Peter pointed to the field near the outskirts of the jungle. He smiled boyishly and spoke a few words to the driver of their vehicle before he departed.

"On foot? I can't believe it!" Rita exclaimed.

It made sense to Nicky. The most important finds were usually in places that people only got to on foot. A spark of excitement began to grow inside her as she contemplated the trek ahead. Although she had renounced this way of life, it did call to her on a very primitive level.

"We're really going to walk the rest of the way?" Rita had apparently not had a very accurate perception of what the trip would entail.

Without a word, Nicky picked up her gear and walked toward Eric who was standing alone, looking over the jungle in front of him. She was still smarting from Rita's uncalled for accusation. *Perhaps she's the one who's interested in Harry.* Looking behind her, she saw Rita struggling with three pieces of baggage and smiled at the sight. *Surely, she must have gotten the memo about packing light, especially in this terrain.* Unable to suppress the smile spreading across her face, she didn't catch the sneer that Rita gave her as she turned away and walked over to her uncle.

He grinned as he pulled her into his wide shoulder with his arm around her own much smaller ones. "Hey, Sprite, how was your trip?"

"No problem," Nicky lied. She didn't want any trouble and by talking about Rita's snide comments someone might construe into meaning she cared about what Rita had implied.

He waved his free hand toward the dense stand of trees before them. "It's a beautiful sight, isn't it? I miss all this, Nicky."

"Yes, it's very beautiful, and I know you miss it, but you're here now and the odd occasion is better than none at all." Nicky had known the man all her life and it always seemed to her that one day, when he was ancient, he would just fail to come back from one of his trips. That hadn't happened; he had found out that a heart condition would severely curtail some of his more adventurous journeys. It surprised her that he had been selected for this particular trip, but she figured the company knew best.

"I never thought I'd have to go back to what they call the civilized world, you know. I expected that one day I just wouldn't make it back."

Nicky quickly looked at him. *Is he reading my mind?* Then she gave him a warm hug of understanding.

"What about you, Nicky?" Eric didn't glance down, he didn't need to. He knew that she was looking anywhere but at him.

There was no use prevaricating, she knew what he meant and, to the best of her knowledge, she had never lied to him. He had always been a very caring man and was there for her when she was a child. Often times when her parents were preoccupied with some new find, he would listen to her when she needed an adult to talk to. Then, as Abby became older, she became the adult figure for Nicky. Now she was alone and had to provide her own counsel.

"Sometimes I miss all this," she admitted, waving a hand at the jungle. "Then I look at what I have and the stability I've found, and it reminds me of how unpredictable my life was back then."

Eric Lasser smiled; he knew she was trying to convince herself that was the truth. He had seen enough in his life to know when someone had explorer's blood running through their veins. Her parents bordered on the fanatic, and he knew Nicky was close to that even if she didn't see it. When she'd left the camp for the last time ten years earlier, they had never expected her not to return...after all, it was just a phase she was going through. Her parents still held a glimmer of hope that she would return one day, but as the months stretched into years, that hoped dimmed to a tiny flicker. *This will be an interesting trip; maybe the exploration bug will hit again. Perhaps when Nicky finds herself at home, it won't be an apartment in a cement jungle, but in Mother Nature's jungle.* "Some people thrive on the unpredictable, Nicky. Take Harry, for instance."

"Harry?"

"Yes, Harry. She lives in the world of the corporate jungle where jackal eats jackal, although I think in Harry's case, she might actually be one of the few true lions of that breed called executives."

Nicky laughed softly as he described the commercial world in the only way he knew, as nature had set it up. Actually, if she thought about it, there was a great deal of truth in the scenario...except maybe Harry. She saw her as a panther, with sleek lines that could outrun everyone. She shook her head as she wondered where that thought had come from. *Must be the heat.* "I guess I'd rather have the sedate these days."

"You might change your mind." He grinned down at her as they heard someone approaching. Turning, they came face to face with the feline herself, Harriet Aristides, who was looking none to happy.

"Eric, why didn't you tell me that we were going some of the way on foot and that I'd have to carry my own baggage? Do you know how long I'm going to last in this heat?"

Nicky had to glance down at her feet again and reprimand herself for laughing, but she couldn't help it. The other woman's face was a picture. *Yep, it's evident that Harry isn't on speaking terms with Mother Nature.*

"You find something funny, Ms. Ralston?"

Nicky looked up when her name was mentioned and was immediately snared by cold blue eyes. It only made her snort in laughter as she thought of what Rita Lawrence had said about her and Harry. *Not a chance in hell with the look she's giving me.*

"Why, nothing, Ms. Aristides."

Harry flicked back a stray bang and turned back to Eric in disgust.

Eric gave her a smile. "Didn't you read the notes that were given to us before we left?" He waited as he saw the concentration flood her face, as she tried to decide whether or not she had received the information.

"I wasn't...that is, I don't recall having any notes."

No one spoke for a few seconds then unexpectedly, Nicky did. "Ms. Aristides, it was from Seth Roland marked 'team essentials'."

Harry gave the younger woman a perplexed look and considered what she'd said. She had received an envelope marked *team essentials* but she had been so preoccupied with ensuring that everything would run smoothly in her absence, she had basically dismissed it as irrelevant to her as she was an observer only.

"I see. Then of course, yes, I did. Obviously, I did not read it." She gave both Nicky and Eric a long glance and then shrugged. "I'm sorry, Eric. I think I've over packed."

The large man gave her a wide grin, stroking his chin as he exaggerated his contemplation of her problem. "Looks like you're in luck, Harry, Nicky and I packed light, as all well brought up explorers' children learn from...two days old, I think. Isn't that right, Nicky?"

"Yeah, goes with the territory." She smiled at him, knowing that she was being asked in a discreet way to help.

"I don't expect you to carry any of my baggage!" Harry's voice raised just a fraction in annoyance for being less than efficient in reading her mail.

"Really? Well in that case…." He turned away and heard her snort in disgust at her predicament.

"I guess I could do with a hand or two, thank you both." Harry's eyes reflected her genuine appreciation.

"We had better deal with that now, then. I suspect Peter and Roja will want to move on quickly."

Harriet never accepted help readily from anyone and yet, all at once she had to accept it from two people. *Abby was right; I'd never make a decent field person.* Standing in the clearing of the jungle on the anniversary of her beloved's death, the memory hit her hard, the loss, palpable. *Why take her away? She was so young, had so very much to live for.*

"Ms Aristides, are you…" Nicky stopped as she saw the pain throbbing in the pale blue eyes of the woman who appeared, to many, invincible. What people tended to forget was that whatever one did in life, they were still human and everyone pretty much ran the gamut of the same emotions and experiences, just in different ways.

"I'm fine!"

Nicky knew differently and she knew why, too. If only she could get up the nerve to talk to Harry about Abby. *I wonder what she would say if she knew? I need to find a way to tell her before we arrive at the site. Oh, Harry, I know your pain. If only I*

201

could let you know. There has to be a way and I'll find it. I must.

Once everyone was ready, the team headed out, with each member lost in his or her own thoughts and expectations. The expedition could make or break any of them, and they all knew it. Soon each of them would hold the promise of a great discovery in their hands. As individuals, none would succeed; only as a team would success be theirs.

Chapter Eight

The trek through the jungle was stressful. For two days straight they encountered dense foliage and bug infested swamps. Their boots were soaked through with the dampness of the rainforest, and insect bites could be found on every part of their bodies. Add to that the heavy luggage, and one very tired, cranky team emerged.

Harriet closed her eyes briefly as she tripped over the root of yet another enormous tree. The damn things were gigantic, with invisible tops which allowed light to only dapple through, like a spotlight on a stage. Even that small amount of light made the forest less frightening. *Whatever possessed me to come on this trip? Oh yes she had her reasons two-fold, and each had a sway on her emotions in totally different ways. Except for one aspect that they both may administer, either way she'd probably end up with an ulcer, all the silent worrying she was doing.* Fortunately, she at least had privacy at night, as she was the only one with a tent of her own. The others all had to share, except for Roja and his compatriot, who appeared to sleep under the stars.

The help she was receiving from Eric Lasser and Nicky Ralston stuck in her craw. She really didn't mind Eric's help because he was a pro in this terrain. She did, however, feel inadequate compared to that slip of a girl Ralston, who seemed to be at home in the jungle, as well. *What was it Eric remarked about explorers' children? Is that why she was so adamant at first about not coming?* The only jungle Harry knew was the corporate one, and this certainly was not functioning within those parameters.

203

Mopping the sweat from her brow for the umpteenth time, Harry speculated about the people walking with her. Neil Jenson, Rita Lawrence, Peter St. Clare, and their guides were walking quickly and confidently, obviously not having the trouble she was. Roja was making a play for Lawrence, which made Harry chuckle, as she was certain he was most definitely not her type. The woman's not so subtle advances toward her over the last few days clearly implied that.

Jenson was a quiet man who didn't say much at all. He was the type that considered all his words carefully before he spoke. Hopefully he took that approach in making his determinations with experiments, as well. She was relying on positive results.

She didn't need to turn to know that St Clare was right behind her... she could smell him. His penchant for a very powerful aftershave didn't exactly go well with the sweat of the day. She smiled briefly. *I wonder how he manages to keep the bugs from attacking him; maybe I'll try using some of his aftershave.* According to Roja, if they kept up the same pace, they would reach their destination in three days.

As with the previous days, the stragglers were Lasser and Ralston, and Manuel, the other guide. Fortunately, it was Manuel who was watching their backtrail, as the other two constantly talked while they walked. Occasionally they would stop and take in certain parts of the terrain with more interest than other places. Harry didn't understand the fascination these scientists seemed to have with the flora and fauna, or why they found this kind of challenge exciting. On the first day, she worried that it was her extra baggage holding them up, but she soon realized they were simply enjoying the world of Mother Nature around them.

Just then, all Harry wished for was evening, and settling down to a nice hot drink and a meal. Eric and Peter were pretty good basic cooks and at the end of the long day, she was glad for anything. *Maybe that's exaggerating. Bugs and such wouldn't be welcome.*

Her mind was so preoccupied with thoughts of a warm meal, she didn't see the enormous tree root gnarled up like a lasso until her boot was caught in its grasp. She found herself being propelled awkwardly and heavily onto the mossy jungle floor. The crack she heard and the excruciating pain that followed were unmistakable. Her shout of pain stopped everyone in their tracks, except for the birds, which were startled into squawks and took off through treetops and rustling in branches.

St. Clare, the closest to her, rushed to her aid. "Ms. Aristides, are you okay?"

Is the man a bloody fool? No, I'm far from okay! "Does it look like I'm okay?" she growled. The intense pain radiating from her ankle caused such a churning in her stomach that she was fighting nausea as well.

A ring of bodies circled her as if she was an attraction at a freak show in a circus. "Give her air for God's sake," Rita Lawrence exclaimed as she knelt down on the damp ground to inspect the injury. "This might hurt."

The expletive that followed made the others step back. With the swelling, which was already evident, it didn't take a qualified medic to know something was seriously wrong with Harry's ankle.

Ten minutes later, the ankle had been securely wrapped and Harry was propped up against a tree with her leg elevated. Not too far away from her a discussion was going on about what to do next.

"She needs to rest, Roja. Perhaps it isn't broken and the swelling will subside...then we can continue in a few hours." Although she had to say something to appease the obviously aggravated Roja, Doctor Lawrence knew that it was unlikely. The painkillers she had administered would knock out an elephant.

Roja wasn't happy about the delay. If it had been anyone but his employer, he would have been cursing verbally instead of silently. "We need to keep moving. It is not healthy to stay in one place in the jungle for long periods."

"We're talking maybe the rest of the day, that's all." Roja was really irritating Rita. *Doesn't he have a heart?*

Muttering under his breath, Roja stalked off. St. Clare pulled at his chin, contemplating the problem. He was, after all, team leader, and it was his responsibility to decide what to do. Not affected by their boss's predicament, the main team could easily continue. The question then became—what to do with Harry, They couldn't leave her there alone.

Eric, Jenson, and Nicky waited patiently for a decision to be made, each with their own thoughts on what the best course of action would be

Nicky saw the pain etched in Harry's face. The ankle, swollen to twice its normal size, clearly had a bone out of place. She had seen enough broken bones in her life to know this one needed to be set, and the sooner the better. Her eyes scanned the small snippet of visible sky above the foliage. A rainstorm was on the horizon and it wasn't looking good. She didn't need to look to smell St. Clare approaching her. He gave her a rather sheepish look before speaking.

"Hi, Nicky, how are you doing? I was hoping to have a chat with you and maybe ask the boss her opinion on my plan of action."

She knew what was coming next, and she held her hand up before he could even start his spiel. "The boss isn't in a fit state to make any calls right now. I'm guessing you want me to stay with Ms. Aristides, am I right?"

He grinned as he nodded. "Guess you saw that one coming. Of course, Manuel will be here with you, and when the boss feels able, you can join us. According to Roja we're two days away at our previous pace."

"I understand the mission comes first, and Harry and I are not the first team." Nicky glanced across at the woman under discussion, who was struggling to keep her eyes open. Once the drugs Rita gave her started working their magic, she would rest easier. "She has broken the bone. She won't be in a position to walk unaided. Will you send Roja back to help?"

"Yes, yes of course. As soon as Roja has seen us to the base camp, I'll let him rest and then come back to help. Worst case scenario, Nicky, you'll be three days behind the rest...four at the max."

Nicky turned to him, her green eyes serious, "Harry isn't in a condition to stay out in the open in unpredictable weather conditions. A storm is coming."

Peter gave her a puzzled glance. *Roja hasn't mentioned a storm brewing. Perhaps it's her imagination.* "Nicky, I doubt there's a storm around the corner. Besides, Manuel will take care of you; he's supposed to be a fine guide."

"Okay, see it your way. But I'd keep your rain gear close by." She saw him wink at her and knew he didn't think she knew what she was talking about. *We shall see,* she thought, smiling at the clueless man.

He left to gather the rest of the team and explain the situation. As he did, Eric took his place at her side. "You okay with staying behind, Sprite? It wasn't my idea. I thought we should take turns carrying her on a makeshift hammock."

As she felt the comforting arm close around her, she smiled up at him. "Hey, Uncle, when have I been afraid out here? This is my backyard, remember?"

He smiled at her. He knew that she had never been afraid, not even as a toddler. She had been fascinated. She was always inquisitive and nature took care of her in return. "You could always have that chat with Harry, since you'll have some free time together."

"Please give up on that topic. I don't think a discussion about Abby at this time would be a good idea. She's hardly in any condition to handle emotional issues."

"Perhaps not, though when will there ever be a good time to talk about Abby with her? I really think Harry expects Abby to come walking into the house one day as if she never left. Who better to talk to her than someone else who loved Abby deeply but has allowed herself to move on? It's the circle of life, Nicky."

"We'll see. Now you'd better move along or they'll think you've decided to stay with me."

Laughing the deep belly laugh she would always associate with him, he kissed her cheek, hugged her tightly, then released her to join the others.

Nicky decided she had better see how Harry was and talk with Manuel. *I don't care what anyone else says, that storm front is going to hit in a couple of hours.* Looking over at the now sleeping woman, Nicky was once again struck by how fragile she was. *So much for my plans to come here, do my job, and go home. Guess I was fated to be here to help Harry.*

"We will get through this Harry, I promise you," she whispered.

∞

Just as Nicky predicted, the heavens opened three hours later. The torrential downpour not only soaked everything in sight, but also raised the humidity to a stifling one hundred percent. Nicky gave herself a silent pat on the back for her accurate prediction, considering she hadn't been in this part of the world for almost ten years. Prior to the storm, there had been a flurry of activity as they built a tent for the two women around Harry and a smaller one nearby for Manuel. Harry's height had made it tricky to set up the tent so her feet didn't stick out, an amusing fact she and Manuel laughed about during the whole setup. Fortunately, he spoke a dialect that Nicky was fluent in, which was a bonus for them.

Now, listening to the heavy raindrops splattering on the canvas of the tent, she gazed at the sleeping Harry. Nicky was certain the rain would continue at least through the night, and she wondered how they would travel through the thick, wet jungle with Harry incapacitated. At the best of times, travel was precarious; for someone with a foot injury, it would be nigh unto impossible. For now, they were stuck in place until help came or Harry was able to travel.

As her mind drifted to her family a scant two days away, she heard a small cry from the sleeping woman beside her. Turning, she saw the flickering of the eyelids going so fast that she was sure Harry must be dreaming. Although she wasn't thrashing about, those small incoherent sounds became a little louder each time. The drugs Rita had administered were powerful. They should be enough to give Harry a decent rest through the night, although there was the possibility for one hell of a headache in the morning.

"Hey, Harry, everything is going to be fine, trust me." The words she knew Harry couldn't hear were spoken softly. She pushed back errant bangs gently as she checked for a rise in her charge's temperature. Fortunately, she didn't seem any hotter and the stroking of her hair seemed to have a soothing effect. Nicky couldn't stop the tears that fell unashamedly as she heard, "Abby, I love you and miss you so much."

Trying to clear her eyes of the tears, Nicky gulped back the sob that threatened the silence. The rain now cascaded heavily, and a sharp crack of ear piercing thunder was followed immediately by lightning zipping across the sky. Even through the heavy vegetation, it lit up the interior of the tent, making the small lantern in the corner pale by comparison.

Nicky knew she should get some sleep, but stormy weather had always kept her awake, even as a child. Never did it frighten her, far from it, she always wanted to run out and bathe in the coolness. The sheer power of the storm excited and stimulated her. Her parents were aghast when she would sneak out of the cabin or tent and run around in the mud, splashing in the large pools of water that quickly formed as the torrential rains came.

A smile lit up her face as she recalled a time when Abby had found her standing in the middle of a glade, washing her hair in the rain. It took only a few moments before they were both covered in shampoo bubbles, giggling and laughing together. Harry's deep, rather melodic voice shook her from memories of her childhood.

"Hi, how long have I been asleep?"

"Oh, Harry…ah, sorry, Ms. Aristides…almost three hours."

"Harry's fine. Three hours? Where are we?" She sounded puzzled and disorientated, and the look on her face was one of bewilderment. As she tried to focus her eyes, Harry kept shaking her head as if to clear out the cobwebs.

"Yes, three hours. Doctor Lawrence gave you pills to help with the pain and relax you. I think she thought they would help you sleep the day away." Nicky rushed out an explanation and then moved to open the flap of the tent for a moment to allow Harry to see the weather conditions.

"I see. I don't recall anyone putting up a tent. How did I get in here? That's some storm out there, are we safe?"

"We are quite safe; the foliage offers us some protection. If we moved further in, we wouldn't see any rain. As for the tent, we built it around you as you slept. We thought moving you wasn't advisable."

"We?"

"Manuel. He's in the tent next door. Want me to fetch you a bowl of hot soup?" Blue penetrating eyes looked deep into her soul. Nicky wasn't prepared for the fluctuation in her heart rate at the concentrated gaze. Then amazingly, Nicky's heart did a tremendous flip as she was given a wide, bright smile. "Sure, I'd like that."

Nicky couldn't help it, she grinned like a foolish teenager and without a thought for the weather, dove out of the tent into the pouring rain to seek out Manuel and the hot soup.

As Nicky disappeared without any rain gear, Harry attempted to stop her, but the movement caused a sharp pain in her ankle. She sucked in a deep breath, trying to concentrate on not screaming out. She closed her eyes and concentrated on the pain, talking to it and challenging it to beat her. It was a tried and true method she had employed in the past to combat the horrible headaches she'd had after Abby's death. Gazing around the small confines of the makeshift, compact tent, Harry wondered what had happened to the spacious one she'd had the night before. This one only had enough room for two average sized adults, and she wasn't exactly average. Then again, she was sharing this one with Nicky and she was on the small side. *Yes, this will work out just fine. I wonder what happened to the rest of the team.*

Nicky found Manuel sitting under the lean-to, stoking the fire and enjoying the peace a storm brings to the jungle. The soup was simmering in a pan over the open fire. Speaking quietly, she told him that Harry was awake and wanting some soup. He ladled some into a flask, handed Nicky a tin cup, and asked if the woman was going to recover enough to travel soon. He added a few ground leaves into the flask from a special plant his mother always used when someone was injured. Nicky smiled and thanked him; she had seen her own mother use the same herbs for that purpose in the past. Clutching the cup and the flask, she ventured out into the wet night.

Walking back to the tent, Nicky wondered if Harry would be awake enough to eat the soup. *Maybe I will have to spoon feed her.* That thought brought a small smile to her face. *We'll find out soon enough.* She pulled open the tent flap and a stream of raindrops following her inside.

"Here you go." Nicky grinned like a Cheshire cat. She was sure Harry was going to chastise her for going without a coat. Her clothes were soaking wet and her hair was dripping with rivulets of water.

"Thanks, but I didn't expect you to go out in that!" Harry wrapped her hands around the hot cup, trying to chase away the cold and damp caused by the rain. The aroma of the soup reminded her of how hungry she was. *Wasn't I thinking about a hot meal just before I tripped over that damn root?*

"Mmm this tastes good. I didn't realize how hungry I was. This was very kind of you, thank you."

"No problem, it was my pleasure. I love this weather. It brings you as close to Mother Nature as anything."

She was so enthused that Harry was taken with the words that sounded so naive and innocent. *How does one retain innocence at her age while living in the city?* "Personally, can't abide it, but to each their own." Harry saw the twinkle in the eyes of the younger woman and it brought a brief smile to her lips. *Thank God her shyness has evaporated. I can't imagine what it would be like being stuck in this tent with a Nervous Nelly.*

Nicky changed the subject rapidly. She didn't want to talk about herself, as it might get complicated. "How's the ankle?"

"Hurts like hell! It was my own fault, of course; I should have watched where I was going." The words were clearly tinged with resignation at her stupidity.

"We all lose concentration occasionally and don't always look where we're going."

"I suppose. Do you? I noticed that you and Eric were always the stragglers."

Smiling as she thought of Eric Lasser, Nicky hoped that he had heeded her warning and had the rain gear ready. "Yes, I do; who doesn't? Eric and I get lost in conversation about what we see around us. It can be fascinating to watch nature work her miracles along the way."

"You sound like an idealist. Are you a member of Green Peace?"

"If being an idealist helps to conserve nature while at the same time using it sensibly to help people, you can call me what you want. I understand their ideology, although I'm not a member." Nicky looked down at her sodden shirt and trousers. *I really need to change, but that's going to be difficult in the confines of this tent.*

"You sound like Lasser. Is he really your uncle?" Harry wasn't usually nosy, but Lasser had been a surrogate uncle to Abby too. She wondered if Abby and Nicky had ever met, or known each other.

"I consider it a compliment that you think I sound like him. He's a wonderful man. If I become half the human being he is, I'll count myself lucky."

Harry noticed she didn't mention how their relationship had come about, and she thought that maybe her question had been out of line until Nicky continued.

"Eric is a good friend of my parents. He never had any children of his own; however he did go around adopting as many kids as possible." She chuckled as she thought of the numerous native children that Eric had sponsored over the years, even sending some to university.

"I know he's a special man. He's been with the company for over thirty years...one of the old school who have it in their blood to explore, I guess."

Nicky was intrigued since that's exactly how she considered him, as well as her parents. Precisely what she'd thought she was going to be once, long ago. "Oh, you think of him as an explorer."

"Yeah, we have explored, travel wise, most of the globe. We have even gone out into space and explored childishly there. Today the explorers are men like Eric and people like the scientists we will meet at the base camp. Somewhere along the line, we forgot about Mother Nature and how much we still have to learn and what she can teach us."

Nicky considered the statement. She had never thought a corporate executive, especially someone like Harry, would have such romantic notions. *But why not? Surely they must have secret dreams. And being with Abby...she would have had some influence those years they lived together.* "Did you ever want to be anything other than what you are today?"

"Me? Oh I don't know really. I suppose as a child I wanted to be a doctor or nurse, something like that." Harry shrugged and the slight movement caused her to wince in pain but she tried to mask it.

"I wanted to be like Uncle Eric and...see what he's seen." She'd almost said like her parents, too, catching the words before they were spoken.

Harry felt the drugs taking over again, and she lay back down on the pillow and pulled the sheet around her. "Why are you in the lab? You're more than capable of being like Eric. I've seen you...I mean...we've spent time together...you know...out on the field already...um...you know what you're doing..." Her words were becoming disjointed.

Nicky heard the suppressed yawn and smiled wryly. Harry would be asleep shortly, giving her an opportunity to change out of her wet clothes. "Someone has to do the lab work."

"I guess."

Those were the last words Nicky heard as Harry fell asleep, looking so young in repose. *Is she really forty?*

Peeling off the soaked shirt, jeans and underwear that clung to her body, she made a mental note that it would be pointless to put on fresh clothes until they were on the move. Earlier she had noticed a small stream nearby where she could bathe and wash her clothes. Grabbing a T-shirt from her bag, she slipped it on and settled herself down to get some sleep.

As her eyes closed, an image of Harry's smile filled her mind, and once again, warm, wonderful feelings erupted inside her. She now had an inkling of why Abby had fallen for the woman; it would be so easy to do. Finally, with thoughts of Harry filling her mind, sleep took her.

∞

After a night of fantastic dreams, Nicky woke up feeling elated. Smiling as she stretched, her eyes wandered over to her sleeping companion. Once again, she was overwhelmed by remarkable feelings of tenderness towards the woman.

Harry's eyes began to flutter as she stirred on her cot.

"Good morning. How are you feeling?" Nicky's good mood couldn't be contained.

Shaking her head Harry tried to focus on where she was and why. "Aren't we Miss Cheerful first thing in the morning?"

"Ms. Aristides, aren't you a morning person?"

"You know, Nicky, if we are going to share this tent and campsite, I think you should call me Harry, don't you?"

"Of course, you're right, Ms. Ari…Harry." For some reason Nicky blushed when she used the familiar form of address.

"Thank you, and good morning to you, Nicky."

"How would you like something to eat? I'm not sure what Manuel has made…maybe some native feast of bugs and monkey meat." Nicky had to contain her laughter as she saw Harry's eyes bug out.

"You are kidding, right?"

"Yes, I am, Harry. Not to worry. I think there's coffee and eggs, and maybe bread, if we're lucky. Do you want to wash up and try to use the bathroom?"

"Just how do you suggest I do that?" She motioned to her ankle. "As you can see, I'm not all that mobile."

"Out here in the field, there are ways, if you'll trust me."

"I'm in your hands then, Nicky, thank you." Stress and pain were evident on her face.

"Can you move, Harry?"

"With difficulty." As she tried to get up, the pain shot through her ankle. *The damn thing is undoubtedly broken.*

When Nicky opened the tent flap, Harry could see that the rain had finally stopped, though Nicky warned that in a few hours it would be back, probably worse than the night before. That alone was enough to make Harry wish she had never had the foolish idea of meeting Abby's parents. *Good idea, my ass, more like a disastrous one.* She struggled to make her way out of the tent. Glancing around the makeshift camp, she saw Manuel staring out into the forest, a rifle held casually in his arms. A smaller tent and a lean-to with a table and stools in front of it sat next to her tent, and off to one side was what appeared to be a shower or perhaps a bathroom.

Standing next to her, Nicky had a towel around her neck and a bag with clean clothes and toiletries in her hand. "We'll go over there so you can clean up."

"Just how do you think I am going to make it over there? Fly?"

"No, silly, you just lean on me and use this on the other side." She held up a sturdy tree branch with a vee at the top that could serve as a crutch. Noticing the doubting look on Harry's face, she added, "I promise nothing will bite unless you want it to."

"I think I might be too much for you to handle, Nicky, I am rather bigger than you."

"I'm a lot stronger than I look. Please, everything will be fine."

Reluctantly, Harry put her arm around Nicky's shoulders and allowed the smaller woman to assist her toward the makeshift bathroom. The distance couldn't have been more than twenty feet, but for Harry it was twenty feet of agony. When at last they arrived and Harry pulled back the flap, she couldn't believe what she saw. There before her was a campstool with two buckets of water next to it and not far from there, a hole in the ground. "My God, what's this? You're joking, right?"

"I'm sorry, it's the best we could do. The water is hot, so that's a plus. I can help you so you can keep the weight off that ankle."

"I think I can manage to go to the bathroom and wash myself."

"Okay, but if you need any help, I'll be near by."

Leaning on the tree limb crutch, Harry worked her way over to the hole. *How on earth am I going to do this without help?* She made up her mind that she would. *It's bad enough to let an employee see me vulnerable without having to degrade myself, too.*

Nicky looked toward Manuel as they heard one oath after another come from the crude bathroom. Shrugging, the young blonde smiled as another robust "God dammit" was heard.

A frustrating hour later, Harry was somewhat fresher, although all the movement had made the pain increase. She was surprised as she exited the 'bathroom' to find Nicky right there.

"How did it feel to clean up? I find feeling clean sometimes makes me feel better. Want me to check the dressing and see if the swelling has gone down any?"

Smiling as she looked up into the green eyes that had specks of silver that made them sparkle at close range, Harry said, "Why not? Thanks, Nicky."

"Great. Do you think together we can make it over to the table and some breakfast? I can check your ankle while you get some food in you."

Once again, Harry leaned on Nicky as they made their way to a waiting chair and some much-needed food. The aroma of coffee perked Harry up a bit. "Hmm, that coffee sure smells good." She felt her stomach rumble and realized she hadn't eaten anything since yesterday. "All of a sudden, I'm starving," she said as Nicky helped her down onto the stool.

Nicky had seen the pain cross the woman's features as she sat down and knew that proceeding right away would be out of the question. Manuel brought over a plate of eggs and a steaming cup of coffee and placed them in front of Harry, then moved quickly away.

"He's in a hurry. Was it something I said?"

"Well...he did hear your expletives from the bathroom." Nicky laughed again when she saw the look of horror on Harry's face. "Not to worry, he doesn't understand English very well. Go ahead and eat, and I'll check out this ankle."

Harry sat there, unable to comprehend what was happening to her. Not only did she have to rely on Nicky for almost everything, but now Manuel was a witness to her helplessness as well. *What is that they say...pride goeth before a fall? How very true.* She was drawn from her thoughts by an agonizing pain shooting through her ankle. *No way I'm going to cry out and let them see any more weakness.*

Nicky knelt to remove the bandage and was careful not to move the ankle unless she absolutely had to. Hearing the sucking in of a deep breath as she gently probed the area, she spoke soothingly, "Manuel mixed up a poultice of bark, berries, and leaves that should relieve the pain and swelling. I'm going to lather it around your ankle, then replace the bandage. Okay?"

Her breakfast and coffee were forgotten as she fought the need to cry out in pain. "Sure, why not? I read somewhere that the natives have all kinds of medicines for everything from headaches to menstrual cramps."

"Actually headaches are rare in this region. The jungle is nature's pharmacy if you know where to look."

As the young woman took tender care of her ankle, Harry was struck by the way Nicky talked to her in a soothing tone. Perhaps she had chosen the wrong career altogether; she should have been in medicine rather than research.

Nicky had lived the first seventeen years of her life roaming from one remote spot to another. Something she'd learned quickly was how to take care of injuries and to know what could and couldn't be expected of them. Breaks were what everyone dreaded—they could cause the injured person to hole up in a remote and potentially dangerous area for days, possibly weeks. Nicky completed her examination, she settled down on her haunches, and stared directly into her boss's pain creased features. "The swelling hasn't gone down any, I'm afraid. I'd hazard a guess that you won't be fit to move around until we can get it in a cast."

"Are we stuck here until help comes, is that what you're saying? Can't you do something with it, like make a cast out of magazines?"

"Well, we're fresh out of magazines. I wish I could, but the bone needs to be set. If I set it incorrectly, you could be permanently disabled. I don't want to chance that."

"Neither do I, although I hate the thought of being stuck here for who knows how long." Harry had a thoughtful look as she fixed her eyes on the jungle's foliage. "Certainly there will come a point when it will become dangerous for us." Nicky's gaze confirmed Harry's earlier description of the eyes—they did hold a few slivers of silver, quite unusual and very spell binding.

"We'll be out of here before that, Harry. Right now, I'm concerned with the skies that are becoming heavy again. I think we'll be lucky if it holds off for more than thirty minutes. Let me get Manuel so we can both help you back to the tent. That'll be quicker." Nicky smiled as she stood up and went in the direction of the man who turned as he heard the rustle of leaves underfoot.

Harry watched the confident gait and for a brief moment, it reminded her of Abby. She had always had that kind of swaggering gait, full of confidence; it had been totally endearing. As she thought of Abby, Harry smiled slightly. *You would have had a field day at my expense if you could see me in these circumstances.*

Nicky approached Manuel and explained the situation. He gave her a look of understanding, nodding his head in concurrence. Discussing the changing weather front, both agreed that they must quickly put everything securely away and shore up the tents. They both returned to the seated invalid, who looked somewhat morose.

It was quite disconcerting for Harry to be helpless and at the mercy of others. Thinking back, she could not recall a time in her life when she felt so dependent on others, not even as a child. "What next?"

Nicky grinned and laughed when Manuel said something in response. "We're going to move you back into the tent, settle you down, and then make sure everything is secure before the heavens throw another downpour at us."

"You understand Manuel?"

Sheepishly, Nicky allowed herself to gaze into the blue quizzical eyes below her, "I'm a little rusty, but yes, generally I know what he's saying."

"Another hidden skill," Harry didn't have time to elaborate as the two gently swung her into a cradle position moved her back into the tent with relative ease.

As predicted, the rain came, heralded by crescendos of thunder and huge pebble-like drops of rain. As Harry listened to the force of the storm against the canvas tent, she wondered what had happened to Nicky. She could hear them still clearing away the few items they had left outside, and she wondered if the lovely bathroom was being rescued. *How long does it take to stow things away, and why not leave them? What does it matter. Surely keeping dry is more important.* Her thoughts kept her from facing the fact that she was actually worried about Nicky.

Ten minutes later, a dripping wet Nicky Ralston rushed into the tent and closed the flap quickly before the rain could find its way inside. Harry watched in fascination as she saw the woman flick her dripping hair back behind her ears. She was surprised to see that the young woman's face was a picture of exhilaration not irritation. Nicky's scant clothing, a pair of khaki shorts and a matching T-shirt, were drenched, molding to her well-formed body like a second skin. "May I ask, do you actually like this type of weather?"

Nicky laughed at the sardonic expression on Harry's face. "Oh yes, give me a decent rainstorm any day."

"I've never met anyone who really enjoys this type of climate."

"Lot's of people do, Harry. Maybe you would too, under the right conditions."

"How can torrential rain ever be the right condition?"

"Trust me, it can." Nicky cringed at the words that seemed to flow from her mouth. She wanted to run and hide in embarrassment, realizing that her words sounded so...so adolescent.

"You need to change your clothes or you'll catch a chill."

"I'll be fine," Nicky said, shrugging off the need to remove her clothes. Somehow, it made her flush, the thought of Harry seeing her unclothed.

Harry saw the faint tinge of red stain Nicky's cheeks. *Ah, but of course.* "I promise to close my eyes, how would that be?"

"It isn't...that is...I didn't mean for you to think... I guess if you turned your back," she said, finally admitting her embarrassment.

"You got it."

Nicky had to smile in genuine affection as Harry shifted her position. The flinch of pain that flashed across Harry's face made the gesture all the more endearing. "Thank you, Harry."

"Anytime, Nicky...anytime." Harry smiled inwardly as she felt herself warming to the pint-sized woman with the compassionate heart. It had been too long since she had let the sun shine in her life, and Nicky Ralston was definitely a ray from the sun.

Chapter Nine

The base camp was like many other scientific sites. Any outbuilding used for research was specially equipped and state of the art for the jungle. The housing for the scientists and other participants might appear primitive to the casual observer, but was remarkably comfortable.

The team had been welcomed and shown to their new residences and workplaces. After settling in, Eric went in search of his long time friends, Eden and David Martin.

"She's coming here, Eric?"

Eden Martin was astounded but ecstatic at the same time. Over the years, they'd practically given up hope of ever meeting Harriet Aristides.

"Oh yes, and I think you'll be surprised."

"I don't think so, Eric. We've had reports, remember."

"Ah yes, I forgot. That would be from... me." Eric grinned as he watched his two old friends. How he had missed them! They had many memories that bound them together, more so than blood ever could. Somehow, the feeling of coming home was never more acute than now in their presence.

"I thought I was the absent minded one, Eric." David Martin tapped his hand on the larger man's shoulder in a friendly gesture as he looked around for his pipe.

"My friend, I believe it's called selective memory loss."

"Oh, Eric, really. David remembers nothing but his botanical finds. How he remembers to come home each evening, I'll never know," Eden remarked as she looked over at her husband of thirty-five years. In her eyes, he hadn't changed at all. He might not be the best looking man around and he certainly never recalled a birthday or anniversary, but he was hers. She had fallen for him the very first day she'd met him in college. Fortunately, he'd been smitten as well.

"Precisely my point...selective."

Eric recognized that Eden and David Martin were far from the classic match. Most would say they were mismatched in many ways. Eden was attractive, outgoing, bubbly, and planned things studiously. David, on the other hand, was plain in looks, shy, and extremely absentminded. Opposites apparently did attract, and they did so in a very loving way.

"What do you make of the others in the party, Eric?"

"Jenson is a good guy, a little slow on the uptake but capable. Lawrence could be difficult in the wrong conditions, hopefully we won't have those." The Martins both gave him a quizzical glance.

"Hmm, how should I put it better? Well, why not wait for the others and then you can make up your own minds."

"Okay, who else is there, my friend?" David asked, perplexed by the evasion.

"Tremayne is young, but knows his stuff and is willing to learn. St. Clare is finding his feet but enthusiastic."

"I see you have Roja as your guide. Who chose him?" Eden asked suspiciously.

Eric heard the slight bitterness in Eden's tone, but he refrained from asking what caused it. If she wanted him to know, she would tell him. "From what I gathered, he came highly recommended and so far he's done what we needed."

"Yes, to a certain extent he would do so but I'd watch out for him. He'll sell you out to the highest bidder."

Eden walked over to the cabinet and retrieved the pipe her husband was looking for. He never managed to find it on his own. God blessed her with a loving child in adult's clothing. Her husband needed her and she would always be there for him.

Eric looked around the comfortable room and was once again amazed at how adept the Martins were at making something so temporary into a home, in every sense of the word. It had crossed his mind more than once that they were born to be nomads with the understanding of what was needed to make that work. His eyes then shifted to the photographs that stood proudly on the bureau. *A lifetime in photographs in more ways than one*. He looked at the last one taken of Abby when she was nineteen.

In that long ago time, life had been so different for them all, so simple. Happiness had flourished in those days as the sun shone brightly and love was everywhere. Laughter had been replaced with a sorrow for those departed and those lost. Eric wondered if life could ever be that simple again.

Chapter Ten

Over the next few days, as Harry took some time to heal, she and Nicky began to know and respect one another for their depth of feelings and knowledge. Nicky found Harry to be quick and quite funny, while Harry found Nicky to be kind and compassionate. Each woman accepted her role in this newly forged union of survival. They had discussed various subjects, though nothing too personal, finding out that they supported opposite political groups, weather conditions, food and clothes. Laughter also mixed with many in-depth conversations about ecology and research. Overall, they were opposites in every way. However, that hadn't stopped the tendrils of tentative friendship from taking hold.

Harry had dug out a bottle of Scotch, which they were happily consuming at a steady pace. "Who taught you how to play cards so well?" Harry chuckled as she lost for the sixth time in a row that evening.

"Oh, I was brought up on them." Nicky cocked her head. "I don't think there is a card game in existence I haven't played…but I'm willing to be taught new ones." She grinned. The last hour and half had been great. The alcohol not only helped Harry relax, but eased the pain as well. The poultices that Manuel made had done a remarkable job in reducing the swelling, but the pain was another story. *Maybe tonight she'll be able to sleep straight through,* Nicky thought hopefully.

"My uncle loved to play card games. Actually, I think it was the only thing he knew to use to entertain a small child. I used to beat him, but you have me on the run here, Nicky. I'd be bankrupt by now if we were playing for money." Harry laughed as she relaxed into the moment. *It's been a long time since I've felt this...happy.*

"Oh, I'd let you bet your shirt." The off-handed remark was out before Nicky could stop it, and she blushed at the mental image it produced.

Harry laughed at the comment. Although she knew that it was meant innocently the blush on Nicky's face lent it another meaning altogether. "Ha...I didn't realize we were playing strip poker. Now that would be a game of cards I've never played. What about you, Nicky?"

Nicky was flabbergasted. *How do I answer that one?* "I...I...I've never played it either."

Harry grinned, wiggled her eyebrows, and watched as the younger woman shifted under her gaze. *Maybe I'll play with her a little longer...it's harmless fun, after all.* "Well, how about it? You up for a game you've never played? I'd call that challenging, wouldn't you?"

"I...I don't think..."

"You chicken?" Harry couldn't resist the teasing. Nicky was so easy to tease, and although she wasn't going to go through with the game, it did have its appeal.

Nicky was glancing anywhere but at Harry. The close confines of the tent seemed even closer as she felt the heat of embarrassment surge through her. Then she felt a bubble of laughter at the absurd suggestion. *It's a joke...it has to be. Well, two can play this game...let's just see what she's made of.* "I'm not a chicken...I'll play if you will."

Harry was caught off guard at the offer, not knowing whether to proceed with the joke or dismiss it as such. Her voice took on a sultry, seductive tone. "Will you really?"

Nicky found herself hoping that they would play the game. "Why not? I can't lose. If your current performance is anything to judge by, I have a better chance of keeping my clothes on than you do." The heat rising in her body was not from embarrassment, but desire. The thought of Harry buck naked in front of her was very stimulating.

"Okay, Ms. Ralston, let's play. And if you don't mind, you may top up my glass. And don't forget your own. I don't want you to have an advantage by not drinking as much as me."

"At your service, Ms. Aristides." She did as requested and the two sipped Scotch as the new game began.

"Ha, I win again!" Nicky exclaimed as she showed a hand of twos and jacks. She had won all four games and Harry had removed her socks, jacket and now had to decide between her shirt or her jeans. Although she was feeling light headed from the Scotch, Nicky managed to stay alert enough to win.

Nicky's a real cool customer; wonder when she's going to call a halt to the game. Hell, it's the shirt or the jeans next. Before long I'll be naked! Fortunately, the Scotch was dulling the pain that throbbed in her ankle and the humiliation of defeat.

"I'm waiting, Harry." Nicky sat back with a smug smile on her face, waiting for the woman to indicate which garment she was going to lose next.

"You can't really expect..." She didn't finish when she saw the raised eyebrows. Those wonderful eyes were undressing her, of that she was sure. *Okay, okay I can do this; I'm sure I can.* "Shirt."

Nicky heard the terse reply as long slim fingers unsteadily began to unbutton the denim. She had to stop herself sighing in anticipation as one creamy shoulder was revealed, then the other until the shirt was thrown onto the small pile of clothes. *Wow! Does she look great without clothes.* The only barrier to seeing her breasts was a tantalizing lacy white bra. *Two more hands and that could be gone too.* "Shall we continue?"

"Yes…yes, of course."

For some inexplicable reason, the next couple of games went Harry's way and Nicky had to forfeit the socks she wore. A smile of satisfaction crossed and remained on Harry's face as she dealt the cards with more confidence.

This time Nicky restored her equilibrium as she won the game and looked pointedly at the jeans cladding Harry's legs. "Want me to help?"

Really, is that necessary? Harry looked at the beaming satisfaction on the other woman's face and contemplated her predicament. "I don't need help removing them," she said before sliding down the zipper and easing her legs out of the jeans. The movement overcame the anesthetizing effects of the alcohol and she felt intense pain in her ankle. She let out a sharp gasp and was amazed when Nicky leaned over her in concern.

"Are you okay?"

Nicky's face was so close to hers, Harry could smell the Scotch on her breath and the faint odor of sweat. Between the throbbing of her ankle and the closeness of the other woman, Harry was finding it hard to concentrate. Her blood began to heat and her body reacted in anticipation of what was to come. She hadn't experienced those feelings for a long time and had thought she never would again. "I'm okay, thank you."

Silver flecked green eyes held pale blue ones and both women felt the tug of emotion.

Quite out of character for her, Nicky found herself falling under the spell of this woman. The need to kiss Harry was overwhelming and she felt herself moving toward the lips she craved.

Harry was powerless to do anything as she felt the vision move toward her. Her body was on high alert, craving the touch, needing the contact, and wanting so much more.

As their lips met, sparks and fire exploded throughout their bodies like an erupting volcano. Harry moved so that she lay flat on the bed as Nicky gently moved with her to lie over her, her legs straddling Harry's waist. The kiss was all enveloping, washing away any coherent thought. For days they had casually flirted with one another, and now the attraction had grown too strong to ignore. There was no stopping as they finally gave in to what they desired.

Nicky was the first to release their lips and she dragged in a ragged breath. Trying to regain her wits, she thought about what was happening. *Am I here kissing Harriet Aristides? Is this a dream?* Pulling away slightly, she was surprised when Harry pulled her back. The blue eyes caught hers, asking her an unspoken question.

"I'm sorry."

"No! Please no, don't be sorry. It's been so long."

The softly spoken words tore at Nicky's heart. Tears began to well up in her eyes as she looked down into blue eyes.

Harry softly wiped away the tears with her thumbs as she held the beautiful face in her hands. "Why the tears?"

"They're happy tears."

Harry gently pulled Nicky to her waiting lips. Once again, they were lost in each other as their tongues slowly and tenderly met and danced the dance of the ages.

Pulling away again, Nicky looked into the blue orbs, "What do you want?"

Harry couldn't believe it. *I'm being offered... what exactly?* Her body craved the contact with Nicky; it was a need waiting to be satisfied. In a moment of clarity, she knew it was more than a physical need. She needed and longed for intimacy and contact with the small, wonderful woman. "I want you."

Nicky's heart began pounding even harder as she realized what was about to happen. It felt right, so very right. She needed to bond with Harry, not only on a physical level but on an emotional one as well. "Then you can have me, if I can have you."

No words were forthcoming as Harry pulled Nicky back for another kiss. Several feverish minutes later, they were both naked as Harry gently stroked Nicky's cheek and looked deep into the eyes that mirrored her soul. "You are so beautiful. I need you, Nicky. I've been so lonely for so long."

The words initially had a sobering effect on Nicky, who tried to pull away slightly. As she saw the tiny frown appear on Harriet's forehead, her misgivings dissipated and she put the memory of her sister to the side as passion overwhelmed her. "Then make me yours, Harry."

Harry's hand moved with tenderness down Nicky's neck and played with the weight of each breast. "Oh so lovely…so very tempting."

The blonde heard herself give a groan of delight as she was thrown into a haze of ecstasy. Her hips ground against Harry's waist, and she was unable to stem the flow of fluid that now traced her lover's belly.

Harry's mouth captured first one nipple then the other as she suckled them to turgid perfection. Feeling Nicky's juices on her belly added to the erotic sensations that were building inside her. "Let me in," Harry mouthed against the left breast, and was pleased when Nicky understood and turned so that her lower body was repositioned for Harry to gain access.

As she felt the long slim fingers invading her moist center, Nicky closed her eyes, delighting in the exquisite feeling coursing through her body. The anticipation of what Harry would do next was nothing compared to what she felt when the fingers deep inside stroked her in small circles. Nicky was desperate to touch Harry and let her know how much she needed her. Reaching for a breast, she fondled it, pulling and squeezing on the protruding nipple. Harry responded with a deep groan of pleasure.

Fingers slowly slid out, searching for the hard nub that was waiting for attention. As she stroked, she heard Nicky's moans and knew she would soon be ready for her first release. Her fingers slowly trailed through the profuse juices, drawing them upward toward a nipple. Harry traced around each erect point, then began to suck as her fingers once again teased the electrified nub. With other fingers, she delved inside and increased the tempo as Nicky's hips moved in time. Nicky's first orgasm was strong and hard, leading up to the next that exploded with such force she trembled for what seemed like forever. The green eyes glazed in passion as Harry held her close.

Still trembling, Nicky couldn't believe her body's response. "Oh my God, Harry, that was spectacular!"

Harry was unable to prevent the smirk that perched on her lips. "I'm very pleased. You're a wonderful inspiration."

Nicky bent down and began placing tiny kisses all over Harry's face and neck before their lips and tongues met in a deep probing kiss. Once again, they were lost in each other, only wanting and needing to please. The kisses lingered on Harry's upper chest, inching slowly toward the enticing targets below.

It was such sweet misery for Harry as she tried to lift her breast up to Nicky's mouth. Then, when she was certain she would die from anticipation, she gasped as she felt lips take her right nipple and suck hard while fingers teased the left. Harry was in ecstasy as attention to each breast was slow and sensual with small kisses. Gulping in a deep breath, she felt a sensual pain as her breasts were subjected to an onslaught of small bites. Although it was more shock than actual pain, she found it to be erotic and completely satisfying.

Harry was in a sexual haze as she felt the kisses move down her abdomen and over her navel before making a path to her mound. It had been so long since she had given herself to someone. Never in her life had she thought she would ever feel this way again. Kisses and sure fingers delved delicately through the forest of hair, while her hips responded to the questing mouth sucking her clit. *Oh, God, if this is a dream, never let me wake up.*

A finger slowly stroked the velvety wetness as a tongue and lips sent all the tiny nerve endings to the edge, only to slow down and start again. Just as she thought she would die an exquisite death, Harry felt a second finger join the first as they plunged into her. The sensual invasion sent her hips into a fury. She was lost in the feeling and wanting more and more. A third finger joined the others. *How much longer can I wait?* Her fingers were entangled in Nicky's hair as she moaned loudly.

The thrusting of fingers and sucking of lips in time with her hips made Harry forget the pain throbbing in her ankle. As she moved her body in passion, all that was important was climbing as high as possible before flying free with release. As the fingers increased their tempo, she felt the waves of ecstasy wash over her repeatedly. The power of her orgasm was so intense that she fell back on the sheets, collapsing in ecstasy. She was amazed at the emotions she felt. Her body had been the biggest surprise, accepting Nicky so naturally. She closed her eyes for a moment before gazing into those green eyes filled with flecks of silver.

Nicky was watching. She seemed to be lost in the moment, an almost angelic look on her face. She tenderly kissed Harry's lips and smiled. Sliding off, she cuddled next to Harry and gently passed an arm under her shoulders pulling her head onto her shoulder.

Harry rested there, shocked that Nicky wanted to stay next to her through the night.

"Go to sleep Harry."

The whispered words made complete sense to her as she drifted off into a deep, easy sleep.

Nicky looked down at the dark head on her shoulder and smiled. *Did we really just make love? My God, I can't believe this happened. Where does this leave us now? What of Abby?*

Her thoughts whirled in chaos as she struggled to keep awake, but the lovemaking and Scotch soon took their toll. *Maybe I will join Harry in a dreamscape.* Soon her mind was hearing Etta James sing *At Last* in time with the rain cascading down the tent. *I wonder when Roja will come back for us.*

∞

Nicky woke in the middle of the night to find herself naked, holding an equally exposed Harry. At first, she wanted to move away before she was discovered, and then it dawned on her that was how they had fallen asleep and why they were lying so. Pink tinged her cheeks as a pleasant feeling of arousal spread through her body. As she lifted her head, the headache that had only been a dim threat, hit like a thunderbolt. *Drinking and playing cards definitely do not mix. Oh my God, what will Harry think of me now? I can't believe I lost control like that.*

Harry moved in her arms and a warm tender feeling overtook Nicky. Reluctantly, she extricated herself, then donned her clothes. Gazing at Harry, who was still soundly sleeping, Nicky sighed as she moved out of the tent as quietly as possible.

The sky gradually became lighter with the heady pinks, pale blues and grays of the rising sun as Nicky paced in the early morning hours. *How in the hell did that happen? What should I say, how should I act? Can I ever look Harry in the eye again? What about Abby's memory?* As she walked around the small clearing, she was unable to come up with any answers.

Now with the dawn heralding a new day, Nicky saw the stump of a tree and sat down on its smooth surface, quietly holding her head in her hands. *Oh God, how can I feel so low and yet so high at the same time?* She had been under the influence the night before, but despite that, as she remembered what they had shared, she was amazed. Over the years, she experienced her fair share of relationships, but nothing was as exhilarating as the feelings she had for Harry. And, she couldn't deny her growing attraction to the woman. *If last night is anything to judge by, it's far more than attraction,* she told herself. *Perhaps it's the setting. After all, we have been out here in the wilds for several days in close proximity.* Of course, there was the obvious. *Good old-fashioned lust. Yeah, that would account for it, lust. Nothing more than raging hormones between two consenting adults.* However, she couldn't lie to herself—she had fallen hard for Harriet Aristides.

Standing, she once again began pacing around the area until Manuel came out of his tent to investigate the noise. Concerned that there was a problem, he asked, "Ms. Ralston do you need anything?" Reassured by her response that there wasn't a problem, he set about making breakfast while making small talk with Nicky about his children.

Their muffled voices woke Harry and she stretched her body to its full length. The movement caused her to wince at the pain in her ankle, and the daggers inside her head vied for her attention. *Just how much did I drink last night?* Her eyes scanned the tent until she saw the bottle of Scotch lying on its side. *Oh, hell.* It was three-quarters empty.

Ugh! I could do with a drink of water or a decent cup of coffee to take away this cottonmouth, and the headache might ease up if I have a decent shower. She looked down at herself and noted first the nakedness of her body, and then the small marks on her breasts. *Either a persistently ferocious mosquito relished that part of my body, or I...oh, shit.* The mere thought jogged her memory and she suddenly recalled everything about the night before.

"Oh my God, what have I done?" Although the words were a mere whisper, they echoed in the tent. They seemed to rebound off of every side of the canvas and return to her a hundred times louder.

Holding her head, Harry contemplated the previous evening and couldn't help the warm feelings that pervaded her body as she recalled Nicky in her arms and the lovemaking they had shared. It had been the first time she'd wanted to make love to anyone since Abby. *Abby! Oh God, I've betrayed our love! How could I do that?* Her feelings of euphoria and sadness were intermingled. *What should I do now, apologize? After all, it was a mutual need, wasn't it? Sex that was all it was...just good old, heart stopping, mind numbing sex.* She shook her head in disbelief as a vision of Abby suddenly appeared before her, then disappeared just as quickly.

∞

Nicky heard noises coming from the tent and was tempted to ask Manuel if he would assist Harry for the rest of the day. But she knew that would be a cop out. She also desperately needed to look into Harry's

239

eyes. *And see what?* Taking a deep breath, she went over to the tent, and slowly lifted the flap, all the while repeating a mantra: *I can do this.* Her heart was pounding so hard, she was sure Harry would hear it. No way was she going to show any sign of the inner turmoil she was feeling. "Harry, breakfast will be in five minutes. Need any help?"

The clipped tone was worrisome and Harry was consumed with a need to know exactly how Nicky felt about the night before. *Maybe it didn't happen. Maybe a hungry mosquito did ravish me. Yeah, right! Damn, she's cute when she blushes. Don't go there, Harry, just don't!*

Blue eyes snared silver green ones, seeking information, but Nicky looked away. *Still, the pink tinge to her cheeks is a dead give away.* "I've dressed as best I can. Would you help me with the jeans?"

Nicky sucked in a silent breath. She really didn't want to—that was how it all started in the first place—but decided she didn't have any choice. *I'll treat this as if it is a lab experiment, in a professional, unemotional manner.* But as she knelt down in front of Harry, it was clear that her body hadn't gotten the message. *Oh my, those legs!* "You know, Harry, you would have less trouble getting dressed if you wore shorts instead of jeans."

"Shorts? I haven't been able to shave my legs, how can I wear shorts?"

"Shave your legs? Harry, we're in the middle of a jungle; who gives a rip?"

By laughing, Harry felt a bit of the tension between them dissipate. "You're right. I'll find some in my bag and put them on. It's too hot for jeans, anyway."

Nicky turned away, busying herself with anything in an effort to avoid looking at Harry. She desperately wanted to retreat to a safe haven...to be anywhere but in that tent.

Harry thought she would play with Nicky and see if she could make her blush again. Besides, she did want to know how Nicky felt. "Nicky?"

The blonde's back stiffened as she turned around. *Damn, why does life get so complicated?* "Yes, Harry?"

"Would you take a look at this and tell me what you think? Are these mosquito bites?" Pulling open her shirt, Harry exposed her breast. When she saw Nicky flinch and turn brick red, she knew it hadn't been a good idea.

Wringing her hands, Nicky hung her head, trying to find the words to explain. "I...Harry I'm...I don't know...it must have been... No, that wasn't it. I'll resign when we get back home. I am so sorry." She felt pathetic.

"Sorry? Was there something to be sorry about?" No longer was Harry teasing; something inside was goading her to be awkward. She was equally responsible for the situation and that irritated her.

"No! No, it was...." *How do I continue? It was wonderful, passionate, and I want to make love to you again.*

Harry had spent years taking apart business associates, and she saw no reason not to use the same tactics for a one night stand. *Was it just a one night stand?* she wondered. *There's no denying I'm attracted to her. Shit, I don't need this in my life now.* "It was...?"

Nicky was upset; she knew she should have remained in control. *What excuse do I have? I wasn't*

241

the one on medication and drinking booze that probably left her vulnerable. How could I have taken advantage of the situation? "What can I do to make it right?"

"Make it right? If I'm not mistaken, Nicky, we were both involved. No one twisted my arm, did they yours?

"No."

Nicky was obviously upset and embarrassed, and Harry felt a rush of tenderness for her, but for some reason just couldn't express her feelings. "Why on earth do you think you need to resign? I'm the one that should be worried about a sexual harassment lawsuit."

Go ahead, keep goading her and see where it gets you, Harry! The words echoed through her head in what sounded amazingly like Abby's voice.

"It won't happen again, Harry, I honestly am sorry." Nicky didn't wait for a reply. Turning quickly she fled the tent, tears trailing down her cheeks.

Manuel watched the young woman come out of the tent crying. He liked this foreigner; she was unlike most of the ones he came into contact with. *Maybe the boss lady became ill in the night; there was much moaning from the tent last night.* "Nicky, is there a problem?" he asked quickly in his native tongue.

"No problem, Manuel, just a female thing, you know."

The man smiled slowly. *Ah yes, a female problem.* He knew all about that, having a wife and four daughters. "I understand. Please, I have eggs for breakfast."

She loved eggs. The guide pushed a plate in front of her and for a moment she forgot her troubles. "Where did you find these? I thought we ran out."

242

"Oh, I know where to look, and the natives were friendly." Manuel winked at her and proceeded to crack another two.

"I think Harry is in pain this morning, Manuel. Perhaps she would appreciate breakfast in the tent, if you don't mind?"

"Sure, Roja should be back today."

"Really? How do you know that?"

"Roja is my wife's brother. He will be back or he will not have a happy life when he returns home. Consuelo, my wife, she would give him an ear bashing, as you say." He laughed heartily as he made the eggs before he placed them on a plate and went toward the tent.

A grin flashed across Nicky's face and then disappeared as the feeling of melancholy washed through her. *How could I have let myself get so out of control? We are both intelligent women; I guess it was the Scotch.* Thinking of how she'd felt touching Harry and making love with her, a warmth and passion began to rise and soon Nicky was flushed with desire. *That has to stop!* She pursed her lips hard. "It wasn't the Scotch," she said with resignation.

Still, the question remained about what had been the instigation, and the only real answer was straightforward — they were in a different place and had been pushed together by fate for many days. And it was certainly better than being incompatible, arguing all the time. *Or was it? Now perhaps we'll never speak to each other with the same ease.* What ate at her the most was that she had made love to the ex-partner of someone she dearly loved. *Oh, Abby, what would you think of me now? Have I betrayed you?*

A rustle of undergrowth made her forget everything as she quickly stood up and scanned the area for signs of life. One thing she could still do, even after all the years away, was to decipher whether or not a noise was threatening. She was staking her life that whoever or whatever was approaching was friendly, because there was far too much noise for it to be otherwise.

"Hello the camp," a voice she recognized as Roja's shouted into the stillness. She shouted back a welcome.

The guide appeared out of the darkness of the trees with a grin as wide as a truck, eyes beaming in satisfaction as he saw the woman by herself. "My lovely Nicky, why this is a wonderful welcome for a weary traveler." Roja quickly crossed the distance between them and stood within an inch of her.

Nicky gave him a brief smile, but before she could say anything, she was astounded by another figure emerging from among the trees. Recognizing him, she rushed toward the figure with childish pleasure and flung her arms around him.

∞

Harriet was going to eat with them or not at all. "Manuel, will you help me? I'll eat my meal outside with Nicky."

"She no happy," he said in broken English

"I know." *I'll take care of that as soon as I can talk with Nicky. I need to explain, make her understand.*

Emerging from the tent, they were greeted with the unexpected sight of Roja, looking somewhat put out at Nicky in the arms of another man. What amazed Harry the most was the jealousy she felt as she watched the two people together. They seemed incredibly happy to see one another.

"I can walk, Manuel. Let me go!" Harry's voice rose sharply as she swung out of the man's grasp.

The pitch of the scream that came from Harry astounded her. *Was that really me, or something in the jungle?* It did have the effect of making her the center of attention as she landed unceremoniously in a heap on the ground.

Manuel crouched down to check on the pain wracked woman, as Roja ventured forward. He spoke quickly in his native tongue, the scowl on his face showing his displeasure at the situation.

Nicky was suddenly there, and for a brief moment, Harry's pain went unnoticed as she gazed into captivating eyes. She was glad to see Nicky, but was curious to know the identity of the man she had been speaking with.

"Harry, are you okay? What possessed you to walk on your own?" The exasperation was clear in Nicky's voice. "Where is your crutch?"

"Can't I even make my own decisions now? Anyway, you seem very engrossed with your new friend."

Abby's voice rang in her head. *Attack, Harry; keep attacking, see where it gets you.*

Nicky looked into blue eyes that didn't waver and were filled with...anger but something more...much more. "Of course you can make your own decisions, but will you wait until you have a cast on the ankle and then, by all means, walk wherever you want."

Harry felt ashamed. In spite of everything, Nicky responded with gentleness as she checked the swollen ankle. She wanted to crawl under a rock, but she let her poorer instincts rule as she petulantly replied, "And your new friend?"

Nicky couldn't keep herself from laughing, the question was so absurd. For some reason the laughter became louder and louder until she felt a sharp sting across her cheek as Harry brought her back to her senses.

I can't believe what I just did to Nicky. Oh hell, what's happening to me? I'm acting like a jealous lover.

Holding her hand to her cheek, Nicky looked quizzically at Harry, the hurt evident on her face. *What is going on here?* "Jacob isn't a new friend, Harry, I grew up with him."

Closing her eyes, Harry slowly shook her head. "I'm sorry," she said softly. She had been an obnoxious heel who had treated Nicky badly.

Abby's voice kept haunting her. *Looks like you found out where pushing would get you, Harry. Are you proud of yourself now?*

Nicky was anxious to get Harry up off the ground and more comfortable. "Manuel, will you help me lift her to the seat near the stove?" she asked in his native tongue.

Roja and Jacob watched the interchange between the two women with interest, each man motivated by his own reasons for wondering about the situation. As Manuel and Nicky moved Harry, Roja came forward with two things he had brought back for them: a brace for stabilizing Harry's ankle, and a pair of real crutches.

"Harry, this brace should help in relieving the pain some. Will you let me put it on you?"

Considering Harry's earlier actions, Nicky thought if prudent to ask permission.

"Of course. You're the best caregiver I've ever had." Harry averted her eyes, chiding herself for the inadequate words. *The best caregiver... Get serious. How lame can you sound?*

Nicky crouched down and gently took the injured ankle in one hand, supporting its weight. With her other hand, she unwrapped the bandage. "Let me know if I move your ankle in the wrong way and hurt you, Harry." She gingerly positioned the brace, never once looking up into the blue eyes above her. Standing up she adjusted the crutches and motioned for Harry to try them. "These should give you more mobility and freedom." The concern in her voice carried a tinge of coolness. "Now you won't have to rely on others as much. I know how you dislike that."

"Thank you, Nicky. I guess I won't be a burden to you any longer, will I?"

Nicky heard the sadness in the tall woman's voice and regretted her business like tone. "Harry," she said genuinely, "never were you a burden...never."

"Nicky?" the voice was soft and earnest. Questioning eyes looked into pleading ones each telling a story without words.

"Yes."

"We need to ta…"

"Ready to go, ladies? If we leave now, we will be that much closer to our destination." Jacob looked at both women. "Ms. Aristides, your carriage awaits you."

"In a minute, Jacob, Harry and I need to finish something."

"No, it will wait," Harry said. "I know everyone would like to get to base camp, so we'd best get started. Thank you for all your help, Nicky. I can't tell you how much it meant to me." With that, she positioned the crutches and headed for the stretcher that would take her to Abby's parents, the voice haunting her every step

Good going, Harry. You really took control of that situation. You have to tell her how you feel; she deserves that.

"Glad to do it." Nicky sighed as she watched Harry retreat.

Chapter Eleven

"They should be back today, especially since you sent Jacob with them." Eric watched the clearing for any sign of the people they had left behind several days earlier.

David Martin frowned as he considered his friend's words. "Yes, the weather has been perfect for Nicky. My daughter loves her rainstorms. It must have known who was coming home."

"I'm sure Mother Nature has missed her as much as everyone else around here. I didn't know that Randy was working in the area too. Is he on a similar quest, or has he found something else?"

"As you know, Randy freelanced for a while, now he's joined the Cole outfit. You remember that one, don't you?"

"Isn't that the group that started to decimate half of the rainforest without government permission a few years ago?"

"Yep, the very same one. They should be declared a hazard to the environment."

"You're kidding me, Dave. Randy wouldn't stoop that low, would he?"

"Nope. He moved with his family to a more civilized area, but quickly found out it wasn't for him so he came back where he felt at home. The Cole outfit was the only one hiring, so he signed on there. Guess he thinks that working for them is better than nothing."

"Yeah, it's hard to leave what you love," Eric said slowly as he contemplated his own predicament.

"I was surprised you had come out again, Eric. Thought you had decided to take that office job."

"So did I, my friend, so did I."

"Eden has gone to the first site with St. Clare and the others. I think she's a little nervous about this visit." David Martin chuckled as he recalled his wife earlier that morning. "She was up at the crack of dawn and started cleaning everything in sight, and some things that weren't. I don't remember the last time Eden was so nervous about a visitor. She's just like Abby was...never letting anything or anyone rattle her." His features became sad for a moment as he thought of his daughter. "You know, most of her life was happy. That's more than most people can say."

"It certainly is, my friend; Abby was a special person. Everyone who knew her, loved her." Eric fell silent as each man remembered Abby in his own way. Finally, he spoke again. "That's rather unusual for Eden, isn't it? I guess this is a momentous occasion in two ways. I think I would be nervous too." He took a deep breath before continuing. "You know, David, when I left her five days ago, Nicky hadn't told Harry about her relationship to Abby. All hell could break loose when she finds out exactly who Nicky is."

"You may be right, Eric." David wrung his hands and began patting his pockets for his pipe. "Right now, all I care about is seeing Nic again. What Harry's reaction will be... Well, we'll see what happens when they get here. It will be cause for celebration when they arrive, don't you think?"

Eric chuckled as he slapped the much smaller man on the back. "Why, David, I thought you would never suggest it."

"It's been too long since you left Eric, way too long."

Chapter Twelve

Nicky chatted amiably with Jacob. With all the years that had passed since they last met, they had much to make up. She had to admit that he had matured into a handsome man and good company, if the two days they had been journeying together were indicative.

"Why did you stay away so long, Nicky? Everyone has missed you, especially your father."

"My father? Oh, don't be silly, Jacob. Dad's head is never out of the clouds and you know it. He's always on the lookout for the next challenge." Smiling, she thought of her father and his single-mindedness when it came to his work. He, more than anyone, would never go back to the civilized world.

"You were his shadow. I think in some ways, he was yours too. He would often comment that you were teaching him more than he was teaching you at the end. He was very proud of you." Jacob took a big breath before making his next statement. "In a way, you broke his heart when you didn't want to come home."

Jacob had watched the small spindly child grow into a small chubby teenager, and now, though her stature would never increase, she was certainly a beautiful woman. Gone was all that chubbiness and in its place a compact body, not thin, but nicely rounded. It suited her. Then, there were her eyes. They had always been mysterious, and now they were even more so. He had been the first boy to kiss her and had wanted to be the first man, but it wasn't to be. She had left before that could happen. From time to time, her parents would comment about the mail she sent,

251

but they never mentioned anything of a personal nature.

His comment stung. "Dad wanted me to have my own life, Jacob; he knew he couldn't live it for me. He had to let me grow up and find what I wanted to do rather than what was offered to me on a plate. I never stopped missing the life, though. It will always be in my blood, I can't deny that. Being here again has shown me that a part of me will always crave this life."

Jacob grinned at her. "Does that mean you might change your mind and stay here?"

Nicky laughed at the absurdity of his comment, then considered that with what had happened with Harry, perhaps it wasn't so absurd after all. "I have a life, Jacob, and I'm happy there, as hard as some of you might find that to believe."

"Oh well, it was worth asking. Who knows, you might change your mind yet."

He threw a casual arm around her shoulders and glanced at the two men behind carrying the injured women in a makeshift stretcher. He wasn't expecting the glacial look he received or the scowl that seemed to be permanently etched on her face whenever he looked in the injured woman's direction. *Can't have been anything I said, I've barely said hello to her.* She and Nicky seemed to have a relationship of some sort, which wasn't surprising, given that she had been Abby's partner. Turning back to look ahead of him, he noticed they were less than an hour out of the main camp. They would all be glad for a shower. He felt Nicky shiver. Was that a reaction to getting closer to her folks, or something else? "Are you okay, Nicky?"

She wasn't. She had felt the fever raging through her body for most of the day. There were times she was so fatigued that she wasn't sure if her legs would keep her upright, and she was certain there wasn't a part of her body that didn't ache. Since they had been making such good progress, she'd decided to carry on without complaining. "Yeah, I'm fine, just a little tired. Of course, I'll be glad of a shower and a nice rest in a decent bed. Sleeping on the hard ground takes some getting used to."

"My God, Nicky, you've gone soft living in the lap of luxury." The man laughed as he hugged her tighter.

Out of nowhere, a sharp, strangled sound came from behind them and they both turned.

Harry couldn't believe it. She had to endure watching that gorilla touch Nicky. Not that it was her business, but his attentions were making her nauseous. Worse yet, Nicky appeared to be enjoying every minute of the man pawing her. *Friends? I wonder if he knows that.* Rage engulfed her.

The voice couldn't leave her alone for even a minute. *You had your chance, Harry, and you blew it.*

Not that she could say anything…she couldn't. She and Nicky had barely said more than a few words since…that night. The brace allowed her to keep the ankle immobilized and left her free to do things for herself. But she missed the small gentle hands that had helped her over the past few days. *And what have you done to thank her for that? Took advantage of her in an alcoholic stupor and then blamed her.* Abby's voice was stronger and clearer now, making sure Harry understood just how foolish she had been. What she hadn't planned on was everyone hearing the expletive she'd uttered as the man hugged Nicky tighter. Now, all eyes were on her.

"Ms. Aristides, are you okay?"

"Yes, thank you, Mr. Roja, just a twinge. That last bump caught my attention."

The last thing Roja needed was for the woman who was paying the bills to be injured again. "Do you need to stop? We can, if you need the time."

"No, no I'm perfectly alright now. Continue please." She hadn't anticipated the arrival of Nicky by her side. The look of concern on her face told Harry all she needed to know. *What an idiot I am!*

"Are you okay, Harry? Do you need to stop? It's not far now, but if you want to stop, it's okay. Isn't it, guys?"

"I'm okay, Nicky, just a twinge. I want to carry on." She couldn't leave well enough alone, so she added testily, "Let's just get there, okay?"

You did it again, Harry. When are you going to learn?

Shaking her head, Harry tried to ignore the voice. *I don't know why I even bother. Damn her for getting under my skin. Why is it that I have no defense against her, I wonder.* At that moment, it would have taken too much energy to be angry and she had none to spare. "Fine," she said in defeat.

Harry saw the dejection, but there was something else: the usually vibrant woman was looking tired and ill. She had been so wrapped up in her own problem that she had totally missed the fact that maybe Nicky was suffering too. *The whole situation surely has to have had a draining effect on her. After all, it isn't every day you make love with your boss only to have it swept under the carpet as if it never happened.* "Are you feeling alright? You look kinda peaky. Maybe I could take care of you for a change…what do you say?"

Nicky stiffened. She hadn't wanted anyone to notice her weakness, certainly not Harry. "I'm fine," she said wearily. "Nothing a hot shower and soft bed won't cure. Jacob said at our current rate we're about an hour away from the camp. It's best to carry on." She turned away quickly before she could be caught by those all-seeing blue eyes.

As she did, Jacob took over the burden of the stretcher from Manuel who gave him a grateful look and took Jacob's place beside Nicky. "You okay really, Nicky? She right, you look pale." He quickly put out a hand before she could stop him from feeling her very hot brow. "You have a fever for how long now?" he asked.

"Manuel, I know what it is; I've had it before. When we get to the camp, I'll have the meds to treat it." Nicky sighed wearily, knowing that she had been a fool to forget to take the necessary precautions against malaria. She of all people should have known better. It had been a long time and the area wasn't high risk anymore, so she had grown lax about observing the safety precautions. *Damn! Why was I so stupid? I'm going to put this little adventure down as my all time stupidity campaign.*

"You sufferer?" the man asked in concern.

Over the few days as she had become close to Harry, she had formed a friendship with the man who was their guide. He understood his land at its very roots, not like his brother-in-law, who worked only for money.

"Yeah. An hour away, Manuel, and I'll be fine. Trust me, the people there will know what to do."

"They better, Nicky. This not good." He walked within inches of her to offer support should she need it. Malaria was not something to treat lightly. It had killed many people, and could kill her too if she didn't treat it soon enough.

Chapter Thirteen

Eden Martin watched the investigative team work to validate her and David's findings, but her mind was occupied with the imminent arrival of the rest of the party. Abby would not have been happy with the situation. They should have met her partner long before five years had passed. Their beautiful, willful daughter, who had such a love of life, would never come home again, and that was still difficult to believe. The feeling of acute loss was overwhelming, and she showed it more so than her husband did. David simply lost himself in their work to hide his pain. She believed grieving was essential, and she had done that for a long time.

In some ways, she blamed the woman who was on her way to see them. At one time, in the early days of her anguish, she had considered leaving the company and moving over to the Cole operation as their friend Randy had done. David wouldn't allow it. He knew it was her grief talking, and that eventually she would see that it wouldn't have been right for them. And she had, although it had taken months since other family issues had come into play during that period. Now, she wondered if fate had intervened by allowing them to focus entirely on their work. If the outcome was what she thought it would be, they had the potential to help improve thousands of lives.

"Eden, would you mind going over a few things with Doctor Lawrence here?" Peter St. Clare asked the woman quietly. He had seen her preoccupation and didn't want to startle her. From all the reports he'd read over the past few days, Harry was going to be ecstatic, despite the injury to her ankle. All they had to do now was get the samples confirmed with a rudimentary synthetic product; then, they would know the exact potential of the find. Nichola Ralston was needed now.

"Sure, I'll be happy to go over whatever the doctor wants."

"Thanks."

As he spoke, a bell could be heard ringing from the main camp and Eden turned to the sound. *They're here at last!*

∞

Nicky felt like shit. Her legs were like lead weights, each step an effort of mind over matter. Only the image of the main camp and what she would find there kept her on her feet.

Manuel had discreetly supported her for the last half hour; without his aid, she doubted that she would have made it. Harry had taken some painkillers and had fallen asleep, so she hadn't seen the pair change from leaders to stragglers. Jacob had given her a concerned glance as he and Roja moved forward. The native guide merely shook his head, presumably at the vulnerability of women under difficult conditions.

The camp was close. Nicky heard the ringing of the bell that indicated visitors were approaching. Not only was the bell useful, but at times, an essential part of the communication process. Harry and the others would be there already. They had moved ahead and out of view a few minutes before.

"Not far now, Nicky. Just around the ridge. How would it be if I carried you?" He spoke in his native tongue and gave her a shy smile. He knew that the young woman was independent and didn't want to show weakness. If she expended all her energy and sapped her strength, she would have difficulty fighting of the effects of the malaria.

"No! Please, Manuel, I can't go into camp that way. It is very important to me, you will understand when we get there." Her voice rasped in her throat, and she felt the perspiration dripping from every pore in her body. Even knowing it was bordering on suicidal, she had to enter the camp under her own power. *I must!*

"Okay. We are near. Just a few more yards and the camp will be there."

The steamy confines of the jungle opened miraculously to allow them into a clearing that held several cabin like buildings and three or four tents. People were getting closer, but she could hardly see them in her fevered haze. Still, she'd made it on her own.

A seemingly friendly native lifted Harry off the stretcher and gently placed her in a comfortable-looking chair. She didn't actually know if he was friendly or not, but at least he was smiling. Her eyes roamed around the camp and saw Eric and another much shorter man looking beyond her to the entrance of the camp. When Harry glanced in that direction, what she saw tore at her heart. Nicky, who had generously helped her throughout the trek, was stumbling into the camp aided by Manuel.

Why the hell doesn't that guy pick her up and help her? The shorter man was rapidly walking towards the two newcomers, while Eric made his way over to her. "Who is that, Eric?" Harry asked, her eyes never leaving Nicky. *What is wrong with her?*

"David Martin," the large man said quietly as he watched the scene unfold. The camp was silent as the others watched as David Martin and Nicky Ralston met face to face.

What happened next Harry was sure she would remember the rest of her life as a moment when she was actually at a loss for words.

"Nic?"

Silver green eyes, glazed in fever, looked into a mirror of concern in matching eyes. "Daddy, I've missed you." The words seemed to echo around the camp as the woman pitched forward into her father's arms. He picked her up as if she was a featherweight and walked with surprising speed toward a cabin, as several natives joined him.

"Daddy? Daddy? Did I hear that right, Eric? David Martin is her father?" Harry was open mouthed. *How can that be? Why didn't I know that Nicky was related? That makes her Abby's...*

Eric felt sorry for the woman beside him going through her own hell as she tried to comprehend everything at once. "Yeah. Nicky is David and Eden's youngest daughter, Abby's sister."

"Why? Why didn't I know? Why didn't she ever say?" Her whispering voice shook in disbelief. Suddenly, the bell was being rung vigorously by one of the natives.

"You need to ask her that when she feels better. Now they want the doctor and Eden. She's going to be livid at Nicky's condition."

"She's not the only one; I'm upset, too. She's my responsibility; even more so now! What could be wrong with her? She was okay a few days ago, even this morning."

"From what I could see and what I heard David say when he spotted her, malaria."

"Malaria? What the hell! How did she get that? We were all inoculated, or so I was informed. Will she be alright?"

"Harry, she is in the best possible hands. Her parents know how to handle this. Nicky has suffered before. Obviously she didn't take the necessary precautions. Knowing that kid, she was out and about in the rain and wasn't protected against the mosquitoes, either."

There was a commotion as Eden Martin arrived at the camp. Someone was speaking to her in a native tongue and what she heard made her ruddy complexion turn ashen. She swiftly mounted the steps of the largest cabin on the site and went inside. Rita Lawrence, her medical bag in hand, followed within a few strides.

"I'll help you to the cabin. You might get some rest yourself." Eric had seen the look of horror pass over her face. *Something is wrong here and whatever it is, I need to find out and make it all okay.*

Harry sat quietly digesting what she knew and what she felt. This woman, Nichola Ralston, had opened a heart she thought was dead. Now she was lying gravely ill, not knowing how much she was cared for. "My God, this just makes it all worse. Oh God, Abby, what would you think of me now?"

Abby's voice whispered to her again. *It will be all right. Continue down this path, Harry.*

"But what if I get lost?"

Chapter Fourteen

Harry spent the next two days sitting on the small porch with her leg propped up and her eyes constantly flitting to the cabin that housed Nichola Ralston. No matter how much Harry badgered, no one had been forthcoming about her condition. Rita Lawrence had been non-committal when she finally encased Harry's ankle in a cast, enabling her to hobble about the camp on her crutches. As she kept her vigil, she read all the notes she could get her hands on regarding the new find.

Roja had set up a chair right in front of her cabin, and time and again, Harry had to listen to him muttering and carrying on. "It was quite careless and stupid of her to have arrived in this climate without inoculations. She should have known better, having been brought up in this environment."

The group was meeting outside Harry's cabin to save her from trekking across the compound on crutches. Evan Tremayne finally voiced what many had silently thought. "Yeah, it was stupid, but it's done now. What we have to do is make up for lost time. Jacob was telling me that the Cole Corporation is close by...or at least someone who works for them in the same field. We might lose the advantage if we don't get on with the investigation."

Harry smiled encouragingly at him. St. Clare should have been the one to state the obvious, not this raw recruit.

"I have rudimentary skills in synthetics. Perhaps I could start the ball rolling until Nicky is well enough to take over," Neil Jenson suggested, then he drank from his coffee mug.

"I didn't know that, Jenson," St. Clare remarked, little realizing he had put another nail in his coffin when it came to review time.

Perhaps Seth Roland is losing his touch, Harry thought, although he had placed a question mark on the man from the beginning. This project seemed to have a black cloud over it from the start. The short notice had meant that not all the top people could join the team. For better or worse, St. Clare was the man assigned to head the team and she would continue to support him in that capacity. "I suggest you take him up on the offer and get to work. Now would be a good time," Harry directed from her seated position, her eyes darting to the main cabin for any signs of movement.

"I will. Sure, I will. Come on, Jenson, let's get moving. Want to join us, Eric?"

"No. Evan and I are going to look over his idea for an incubation area. I'll check in with you guys later."

Harry nodded at the plan. "Good idea, Eric. If you need me, I'll be inside going over the reports. Otherwise, I'll see you all at dinner." Three hours later, she stretched the muscles in her back and neck, then rotated her head. *Oh, what I wouldn't give for a nice massage.* Closing her eyes, she envisioned Nicky working the aching muscles of her shoulders.

The voice was still chastising her. *Now why would she want to do that for you, Harry? You have been nothing but awful to her.*

The opening of the cabin door drew her from her thoughts as she looked up into eyes that made her catch a sharp breath. Abby's eyes were looking down at her with a cautious expression in them. *Get a grip, Harry.*

Eden Martin had been remiss in failing to greet the newest of her visitors to the camp, especially this visitor. Not only was Harriet Aristides in charge of the company they worked for, but more importantly, she was the woman Abby had loved and the last person to see her alive.

"Ms. Aristides, I presume." She held out her hand to the woman seated rather awkwardly in the chair her husband always used. "That's my husband's chair. I doubt it is too comfortable for a tall person such as yourself."

Harry broke into a genuine smile. *Yeah just like Abby. Guess my girl was a chip off the old block.* "Well, it's considerably better than what we had in the jungle. Mrs. Martin, I take it?"

"Eden, please. Mrs. Martin was my mother-in-law, God rest her soul."

"Harriet...or Harry...whichever you want is fine."

They shook hands and then Abby's mother drew out another chair and sat down into its well-worn leather comfort. "Harry, I think. That's what Nicky calls you."

At the mere mention of the name, Harry felt her senses sharpen. "How is Nicky? Doctor Lawrence wouldn't say."

"She's is going to be just fine. She gave us all a scare for thirty-six hours, but she's over the worst of it. I guess she forgot about the basics of life here when she decided to come on the trip. David is with her now, giving her a hard time as only he knows how."

Harry gulped back the lump that came to her throat now that she knew Nicky was on the mend. "I was worried about her."

"Yes, I'm sure you were." The frank admission and the emotion behind it were not lost on Eden Martin. Nicky's ramblings were interesting but didn't know if they were true or just the imaginings of a woman who was less than lucid. Watching Harry's composure slip at the mention of her daughter, Eden surmised that there must be some truth behind the ravings after all. "My baby has grown. I wouldn't have recognized her in a crowd."

"I…that is, I didn't realize she was your daughter, not until we got to camp," Harry said wearily. The lack of sleep and worry over Nicky's condition was finally catching up with her.

Eden gave her a measured glance, taking in Harry's posture, softly spoken words, and tired features. "Eric told me. I find that very strange, although when I think about it, perhaps not with Nicky. She takes after her father in many things, and keeping personal information close to the vest is one of them. She loved Abby a great deal, and in a child's eyes, you took her away from her family. It was easier to forgive Abby for going away like she did if you were to blame."

The words were quiet, almost absent, as though she hadn't meant to speak them aloud. A mask of sadness visited her features as a fleeting memory tried to take hold.

"She hates me?" Harry almost whispered the response. Her face paled at the unexpected realization.

What did you expect, Harry?

Won't Abby's voice ever stop berating me?

"No! No, Harry, not at all. Nicky has never hated anyone, to my knowledge; she's not built that way. When something is important to her, she can get

265

carried away, but hate...no. She used to cry at night for Abby to come home and I think when we got the message she had met you, it broke Nicky's heart. Abby was her confidant, friend, sister, and someone she loved very much. To Nicky's mind at the time, you replaced her in Abby's affections and she didn't understand. Besides, that was many years ago."

"I see. I guess that makes sense then. Does she understand it now?"

Eden watched the differing expressions flit across Harry's face. She wasn't a conventional beauty, but she did have that inner strength that held you in awe and gave a stunning impression. Abby and, it would seem Nicky, had the same taste in romantic attachments. "I think you should know the answer to that better than anyone."

Harry felt her cheeks warm as she realized what Eden's words implied. *Does she know about what happened between Nicky and me?* Her next words tumbled out in anguish and pain. "I've never cried for Abby. I've wanted to so many times, but I can't!"

"Maybe it's because you haven't let her go," Eden said softly.

"I don't ever want to let her go." Grief was evident in Harry's voice. "She was my life."

"How can you find happiness with someone else if you don't allow Abby to pass?"

"I don't want anyone else..." She stopped as she saw a flicker of compassion in eyes that shone at her like Abby's used to. *Is that compassion for me, or for Nicky*

"Are you sure?"

Harry sighed. "I guess I'm not sure of anything at this moment. Things appear to be changing rapidly around me. For the first time in my life, I'm out of control. Not even Abby's death had that effect on me," Harry admitted reluctantly.

"I'm asking as a mother now, will you do something for me?"

"Yes, anything."

"How about we share a coffee and you tell me all about your life with Abby. I want to hear it from someone who loved her as much as we did."

Something changed in Harry at that moment. Until then, James was the only person she had talked to about the love she had lost in that accident. Yet there in the wilds, with Abby's mother, she wanted to talk. It was the right time to let Eden know about their life together and how happy they had been. "I'd like that, thank you."

"And then later, maybe you would like to see Nicky." Eden wasn't disappointed as a beaming smile flooded Harry's face.

"That would be wonderful, thank you. Nicky and I need to talk."

"Come along then and I'll have Abula make us some splendid coffee. How did you and Abby meet?"

Harry laughed as she recalled the blonde whirlwind that had swirled into her life. "I was working at my desk when a vision of beauty burst into my office demanding I locate her parents. Then...."

∞

The opening of the cabin door startled David Martin out of his contemplation of the conversation he'd had with Nicky. Looking over, he saw his wife and Harriet Aristides, the woman who apparently had attracted both of his daughters. He shook his head.

Strange how fate works. I admit we've lived an unconventional life, but to have both my daughters prefer women... On top of that, they both love the same woman. The odds against that are astronomical.

Eden crossed to her husband and placed a brief kiss on the top of his head. "How is Nicky?"

"She's fine, darling. Sleeping, or was when I left her an hour ago." He gazed at the visitor who was easily recognizable from the photographs Abby had sent. Although he wanted to be angry with her for removing any chance that his eldest daughter might have returned home, he knew he couldn't. His children had to make their own mistakes and earn their own triumphs, and he believed that her life with Harriet Aristides had been Abby's crowning glory in her short lifespan.

"Harry, this is David," Eden said.

Harry held out her hand to the much smaller man who had a warm, solid appearance that made him seem like a teddy bear. Smiling, her thoughts quickly drifted to Nicky, who certainly was a chip off the old block in both size and, she suspected, temperament. "Pleased to meet you, David."

"Harry. We of course know lots about you from our daugh...ters."

"Really? Well I hope at least some of it was good." Harry laughed good-naturedly, her spirits uplifted after the two-hour session with Eden Martin. Reliving her life with Abby had been cathartic in many ways, not enough to cry for her lost love but helpful. For the first time since Abby's death, she felt as though someone understood her pain and grief. Surrounded by Abby's voice and eyes, the intense sorrow began lifting from her heart.

David gave her a long look, his expression of concentration reminding her of Nicky. When anything required any degree of thoughtful contemplation she had that same look.

You miss her and want to see her don't you, Harry? What are you going to do about that?

Eden knew he wasn't happy about something. She placed her fingers on his creased forehead, trying to smooth away the wrinkles that appeared there. "David, really, Harry is family."

"Yes, sorry, Harry. You are also our boss, therefore it can be difficult to decide which hat you're wearing."

Strangely enough, given Abby's descriptions of her parents, Harry had thought she would have a harder time with Eden. David Martin was being particularly unfriendly in a subtle way. *Now why would that be?* Harry had to admit David was right: she was their boss. *Should I tell them the real reason I came here? That it was an excellent opportunity to make contact with Abby's parents I couldn't let go by. Just being here in this place, my heart feels lighter. Would they understand?* "That's true. And actually, my coming here was more personal than business. In your home, I would like you to at least consider me a friend of the family."

"I can do that if you can. Nicky might be awake now if you want to go in. Please let her sleep though, if she gets tired."

Harry tried to suppress her grin. "Thanks. If she's asleep, do you mind if I sit for awhile?"

Eden was astonished at her husband's attitude; it was so not like him. "Harry, stay as long as you want. Nicky will be glad to see you, I'm sure."

Walking slowly toward the door of Nicky's room, she turned and winked at David Martin. "She's in safe hands, I promise."

∞

"David that was rude, I thought we had discussed this."

"I wasn't rude. And *you* discussed it, Eden; I didn't!"

Eden was perplexed. Rarely, if ever, had she seen this reaction from her husband. "Don't try to change things around, David. This is Abby's partner we're talking about. She should be treated as one of the family, not as an enemy."

"Precisely. *Abby's* partner. And she's not taking another Martin scalp for her belt!"

As he kissed her cheek and left the cabin, Eden was too shocked to do anything but watch him leave.

∞

Harry sat quietly watching Nicky as she slept. Her blue eyes took in the pale skin that a few days before had been a healthy color. Although the Martins were confident that their daughter was on the mend, her skin felt clammy.

She is your responsibility now, Harry. What are you going to do about that? Abby's voice was once again taunting her to do the right thing.

What, indeed, was she going to do about Nicky? Nicky, who look looked like a child, the way she was lying in the bed. She had one hand out of the bedclothes and the other under her pillow, tugging it as close as possible. Harry's thoughts dwelled on the lovemaking they had shared. She felt the warm glow building as her body reacted to the memory. *Was it only lust, a desire for sex?* Most confusing were the powerful emotions she felt, not only at the memory, but for Nicky.

It was just another one night stand right, Harry? Keep telling yourself that; it's safer for you.

Shaking her head, Harry wondered why Abby had chosen now to start giving her advice. And there was another aspect to Nichola Ralston...she was Abby's kid sister. *Why the hell didn't I know that?* Her mind methodically checked every piece of information Abby had given her regarding her immediate family, and yes, she knew her lover had a sister. They'd even had a family photo in their house, but it had been taken years before so there wasn't any resemblance between the kid in the photo and the real thing. Abby had never mentioned that her sister was in the States going to college, and Nicky certainly hadn't gotten her degrees in the wild. The puzzle was why Abby never mentioned her or asked her to visit. *Maybe Abby did ask her, and Nicky declined because she was still angry with me for taking her sister away. Damn! What a tangled web we weave, and this wasn't even to deceive.*

Her focus was drawn back to the present when she heard a movement in the bed. Glancing over, she saw wonderful silver-flecked green eyes gazing at her in shock. *Shit, I never thought that she might not want to see me.* Harry smiled nervously. "Hi, how do you feel Nicky?"

"I'm going to be okay." The words were raspy, and Nicky pulled up in the bed in an attempt to reach the glass of water on the small cabinet beside the bed.

Harry was faster. She retrieved it and, with a flick of her eyebrow, indicated for Nicky to rest back on the pillows as she helped her take a drink. Nicky put up her hand to grasp the glass and the touch sent a shiver through their bodies. Both might try to deny it, but the electricity between them was obvious.

"Thanks."

"No problem. It's the least I can do." Harry knew her voice sounded brusque and regretted her tone when she saw the startled look on Nicky's face.

Nicky didn't know what to think, so her mind grabbed on to the obvious. "I'm sorry I've delayed the project. I'll be up tomorrow and get on with the work double quick." All the trauma and events of the previous week overwhelmed her and started to seep out. As tears welled up in her eyes, she gulped back a sob.

"No! Nicky, you haven't delayed anything. It appears Jenson can do the rudimentary stuff. Pity we didn't know that at the time; you would have been saved the trek. You really didn't want to come, did you?"

Not at the time. But now I wouldn't swap this trip, or what happened, for a million dollars. It's too precious. Those moments with Harry are something to remember for the rest of my life. The tears flowed as she realized that Harry was watching her with eyes filled with compassion. It was a certainty that Harry would never accept her overtures again, and she would have to deal with that for ever and always. The thought broke her heart. "Then I'm not needed?" The voice sounded small and unsure.

Harry saw the tears and longed to pull the small woman into her arms and comfort her, but she was afraid that Nicky would think she was being too familiar. She decided to carry on a normal conversation instead.

Way to go, Harry. By taking no chances, you give yourself exactly the same.

Abby was right of course. "Hardly that, Nicky." Harry's tone softened in reaction to her tender feelings for the woman.

Security at the camp had been tightened, and Harry had radioed a message to John Fredericks to put a lid on any communications concerning this research. All correspondence would be marked for his eyes only. Harry was going to return in a few days to eliminate any possibility that Shekia Canning would sell her stake in the company. If everything came right, none of them would want for money ever again. Time was the running out, though.

"If we are to beat the Cole Corporation to the golden drug possibilities your parents have found, we have to do everything at top speed," Harry reassured. "Sources in your parents' camp have indicated that someone who works for Cole is close to understanding the find as well."

At the mention of her parents, Nicky closed her eyes and tears dropped to her cheeks. *What can I say about that omission? That the deception had been well meant, nothing sinister at all? That I was shy? Oh yeah, I'm sure I'd get away with that, after spending a night in Harry's arms making love.*

"I'll get up now and help." Nicky attempted to untangle herself from the bedclothes only to be gently pushed back by the much larger woman. The sparks were once again electrifying the room.

"No, please rest a while longer. Tomorrow, if you feel up to it, go ahead and do your thing."

Startled, Nicky was enthralled at the words of concern and the wink that followed them. "Are you sure?"

"I'm sure, I want you healthy. We leave in two days, and I don't want you to have a relapse on top of everything else."

Harry stood and adjusted the crutches and made her way over to the small window. Outside, several people were scurrying around. It was a good group; they all had tasks to take care of and no one ever sat around doing nothing. Even when the night closed in and everyone was exhausted, she suspected some kept the light burning. With the Cole Company breathing down their necks, time was of the essence.

"Two days?" Nicky asked.

"Yes, I need to go back. It's important now. I have enough information to get things moving forward and if I don't, there might not be a company for me to go back to."

The words were spoken lightly, but Nicky heard the seriousness behind them. "It doesn't give me long."

"No, it doesn't. We can take samples back and you can work in the lab at home."

At home. How I wish I could share a home with Harry. Why was I so foolish as to blow any chance I might have had to make that happen? "I suppose."

The melancholy in those two words was not lost on Harry. "Don't you want to go back?" Suddenly nothing became more important than the answer to that question. It had never crossed Harry's mind that Nicky would not go back with her. The thought brought a distinct emptiness to her heart. Her pale blue eyes caught and held silver green ones as she waited.

"It's not that I don't want to go back."

"What is it then, your parents? I can understand that. Or, is it," her tone turned sharp, "that fellow you call a friend?" *No way could it be that, not after the way she had responded to me with such passion.*

"Jacob? He's an old childhood friend and it was nice to see him again, but I would never stay here because of him. I guess it's my parents, in a way." Nicky wasn't lying, but she wasn't telling the whole truth either. Something more held her back, but the right words escaped her. *Besides, Harry would never understand.* Until she could understand her own feelings and what she wanted, going back and being in close contact with Harry would only make everything between them worse. Of that, Nicky was certain.

"Hmmm, what do you say we continue this discussion tomorrow? As for today…why didn't you tell me that Abby was your sister?" It had been eating at her from the moment Nicky met her father. *Was it really because of me that Nicky and Abby didn't spent time together?* The very thought horrified Harry. *Did I deprive Abby of spending precious time with her sister?* It was impossible to rectify the situation now; there would be no second chances on that score.

"Eric told me to tell you, I just never found the right time."

"Really?" Harry said, arching her eyebrows. "We recently spent some very meaningful hours together, Nicky, and still you didn't think I would be interested in knowing you were Abby's sister?"

Nicky sucked in a deep breath. The headache she had felt niggling away started to pound in her temple as her mind tried to provide her with a suitable reply, and failed. "If I had told you in those 'meaningful hours', as you call them, what would you have said? Would we have allowed our passions full rein, or would you have distanced yourself from me?"

"Does it matter? That particular episode was a mistake on both our parts. The close proximity of the situation and alcohol were the main culprits...producing a mutual stimulating effect on our bodies without emotional involvement. Call it a few hours of lust, sex, a need perhaps. I'm sure you agree." The words were cold; she knew it. No way did she want Nicky to feel that she had to find mitigating circumstances to like her, if she ever had.

Go for the jugular, Harry; make her feel just as badly as you do. That was what you always did when you felt threatened. Maybe it's time to stop running.

Abby just didn't understand...or, did she?

The words, incredibly cruel, cut deep into Nicky's heart. "Is that how you view our relationship?" Was *it only lust? Do I feel nothing for Harry? This is a living nightmare. It must be part of my sickness, hallucinations...yes, hallucinations trying to drive me insane.*

"We are working colleagues, first and foremost," Harry continued. "A personal relationship may have been feasible at one time, had you bothered to tell me the truth. Frankly, to have the information thrown at me like that was a body blow. I'd have much rather you told me alone without the interested eyes of others looking on." Harry had been hurt at the time and had spent the hours of Nicky's sickness going over why. With all the information she now had, she realized that the bottom line was now she and Nicky could never even be friends. That one fact tore at her as no other had since Abby's death.

"I'm tired and have a headache; I'd like to be alone now, if you don't mind."

The eyes that had once held such happiness and joy now showed only sadness. Even if Nicky didn't think so, she had lied to her by omission. Harry was feeling inadequate and floundering in a situation that she had no experience in and was unable to decipher its true impact on her life. "Want me to send in one of your parents?" Harry made her way toward the door slowly, hoping that something would happen to change the situation.

"Not right away, I'll probably just sleep. Harry?"

She turned in hopeful anticipation. "Yes?"

Nicky stared at the woman for a long moment. What did she want to say, what was there left to say? She had lied and blown any chance of their being together. She finally sighed and said, "It doesn't matter."

Gazing at the small woman, Harry felt the grief of knowing there never would be a chance now.

Good going, Harry. Look at her face. Do you see the pain and sadness? You put it there. Are you proud of yourself.

She wasn't…how could she be. *I don't have a choice; it's as simple as that.*

Abby's response almost deafened her. *You always have a choice, Harry, and you are choosing to walk away.*

Harry cast one last glance at the invalid. "Get some rest. I'll catch up with you tomorrow."

Nicky watched Harry leave. She had seen the changing expressions on Harry's face and wondered what kind of drama she had been playing out in her head. Finally, the emotional drain was too much for her and she fell into a fitful sleep.

∞

Entering the main room, Harry saw Eden Martin still inside, pretty much where she had left her. "Hi, Eden. Nicky has a headache. She said to tell you she is fine, she just wants to sleep."

Eden contemplated the tall woman who appeared distracted and unhappy, strained and preoccupied. "Thanks, I'll check on her in a little while then. How did the chat go?"

Dark hair fall across her face as Harry shook her head. Her blue eyes searched Eden's for a few moments, looking for an answer to her thoughts. "Not very well, I'm afraid. I think I might have been judgmental, and it probably wasn't the right time to have any serious conversation with Nicky. I guess I never was very patient when it came to wanting to understand a situation."

"By that you mean, why my daughter didn't tell you who she was in relation to Abby?"

"Yes, precisely. If she was in our part of the world all that time, surely she could have visited. Perhaps she wouldn't have been so alone. I don't understand at all. Was it me?"

Eden stood up and walked toward Harry, clucking like a mother hen over a lost chick. "I assume you didn't ask Nicky that particular question?"

"No!"

"Pity. You might not have to carry the useless baggage of things that can't be rectified if you had been enlightened."

"Will you enlighten me?" Harry asked in despair.

"Sorry, my dear. Nicky has to be the one to explain her motives. Why not ask her when you come over for dinner this evening?"

"Dinner...this evening?"

Laughing softly, Eden placed a comforting arm around the woman's shoulders, "Yes, dinner this evening and I promise you David won't bite."

"Thank you, I'd like that."

"Eric and Jacob will be here too, I hope that doesn't pose a problem?"

Harry thought about it for a brief moment and grinned. It was nice to have Eden fuss over her like a mother. It had been a long time since anyone really cared about her...except for Nicky, of course, and she had just ruined all chances of that ever happening again.

There was no let up by the voice. *What has to happen before you get a clue, Harry?*

Ignoring the taunting in her head, she replied to Eden's inquiry. "Absolutely not, I'll be here. What time?"

"Come around seven and you can break the ice with my husband. Oh, and I can also introduce you to Jacob properly."

"Great. See you then, Eden." Harry hobbled out of the cabin, deciding to check on the progress of Jenson.

Eden watched Harriet Aristides move with slow but remarkably graceful movements toward the lab where most of the team and her husband were. As she turned away, she heard a strangled sob coming from Nicky's room and sighed. She had expected it.

Chapter Fifteen

Knocking softly, she opened the door and was greeted by a tear-stained face. The look of hopelessness in the depths of the silver green eyes tugged at Eden's heartstrings. She quickly moved into the room, sat on the bed, and took her baby into her arms in a warm, loving embrace. "What's the matter, darling?"

"I don't know what to do, Mom, I think Harry hates me!"

A waterfall of tears fell as Eden soothed the blonde hair, whispering into its soft tresses, "Don't be silly, Nicky. Harry doesn't hate you, far from it. Shh, darling, it's going to be okay. I promise." Holding Nicky close, she listened to the heart-rending tears, waiting for her to stop. Perhaps then she could settle her daughter down. Even though she was a grown woman, Nicky was still her baby. No matter how old she was, that would always be the case. As long as she was alive, her shoulder was always going to be there for Nicky to cry on.

"Oh, Mom, what a mess I've made of everything. I feel like I'm in a fog that won't lift. Why can't she and I just talk? I get so defensive, when all I want to do is say 'can we try again'."

"My darling daughter, if I could take away your hurt and pain, I would in an instant. But, there are some journeys in life we must struggle through alone. I will always be here for you—to love you, to listen to you and to give you a shoulder. My best advice for you right now is to step back and not try so hard."

"I don't know if I can, Mom."

"You can and you will. You are Nichola Ralston, my daughter and a fighter. Is she important enough to fight for, Nic?"

"I'm not sure I have what it will take. Perhaps I will step back and revaluate. Isn't that the first lesson of a good resear…" She struggled to stay awake as her eyes grew heavy with fatigue.

"Yes it is, sweetheart. Why not try to get some rest before dinner?" Eden soothed her hair and hummed an old lullaby as Nicky drifted off into a more restful sleep.

∞

Arriving for dinner, Harry looked in through the window and could see David Martin talking animatedly with Jacob and Eric. Sucking in a deep breath, she slowly opened the door and maneuvered into the room. Eden immediately walked over to welcome her and offer any assistance she might need. "I'm a little late, sorry."

"Harry, we are all scientists here and we know that that *sometimes* often dictates your time. I heard that Neil Jenson has done some wonderful things in the time scale."

"Yes, he deserves a raise." Chuckling she glanced around the room. There was a long table laid out for dinner. She almost laughed aloud at the absurdity of being in the wilds without many basic commodities, yet the dining table looked like it had come straight out of a restaurant.

"Let's get you a drink and introduce you properly," Eden offered.

Harry hobbled behind her hostess and smiled at the grin Eric Lasser gave her. David and Jacob, however, just gazed at her seriously while sipping their drinks.

"Hi, Harry, things are looking up, wouldn't you say?" Eric's friendly voice boomed out.

"Yes, better than I thought, Eric."

Eden was talking quietly to her husband, who Harry thought she saw scowling but she wasn't certain. She saw that while Abby was the image of her mother, so Nicky was of their father, but with the softer edges of femininity.

"Ms. Aristides, what would you like to drink?" David asked.

Ah, so that's how it's going to be. I thought we agreed in the Martins' home it would be cordial at least. If that's how he wants to play, it's fine with me. I know that game very well. "I'll have a Scotch and soda, please, Dr. Martin."

At the formal reply, David gave her a sharp glance. "Eric, what about you?"

"Vodka for me, Dave, just the way you know how to make them."

"Right with you."

Eden turned her attention to their younger guest. "Jacob, have you been officially introduced to Harry?"

The man she addressed gave a small smile as his grey eyes sought out her blue ones. Harry's stare branded him like a hot poker and he was struck by the fact that she was quite an intimidating woman. "Briefly, Eden. Ms. Aristides, pleased to meet you officially."

She wanted to be formal too, but having never heard him called anything other than Jacob, it proved difficult. "Pleased to meet you, Mr…"

Eden saw the body language between Harry and Jacob, and it obviously didn't appear friendly. *What a bunch!* "Why is it that everyone has to be so formal? Look, it's Harry, David, Jacob, Eric, and Eden." As the door behind her opened, she glanced immediately to the final piece in the puzzle for the evening...Nicky.

Eden grinned at her and received a small smile in return. "Hey, baby, how are you doing now?"

Nicky's eyes flickered over the group gathering in one corner. "I'm feeling a lot better thanks, Mom. Dad, I'll have orange juice if you're making."

"For you, anything, darling. Go sit yourself down in the easy chair and I'll bring it to you."

Harry watched the exchange, feeling a bit of sadness that she wasn't a part of the family. Something ached inside of her to be accepted as such, but without Abby there were no ties to ensure she joined the family unit; she was just an acquaintance, nothing more.

You pretty much sealed that fate, didn't you, Harry?

"Abby, I never knew you were such a nag," Harry whispered.

David placed her drink on the counter and poured the orange juice for Nicky. "I've got my hands full here, would you mind taking this to my daughter?" He handed the glass to Harry with a shrewd glance, then proceeded to make Eric's drink.

Nicky was instantly by Harry's side picking up the drinks before heading back to her seat. "Daddy, how did you expect Harry to carry one drink, let alone two, with crutches?"

"I would have figured something out," Harry said quietly as she followed Nicky. She was disheartened to notice the small woman still had the pallor that accompanied malaria.

David looked up from his task and shrugged. "Don't know what all the fuss is about. All I asked her…" He stopped in mid sentence when he saw his wife glaring at him.

Harry chose to ignore David's obvious dislike of her and concentrate on Nicky instead. "Are you feeling better?" As she accepted her drink, their fingers touched. Once again, electricity enveloped them and for a brief moment, no one else was in the room.

Nicky looked deep into the pale blue eyes and saw the sincerity there. "I'm feeling much better, thanks. It's surprising what a nap can do for you when you aren't feeling well. Please, Harry, sit and fill me in on Jenson's progress so far."

"Gladly," Harry remarked softly. She sat down in the chair opposite and began to regale Nicky with the events of the day. As Harry talked, Nicky felt herself relaxing and enjoying the simple precise narrative. Nicky asked several questions and before long, Eric joined them in the discussion. Eden followed, and about ten minutes later, David decided, he too, had to give his opinion. Jacob, the only one not involved in the project, stood on the outer circle, watching and listening intently.

The discussion went along with them to the dinner table. The meal was cordial enough, and at some point, the ice had started to melt. Each talked amicably about the project and others they were all participants in. Once the meal was completed, the discussion became more personal, mostly about the Martins and the old days.

Harry sat with her coffee and watched the changing expressions of each participant as they shared memories they had all been privy to. When Abby's name was mentioned, Harry eagerly soaked in the descriptions of her as a child without the feeling of pain she would have expected. In the past, just the mention of Abby's name sent her into a dismal mood; now she could smile fondly as the stories were told. She was also surprised that she couldn't keep from staring openly at Nicky as the youngest reminisced about the days of her childhood. She spoke with great animation and a little of the color came back to her cheeks, causing Harry's heart to flutter. *Nicky really is very beautiful.*

Eden had been watching the woman who had loved her oldest daughter to such a degree she wasn't allowing herself to live life again. There were so many more experiences to be had, some enjoyable, others sad; but the creation of memories that made up the essence of people's lives was being lost to Harry. After their earlier discussion, Eden had no doubt about the depth of the love Harry and Abby had had for each other. However, to starve one's self of love and affection had to be against God's wishes. She didn't have to look to know exactly whom Harry had been intently staring at for the best part of the last fifteen minutes. *How different Nicky and Abby are, just as David and I have been considered a strange match. If Harry met both girls at the same time, would she have chosen Abby? Hmm, an interesting question.*

"Mom, it isn't true, is it?" Nicky was laughing at something her father had said as she asked her mother to verify it.

Lost in her own thought, Eden had no idea what the conversation was about. Falling back on the standard reply in such situations, she replied, "Oh, you know your father, Nicky."

David Martin recognized the gambit and speculated as to the subject of his wife's thoughts. Before he could say anything, Jacob began an anecdote of his own and the answer was lost in the new recounting.

Two hours later, Harry thought it was probably time to say goodbye. She thoroughly enjoyed the evening and was reluctant to leave being part of a family—even as a stranger. It had felt good to her. Jacob had left an hour earlier saying he had to complete a paper he was working on. Eric and David were playing cards, and Eden was clearing away dishes and glasses. Nicky had gone out onto the porch to get some fresh air.

"Before I go, may I help you, Eden?"

"Harry, thank you, but you are somewhat incapacitated right now. Why not say your goodnights to Nicky."

As she turned to do just that, she heard, "Harry."

She turned to face Eden. "Yes?"

"I'm glad you decided to come on this trip."

"Thank you. You have no idea how much that means to me." Smiling, she turned and made her way to the porch where Nicky was. Harry stood next to Nicky, both at a loss as to what to say next. Harry couldn't help but notice how exhausted she looked. "You didn't overdo it, did you?"

Nicky had enjoyed the evening and thought Harry had too. While listening to the night sounds, the thought had occurred to her that Harry was probably just making sure her employee would be up to carrying out her job responsibilities. "I'll be capable of working tomorrow, if that's what you are worried about."

Harry flicked a puzzled look in Nicky's direction. She truly hoped the younger woman hadn't overdone her first time on her feet since her illness, and hadn't expected Nicky to respond so negatively to her genuine concern.

Once again, the voice haunted her. *After how nasty you were to her this afternoon, you shouldn't be surprised at all, Harry. You can give it but can't take it…is that it?*

After listening to the words that Abby spoke, Harry felt the urge to explain her earlier statements, and to find out if she really was the reason for Nicky not visiting Abby when they had been in the same country. Mostly, she wanted to take Nicky in her arms and feel her softness again. Fighting down the instinct, she pulled herself together. *I'd only make more of a fool of myself, and I've already done enough of that on this trip.* "Good evening, Nicky. I'll see you tomorrow," she said crisply before heading out into the warm, dark night as quickly as her ankle would allow. Making her way to her cabin, she was surprised to see Jacob leaving the perimeter. *That's odd. No one should be heading out alone at night. Maybe it has something to do with his work. I'll ask Eric in the morning.*

She was tired, the day finally taking its toll on both her body and her mind. It had been a roller coaster of a day. She wanted to find a place where she could just scream out her pain and let it go. And it was more than just the pain of Abby's death; her chance to love again was gone.

Abby's voice, but a whisper on the wind. *Only if that's how you want it, Harry. Don't settle for less than happiness, my love. You deserve so much more.*

Chapter Sixteen

As she opened her eyes, Nicky stretched her body and realized that she felt better than she had in days. Gone were the headache, the fever, and the pain in every joint of her body. It was time to get busy with the work she had come to do, and then she could head back to the States and her home. *Home. Is that where I belong, or is there some place else I should be?* Ever since her brief, intense encounter with Harry, Nicky had experienced a confusion of feelings of extreme joy and deep despair. Until *that night,* she had known exactly what she wanted for her life and how to get there. Now, she wasn't sure of either. Nicky sighed. *Right now, though, I guess I'd better get my teeth into some lab work, focus my mind on something other than Harry. I've got to do my part for the project.*

Showered and dressed, Nicky arrived at the lab where she was greeted by Peter St. Clare, who looked as if he had been up all night. "Hi, Peter, are you the very early shift or the late one?" She smiled at him.

"Nicky!" His face was beaming. "It's good to see you up and about. How are you feeling? To answer your question, I'm on the late shift. Jenson went to get some sleep about four hours ago."

She grinned at him. *It can't have been easy for him to have his first major assignment as team leader and get the boss along as part of the deal.* "Thanks for pitching in, Peter. Are you an expert we didn't know about too?"

He smiled wryly at her. "No. I just didn't like to leave the lab with all the stuff in the open. You can never be too careful." Nicky laughed as she passed over her black coffee, and he drank gratefully from the mug. "Thanks."

"Thank *you*, Peter, if I hadn't been so careless, no one would have to be doing my job for me."

"Don't beat yourself up about it, Nicky. It's over and done with. Incidentally, Jenson said he would let you have this particular job anytime; it isn't his favorite task. I don't think he minded a bit of a change; but I know he'll be glad to give it back to you. You sure you're okay? I don't want you to push yourself to come back too soon. We'll manage."

"Yeah, I'm okay. Just a little peaky, but my parents will see to it that I don't overdo things."

"The boss said she wants to leave in the morning; doesn't give you much time." St. Clare sat wearily down on one of the lab stools and sipped at the hot coffee.

"Yes, I know. If you'll show me the last of Jenson's notes, I'll get to work and you can get some sleep." After a ten minutes briefing, St.Clare left her to her task.

Two hours later, having been sitting for the entire time, Nicky stood up from her stool and twisted and turned her body to work out the kinks that had settled into it. It was still quite early, but she knew her hunger would be satisfied by something marvelous that Abula would prepare. The experiments were at a stage where they needed time to process, so she headed off to the main house to chat with her parents over breakfast. Before leaving, she secured Jenson's notes and other pertinent information, more because it was protocol than because she thought that anyone in camp would sell them out.

Nicky inhaled a deep breath of wonderfully clear morning air after leaving the lab. She watched as the sun began to rise and start its leisurely trek across the sky. *It's really good to be here!* So enrapt with her surroundings, she didn't see a dark figure steal quietly into the lab.

∞

"She's not going to come with me, is she?" Harry speculated openly as she watched Nicky taking samples and talking animatedly with her father.

Eric was standing in for the exhausted Peter and briefing Harry on the progress of the experiments. "Has she said so?"

"No."

"Then how can you know that? Only Nicky knows if she's decided to stay a little longer," Eric assured the woman at his side. "As for the tests, they are going very well considering we were without Nicky's services for several days." Eric smiled inwardly to himself, thinking of Nicky leaving her shyness behind her and winding up in bed with the boss. It was speculation on his part, but Manuel's account of a particular evening and the sound effects that had come from the women's tent had convinced him that it couldn't be far from the truth.

"If she stays, it will be to the good, I believe," Harry said absently, the thought making her stomach churn nervously.

Eric smiled at her with compassion. "Why not ask her and save yourself the speculation?" He left the pensive woman's side, giving her the opportunity to speak with Nicky.

Balking at the last hurdle, Harry could not bring herself to ask. She needed the extra hours of hope that Nicky would return with her. *If I were to find out now that she's staying, then getting through the rest of the day would be next to impossible.* She turned on her crutches and left the room.

Nicky looked up from her discussion with her father, expecting her boss to venture over and ask questions. When Harry left abruptly, Nicky felt her stomach clench. *Just one more indication that Harry doesn't want much to do with me. Damn! How did things get so out of control here?*

Her father saw the look of sadness in Nicky's face as she watched Harry leave. *Damn woman! How dare she do this to another one of my daughters?* He bent down and kissed Nicky on the cheek. "You're better off," he said before leaving the lab.

"Maybe you're right," she said miserably. Sighing heavily she went back to her microscope. At least she knew the work needed her attention.

∞

Outside, Harry was annoyed at herself for not facing Nicky, but she just couldn't face the rejection.

Hey, way to go, Harry, the voice said mockingly. *Running away has never been your style, my love. Why do it now? Remember, you said no challenge was too big. Face the challenge, Harry, before it's too late.*

Shaking her head, Harry spoke quietly. "There never was a right time. Maybe back home, over time, we could have developed…I'm not sure…something."

The voice spoke once again. *Develop what exactly, Harry? Someone to go bowling with, or a bridge partner.*

"No! More than that."

Then why not face her, Harry, and tell her how you feel? The voice was soft and soothing.

"I can't, Abby; I just couldn't face the pain of losing someone I love again."

Then you are a coward, Abby said defiantly.

Harry had no answer for that; she knew it was the truth.

From her vantage point on the porch, Eden watched knowingly as Harry seemingly had a conversation with herself. "You're your own worst enemy, Harry." As much as she wanted to take her daughter and Harry and shake some sense into the both of them, she knew she couldn't. It was something they needed to do for themselves.

Chapter Seventeen

Rechecking the items he had ready for the journey, Roja glanced toward the main cabin where Harriet Aristides and Nicky were in close discussion, and wondered if he would have a chance to flirt more seriously with the young blonde on the way back. With her parents around, he was keeping a low profile, but once they were away from the camp, it would be a different story. Early the next morning, they were setting off for town, and he would be paid in full. Maybe she would like to spend a romantic evening with him under the stars. Manuel had spent a few days alone with them, but said little about that time. His brother-in-law was never one to gossip, keeping his private life very private. Since he was married to his sourpuss sister, it wasn't surprising. He turned a speculative gaze toward his intended prey. He couldn't hear what the two were saying, but the animation of their exchange was evident.

"Harry, it can be synthesized. I'm sure with the resources back at the company we can make it happen. There's more work to be done here, of course, but I think we have a winner for the company."

Nicky was waving her hands excitedly, and Harry was getting dizzy watching them. She unexpectedly reached out and caught them between hers. "I'm pleased, Nicky, for your parents in particular."

Nicky felt her cheeks grow red as she looked down at her hands. Harry didn't look as if she was going to let go, and Nicky didn't want her to. Her body pulsed with pleasure as she relished the touch, however innocent. The sparks began again. "Yes, it

294

will be the culmination of a lifetime's work, not that they'll see it that way. They'll go on to other challenges, I'm sure."

"That's true, it's in their blood. Nothing short of locking them up and throwing the key away will stop them, will it? And that brings me around to you."

"Me?"

"Yes, you. Nicky, are you coming back with me tomorrow?"

The ensuing silence had both women holding their breaths, waiting for the outcome. The electricity between them was palpable.

Up until that point, everything had been crystal clear for Nicky. But with Harry touching her, standing so close to her that she could feel her soft breath, the decision was not so clear cut. Nicky trembled. She knew what she had to do – Harry had made her feelings quite clear. Lust and desire could not initiate a change; Harry did not want that kind of situation to develop between them again.

"If you don't mind, Harry, I want to stay. You need me, or someone like me, here. As I'm already onsite, it will save you the expense of sending someone else out."

Close to tears, Harry closed her eyes and swallowed the lump in her throat. It hurt…it hurt like hell! She had felt Nicky tremble and for a moment hoped that meant she would be returning with her. Now she was bereft at the thought of leaving Nicky behind.

Tell her, Harry. Don't let the moment pass by, Abby pleaded.

Ignoring the voice of reason, Harry relinquished her hope. "Once I saw you with your parents, maybe even before that, I figured you might want to stay. You love it here, don't you?"

"Yes. It's in my blood, too. When the preliminary reports are done, I'll come back and clear up my affairs. I won't need my apartment."

Harry dropped Nicky's hands, for no other reason than she was shaking and didn't want her to see it as a sign of weakness. "I understand completely. It's in your eyes when you look around and in how you settled so easily into the environment. I wish you luck, Nicky, and if you come back my way, will you look me up? We have the yearly parties for the folks in the field, don't forget."

Nicky heard the tremor in Harry's voice. *Why would she be upset? This is what she wants, isn't it?* Looking into Harry's eyes, she saw a deep sadness. She wanted to take Harry in her arms and never let her go, but something was holding her back. "I will, Harry. Thank you for understanding."

Words had become impossible, and silence enveloped them as they stared at one another. Harry was drinking in the sight of the small woman who had captured her heart. In a short time, Nicky had become more important to her than she thought anyone could ever be again.

Do something, Harry. Find a way to get her to go with you. Don't miss this chance.

"May I ask you a question?" Harry said at last.

"Of course."

"Why are you called Ralston?"

Her soft chuckle broke the charged atmosphere between them. Grinning at Harry, she explained. "I was christened Nichola Davina Ralston-Martin. Abby was a Ralston-Martin too. My mother's name is Ralston, so they double barreled the name. When I went to work for the company, I decided to drop some of the name and simply go by Nichola Ralston."

Harry's forehead creased in puzzled contemplation. She couldn't recall seeing any reference to Ralston as far as Abby was concerned. Admittedly, she hadn't really looked at any official documents recently, and back when she had, her mind had been in a haze. "I guess I forgot. Will you see me off in the morning?"

"Of course. I'll give Manuel the recipe for the cakes that Abula says you love."

Harry laughed. "Yep, I ate a cartload of them; they are fabulous. Thanks. See you in the morning, Nicky. Sweet dreams." She then turned away to tell Roja that there would be one less going in the morning.

That night, each woman's dreams were full of sensuous images of the other, each revealing her true feelings in the only way she could.

∞

The morning arrived and the travelers busied themselves with preparations for their departure. Several men were going along to carry the stretcher for Harry. Roja looked over the equipment as Manuel spoke with Nicky.

Eden took the opportunity to speak with Harry privately. "You take care, Harry. I know my daughter would be upset if anything happened to you."

"I will. Don't worry about me. Roja wants his money and he'll not get it unless he delivers me unharmed. Besides, Nicky is explaining Abula's recipe for the cakes to Manuel, so I guess I'll be fine."

297

"Next time, you'll have to stay longer. I want you to know you will always have a place in our family. David can be a little difficult at times, but he knows how happy you made our daughter."

Harry smiled as she wondered if Eden meant Abby or Nicky. *It really doesn't matter now. They're both gone from my life.* A deep sense of loss filled her as she realized the truth behind those words. Abby was lost forever and Nicky... *I never really gave Nicky a chance.* Struggling to dispel her morose mood, she spoke of her jungle experience. "Next time? Eden, thanks, but no thanks. I suspect that this once was my lifetime limit on remote field trips. What would happen next? I'd probably break my neck." She chuckled, though she was wondering how many people would actually care.

"You know, once the jungle gets under your skin it becomes very alluring. Maybe there will be a powerful reason for you to want to come back."

They both turned to look at Nicky, who was still talking with Manuel. Roja was making his way toward the younger woman, leering suggestively.

Harry nodded her head toward the guide. "At least she won't be subjected to his advances. The man makes my skin crawl with the way he looks at her." Anger began to seethe inside her as the smarmy man closed in on his target.

Eden watched as Harry's eyes narrowed on Roja. "Don't worry about him, Harry, Nicky knows his type and how to handle him."

"Yes, I know she can. Who knows, you may be right. I may find my way back here one day. Thank you for making me feel welcome, Eden, and for helping me remember Abby without feeling the bitterness I have in the past. After our talk, I felt as though a weight had been lifted from my heart."

After she gazed into the sincere pale blue eyes, Eden smiled warmly before pulling Harry in for a hug. No one was ever too old for a good hug and she suspected Harry would benefit from one. "Harry, you're welcome, and thank you for allowing Nicky to stay. It means a lot to us, especially her father. He couldn't believe it when she told him last night after she spoke to you. I thought the champagne was going to pop."

"It's Nicky's decision totally, always was, always will be. She belongs here with you." A far away look filled Harry's eyes. "She's happy here. Guess that's something the big city can't offer her." She sighed and wiped an errant tear that was forming in the corner of her eye.

Before Eden could respond, they both heard Nicky call out while heading their way.

"Are you ready to go, Harry?" she asked as she bounced up to them, her stance lively.

Obviously, my leaving doesn't matter to her at all. Harry's heart dipped dangerously low.

What else can you expect after the way you treated her? When will you learn, Harry? It's not too late to make things right. Don't be stubborn, my love. Now is not the time for that.

Harry ignored the voice. *What's done is done and there will be no turning back.* She needed to distance herself from the camp and especially from Nicky. *I guess she can't wait until I'm gone so she can go on with her life.* "Yes, as ready as I'll ever be. You take care in the rain, Nicky, and please try not to get sick again. You wouldn't want me to have to come out here again to see what's happening with you." Harry

tried to make light of her leaving but both knew her
threat to return was hollow. She looked expectantly
into Nicky's eyes hoping to see a positive reaction to
her words and saw none. "Okay then, guess I should
be going. Who knows what large root awaits me in
the jungle. I'll expect reports on my desk frequently,
Nicky."

Eden listened to their exchange, realizing that
each heart was aching for the other while at the same
time each heart was afraid of breaking. *How can it
end like this? It isn't right.* She said her goodbyes and
left the two women alone to say their final goodbyes,
hoping that one of them would finally speak her true
feelings.

Nicky felt like a teenager on her first date saying
goodnight. "Don't go falling again, Harry. I won't be
there to take care of you, which means you'd have to
rely on Roja." The both laughed. "Somehow I can't
see it, can you?"

"Nope. Roja is certainly nothing like you at all,
so I'll stay upright. No more malaria scares, deal?"
Harry tired to act casual, but her heart was pounding
so hard she was sure Nicky would hear it.

"Deal."

They stared at each other for a few precious
moments and then Harry pulled Nicky in for a hug.
As their arms tightened around each other, the sparks
flew all around them. Being close one final time was
as essential as the air they breathed. Nicky couldn't
stop herself as she leaned in and kissed Harry,
tentatively at first. Her lips moved softly over the
eager lips of the woman in her arms.

Though Harry's mind refused to admit it, her
body craved the touch. In one brief, bittersweet
moment, all her dreams were coming true. Then, she

realized it was likely to be the last time she would ever experience this with Nicky. She deepened the kiss, trying to convey all that she couldn't or refused to say.

"I know why Abby loved you, Nicky." The words, barely a whisper, floated between them.

"I know why Abby loved you, Harry…"

They broke apart quickly as they heard the two men approaching. Roja was annoyed enough at having the plans changed at the last minute; it wouldn't do for him to see them in such an intimate embrace. From a moment of total bliss to absolute abandonment was how it felt releasing from the hug. Each was too afraid of rejection to express her true feelings, having to let go but aching for more. The same thought echoed through both minds: *how can this be happening?*

Within minutes, Harry was on her stretcher and the travelers left the perimeter of the camp for the jungle. Tears threatening to flow, Harry turned back and waved to Nicky.

Abby's voice was loud and clear in her mind. *Don't do this, Harry! Go back for her.*

"Abby, I can't. I need time away to figure out what I feel." The litter bearer was looking at her, wondering if she was talking to him.

Oh my love, you already know. Go with your heart.

As she heard the words, Harry's tears flowed freely.

Nicky couldn't believe Harriet was leaving "I know why Abby loved you, Harry, because I love you too." Too late, the words tripped off her tongue as she turned to be engulfed in a loving embrace.

Eden was there to console her daughter, whom she knew hadn't wanted Harry to go.

Chapter Eighteen

In the ensuing six months, both women worked feverishly on the project as one snag after another threatened to stop everything. Nicky had been so involved that her planned return to the States to settle her apartment never materialized. For her, the isolation in the lab and non-stop work kept her mind off Harry. On the occasions that she allowed herself to think of Harry in more than a casual way, her mood changed drastically. She became sullen and withdrawn, burying herself deeper in her research.

Trying to forget the small woman she'd left behind, Harry became so engulfed in her work that everyone around her was on edge. Absolutely no one was immune to her wrath and almost daily tirades.

Harry paced her office like a caged lion. "What do you mean Cole Corporation is taking a new drug like ours to the federation before us! How the hell did that happen?"

John Fredericks felt the full brunt of her frustration and rage. "Harry, I'm just telling you what the head of that particular panel told me. I thought we had the lead on this."

"We did. As far as I know, we do. This is unacceptable, John. I will not allow all our hard work to go down the drain because some bastard is selling us out!"

She jabbed the button of her intercom with such force that it bounced across the desk. "Sally? I want to speak to the last person who came out of the Martins' project with information. No! Strike that. I want to see all available personnel who have provided information in the last six months. Now!"

Sally had been waiting for this major eruption ever since Harry returned from her disastrous trip out in the field. Her boss had been preoccupied, quite often harsh, and very engrossed in the new project. She even inspected the personnel assigned to the teams that were rotated every three months. Her scrutinizing of every operative in minute detail had Seth Roland paranoid that she was going to let him go.

"I want Guy Cole in for a meeting this week, John. We've held him at bay long enough. Let's see what he's been up to, shall we? If he's indeed the frontrunner in this, then Shekia will go over to him once she knows. Deal with it!"

John Fredericks had seen the deterioration in her mood for weeks. At first, he had attributed it to the broken ankle, but that was now completely healed. Unfortunately, her mood was not.

Fredericks left and Harry picked up the last report from the project containing Nicky's precise script. After the initial snafus, everything was progressing ahead of schedule. David and Eden Martin and their daughter Nicky were the only people that she could trust completely; they had the most to lose. *What the hell does this all mean? Who is the mole in my operation giving away the secret to Cole?*

As she looked at the written words, she felt closer to Nicky. Sometimes she would read the reports repeatedly, picturing Nicky narrating the contents. At first, she would see those silver-flecked green eyes mysteriously appearing out of nowhere. Over time, the image changed to a very sensual one: Nicky naked in her arms and passionately wanting. The images and the effect they had on her body were driving her crazy. If she were going mad, it would be her penance for leaving Nicky behind and refusing to admit she had feelings for the young woman. With pen in hand, she dashed off a quick note.

Nicky,

Your reports have been extremely valuable to me. Thank you for keeping me well informed about the goings on there.

Diane asked me if you would be returning, as everyone in the lab misses you. I do too, Nicky. I wanted to tell you so much, but I never seemed to find the right words or moment. Perhaps when and if you return, we could have a long talk.

Take care of yourself, Harry.

She sealed the envelope and smiled as Nicky's face appeared, bringing her, for the moment at least, some sense of calm. *If the Cole Company takes over, what will happen to Nicky and her parents? All their hard work on the project will be worthless if that company gets approval first. I simply can't let that happen. Nor will I allow my life's work to go down the tubes.* This was her company, the place she'd worked in since leaving college at twenty-one. No one would take it away from her or harm those she cared about without a knock down, drag out fight.

At that moment, Sally walked in with a cup of freshly brewed of coffee in hand. "I think you need this, Harry."

"What would your reaction be if I said Cole has the same drug up for assessment before we do?"

"Hey, don't joke about a thing like that, not with all the work everyone has put in on the project."

"Might not be a joke, Sally."

Without being asked, Sally dropped into a chair opposite Harry. "Really?"

"Yes. God knows how, but he's pulled that rabbit out of the hat. And we have to find out how."

"You think he's stolen it from your project?"

"I wouldn't put it past him to have one of his people on the inside, but we might never know for sure. Cole is very astute and he would have covered his tracks well."

"If you can't prove it, what will happen?"

"He'll get the company, if he wants it at a knock down price. Shekia needs the funds and I can't blame her. Her father was the one with allegiance to the company; she's actually stayed with us longer than I expected."

"Yeah, because you charmed her. She likes you, Harry, everyone knows that. I guess they have always banked on it."

"Things change, Sally, unexpectedly sometimes."

There was a hint of defeat mixed with tiredness in her voice. Sally knew it wasn't just a conversation about Shekia Canning. There was more to it than that.

"How's that young woman that you left behind at the project getting on? She didn't even want to go at first, if I recall."

"Nicky? Oh, Nicky's fine. She was Abby's sister, Sally, and I never knew. All those wasted years when we could have talked about her sister, she never said a word."

Sally realized what the problem was and it had a great deal to do with the pint-sized Nichola Ralston. *Strange, no way would I have guessed that Abby and the women I met that day in the conference room were sisters.*

"That must have been a big surprise. Why didn't she ever tell you? Come to think of it, why didn't Abby say her sister was in town?" Sally wished she were anywhere else at that moment. She realized she had said something vaguely detrimental against her boss's partner. Abby was on a pedestal it would take a Titan to remove her.

"I don't know, Sally, I really don't. Maybe Nicky didn't have a good impression of me. I guess it's something I'll never know."

The words were so plaintive they cut through Sally's tender heart. "I don't think it had anything to do with Ralston not liking you, Harry. Otherwise when you asked her to go on the field trip, she would have definitely said no and stuck to it."

Harry had never considered that aspect. If Nicky had wanted to hurt the project, and Harry by default, the young synthesist would have stayed behind. She didn't know it was her parents' project until she was on the aircraft. *Why did she change her mind? Nicky was never difficult; in fact, quite the reverse.* "I think you're right, Sally. I never looked at it like that."

"Harry, did you feel better after meeting Abby's family?"

No one had asked her that question, not even James who was now embroiled in a long term relationship and with it, the prospect of leaving old friends behind. "Yes, I did."

Satisfied with the answer, Sally went back to business matters. "What's the next step with the Cole situation?"

"We have it all out in a meeting, the sooner the better."

"He might be awkward."

"Not if the stakes are high, and I'll make them the highest."

Sally wasn't sure what she was hearing. *Is she issuing a challenge? Does the victor collect all the spoils and the loser leave with little more than the shirt on their back?*

"What do you mean, Harry?"

"Wait and see, Sally. Wait and see."

∞

"Have you seen Jacob recently, Nicky?"

"No, Evan. He had to go into the town on business, but he should be back in a couple of weeks or so. Anything I can do?"

"He was going to loan me a couple of books, but no problem. I can wait until he gets back. He's not having any trouble, I hope."

"No, if everything goes well on this trip, he should be fine."

"I know he has a problem, Nicky. We've talked a little about it."

Nicky smiled. Evan had declined to be posted back home and had stayed the entire six months to continue his work. Now he was on his second stint and seemed to love every minute of life in the interior. She did think that Jacob might have something to do with it, probably a lot to do with it.

"You've really settled here, Evan. The company will be hoping no one else poaches you."

"Oh, I don't know Nicky. I love the job, of course, but something else keeps me here."

"It does? What?" Nicky was interested, although she thought she knew the answer. Rita Lawrence had gone home disillusioned but well paid. Neil Jenson had signed on to come back in a couple of weeks. He wanted to be home for the birth of his first grandchild, otherwise he would have stayed longer. Peter St. Clare had managed to survive a dressing down from Harry after the first three months, and had been given the project for the next year. Nicky did wonder if the letter she had sent with Peter had helped his cause. But she couldn't second-guess Harry at any time, she really didn't know her that well…the business side of Harry at any rate.

"The people…one person in particular," Evan admitted ruefully.

"We admit to being friendly natives, Evan." Nicky chuckled as his face turned red. *Oh, so it is what I had originally thought.*

"Yeah, you sure are."

Nicky didn't want to pry, so she slapped Evan on the back and went back to her analysis.

Six months had passed since Harry had left. It hadn't been easy at first, and Nicky had wanted to follow her boss back to civilization. However, the pressures of getting the job done correctly and quickly became the overriding factor. Waking up at the crack of dawn and working until sunset helped. By the time her day ended, Nicky was too tired to do anything but eat and chat for a short time with her parents before she hit the hay. It was all a diversion, but it didn't eliminate Harry from her subconscious. The rare times she allowed herself to daydream, she would picture Harry in her arms, needy and passionate, with Nicky fulfilling every need. Who cared if it was just sex! At the end of the day, she was sure they had felt more than that. *Now we will never know. Mom said time is a great healer, but time is infinite isn't it? Can I wait that long?*

Leafing through the mail, she recognized Harry's distinctive writing. *It's addressed to me!* Ripping open the envelope, tears flowed freely as she read the words. *She does care.* Sitting down with pen in hand, she wrote the words she had wanted to say, longed to say.

Dear Harry,

Everything here is progressing on schedule and we should have a finished product in the near future.

I miss you too, Harry. Many words were left unsaid by both of us. I'm not sure why we both found it so difficult to express ourselves with something other than defensiveness. You are right; a long talk is in order. I'll be back; that's a promise. So watch for me to pop up when you least expect it.

Love,

Nic

As the image of Harry came to mind, she smiled and sealed the envelope. With a skip to her step, she went to find the runner to take it into town and post it.

Chapter Nineteen

"Cole, we both know why we're here. I see no point in prevaricating, do you?"

Guy Cole was a large man, about six foot four, with short dark brown hair and a well developed body of a weight lifter or possibly a football player. In college, he excelled in sports and went on scholarship as a soccer goalie. That fact alone explained his *take no prisoners'* attitude when it came to business. The company he spearheaded was swallowing everything. Harry's company was small potatoes in comparison to what he already had under his belt. Shekia's support was the final obstacle in his path, but he knew he held the trump to that ace in the hole.

"Get on with it, Aristides. You have tried my patience a little more than I usually allow."

Harry knew the man was out to make as much money as possible. People meant nothing to him. The only thing that mattered was the bottom line, making a deal.

"I think the new drug you're submitting for approval is a rip-off of one we have under development."

He didn't flinch. He gave her a long thoughtful look out of hooded dark eyes. "Prove it, Aristides, and then we'll talk. Is there anything else?" He was baiting her, hoping for an angry confrontation.

I wonder if we were given false information and were just too late on this one! No! No, we were there first and I'm going to prove it, somehow. Harry's blue eyes held the man in an icy gaze. "If there is a mole in my organization, I can assure you I will find out who it is, Cole. Perhaps then you might be a little less arrogant."

"Provide evidence, Aristides, then you can point your finger in my direction. But be careful, I might bite it off. Do I assume that is the sum total of the reason you requested a meeting?"

"For now."

Guy Cole stood up and walked over to her, capturing her eyes in a look of undisguised contempt. "Next time, I'll call the tune, and you, Aristides, will be dancing like you've never danced before. I think you'd better learn a few steps…the groveling kind; I hate a poor show." His smile was cruel as he left the room.

Totally drained, Harry sank down into her seat. If she didn't find the evidence, she could say goodbye to her career. Pressing the intercom, she called for John Fredericks, his PA, and Sally. There wasn't much time left to salvage, not only the company, but also all the people who depended on them. *What we need is a benefactor who can buy up Shekia's shares and give us a reserve of cash. It would take a miracle to find someone who would do that with Cole snapping at our heels.*

While waiting for the others to arrive, she picked up the mail she had been neglecting for a while. Sally had placed one particular piece of mail on the top. *It's from Nicky!* Harry smiled, feeling the warm rush of blood she had every time she thought of the petite blonde. The one word she focused on was "love". *Does she mean that? Is there a chance for us?* The very thought sent Harry's senses reeling. And, for the first time since she had returned, Abby spoke to her.

The only way to find out, love, is to ask her.

Smiling, Harry answered, "As soon as this is over, I will do just that."

Chapter Twenty

For the next three months, Nicky worked tirelessly toward the completion of the project. Her nerves were frayed. Harry had sent a message that no more transmissions were to be sent. All research processes and results were to be sealed and locked up, with an armed guard if necessary. There had been no explanation, but the directive had been enough for her parents to react immediately. The project had been jeopardized, that was all they needed to know.

"I made a pact with the devil, Nicky. Now I hope I'm going to redeem myself." Jacob spoke clearly, but the volume was only enough for her to hear.

"I don't understand, Jacob."

"You wouldn't; you never will…it's not your nature, Nicky, and thank God for that."

"Please, Jacob, what's going on?"

"You wouldn't understand my reasons, Nicky, and I'm glad. Glad that you came back, and happy that you have settled in so well again. Although I have seen a loneliness and longing in your eyes."

Nicky drew in a deep breath and exhaled it as she spoke decisively. "Cut the bullshit, Jacob. What the hell is going on? Are you the reason we're almost under house arrest?"

"No! No, I would never betray any confidences. You have to believe that. Not directly, anyway."

"I do believe you, Jacob." She smiled at him and pulled him closer until they lay forehead to forehead as they had as children.

"I fell in love, Nicky, and it reminded me that a good life was worth working for rather than selling out for the easy buck. I had to make up my mind what *I* really needed in life, not what others wanted."

"I knew that."

Jacob smiled and saw the matching smile of his friend. "You did? And how would you know?"

"Oh, I'd know, Jacob; I'd know. When are you going to admit that to the love of your life?"

He grinned broadly. "You make it sound so...so theatrical."

"Love can be, didn't anyone tell you that, Jacob? Mine was."

"Ah, but you never admitted it, did you?"

Nicky gave him a sharp glance, the sadness evident in her eyes. "No, I never did."

"It's never too late, Nicky. If that person loves you, they'll still be waiting."

"I can only hope, Jacob. Someday maybe, who knows. It does make for a good story, though."

"Nic, you've always been a fighter. Why stop now?" He wanted to see her completely happy.

"We'll see. Give, who's the love of your life?"

"Oh no, you tell me yours and I'll tell you mine." The tension in the man eased a little.

Nicky said, "It's a stalemate, then."

"Guess so.

They both smiled, having a very good idea who the respective loves were. A telepath going by at that moment would pick up on two names: Harry and Evan.

"You'd better spill the beans on your problem, though, Jacob. I might be able to help you."

Chapter Twenty-one

For three months, Harry and her lawyers had employed every stalling tactic they knew to keep their rivals from filing for approval with the federation. Their basis was the preliminary reports and the documentation that verified when Global Research Pharmaceuticals first began experiments. The failure of the Cole Corporation to prove that their findings were independently obtained at an earlier date gave Harry's company a much needed reprieve. Despite the temporary victory, Harry knew that Cole's registration was only a matter of time if they couldn't find the leak.

Harry pored over the reports, and the people who had provided them, for the hundredth time. *All of them appear to be squeaky clean, but that can't be. I'm missing something; I know it. What could it be?* Something niggled at her...a memory forgotten but not gone. It was back in the jungle when Nicky was tending to her ankle and Harry had asked her how she knew it was going to rain. Nicky replied, "You must look beyond the obvious, Harry. Never rule something out just because you can't see it."

Have we ruled people out because of who they are? Are there other circumstances we don't know about? Time, I need more time and I don't have it. Damn it. There must be something I can do.

Her eyes drifted to the picture of Abby and she smiled for the first time in hours. "What would you advise me to do, Abby? I could use a miracle. If you have a message from heaven for me, please share; I'd love to hear it."

Stretching the aching muscles in her neck and shoulders, Harry considered that she might be staring defeat full in the face. Her team had worked long and hard to uncover evidence that someone from the camp had divulged information to the Cole Corporation. Nothing, absolutely nothing had been found to cast even a fraction of doubt on anyone. If she didn't find something by the morning, she would have to make the call to the authorities. Their stay of execution would be over and they would accept Cole's validation. At that point, Global would fall to Cole and his predatory ways.

Harry looked at her watch. It was eleven in the evening and she knew that even if she spent the night going over everything again, it would produce nothing. What she needed was to go home and sleep, if possible. Tomorrow would be a long day of meeting after meeting, culminating in possibly her final day as president of the company. She glanced around her office. It had been her home for the past three years and she would miss it a great deal. She would also miss the people she had worked with, particularly Sally and John. They would be kept on, she was sure. Cole wasn't stupid; it was common knowledge GRP recruited only the best.

With a deep sigh, she got up and gathered up her jacket, purse, and briefcase. She opened the door, switched off the light, and headed down the small corridor that fronted John's office as well as those of both of their PAs. She moved toward the elevator and was surprised to see that it was already moving upwards. *Security guard doing his rounds probably*. As the elevator doors opened, she was shocked to find someone completely unexpected.

"Ms. Aristides, I need to talk with you."

Harry knew she was standing open-mouthed, just inches from Jacob. Finally finding her voice, she said, "Why would I want to talk with you?"

"When you hear what I have to say, I think you will be more than happy to talk with me."

"There's nothing you can say to me that I would want to listen to. And, frankly, isn't it a little late in the evening for you to be coming here and asking for an appointment?"

"Okay, I know we didn't exactly hit it off. Nicky said to tell you that you will want to speak with me. She gave me this note to give to you, if you were skeptical." He passed over a folded piece of paper.

Harry opened it and scanned the contents. The note was brief, but was definitely in Nicky's handwriting:

H, Jacob has valuable information. Please listen to what he has to say. He had to come himself, as I couldn't trust anyone else. N

"Jacob, this better be good." Harry waited for clarification.

"Oh yeah, it is good. In fact, I'd go one better and say it might be a life saver."

What could he know that would be of interest to me and would warrant Nicky being involved? She looked at him skeptically, back at Nicky's note, then turned away from Jacob. "You'd better follow me, then."

He grinned as he walked quickly to keep up with her long strides and followed her into her office.

Chapter Twenty-two

Eden Martin was shocked at the information her daughter had given her. *Who would have thought it?* It was family cheating on family, and that brought its own measure of pain in addition to the betrayal itself. "Jacob went of his own free will, Nicky? When Harry decides to press charges."

"I know, Mom. I'm certain he had already decided it was the right thing to do before he told me. I still can't believe it. All these years you've trusted him with all our secrets and what a way to pay you back."

"I would like to be the one to tell your father, if you don't mind."

Nicky knew her father would be gutted at the betrayal from such an unexpected quarter. They had never suspected, and why would they? There had been absolute trust between them for years. "Thanks, Mom. I'm afraid I wouldn't have had the words. They were so close, Dad will never believe it."

Eden looked at the family pictures and saw the turncoat having fun with Nicky and Abby; they had been happy. Back then, who would have thought that one day their friendship would be traded for money, the years of hard work and sacrifice stolen away. "Harry might not listen to him, or believe that he's telling the truth."

"She will, Mom. I sent a note. Harry will listen, I know it." Why she was so sure, Nicky couldn't have explained. Her gut feeling was that Harry would at least listen and decide for herself—Harriet Aristides was one astute woman.

Now that mention of Harry had come up in conversation, Eden broached a subject she had never found the opportunity to do since Nicky's return. "Why didn't you tell Harry who you were? If not when you first went to work for the company, why not when you and she were... thrown together, shall we say?"

I wondered when we'd get around to that question. I'm surprised it took her so long. I suppose that now is as good a time as any. "I was going to. I even tried to make an appointment to see her when I first started working at the company. But after Abby's death, Harry went abroad and didn't come back to the office for any extended periods of time for a couple of years. By then I decided that it was pointless to open old wounds, Abby had been gone for over two years. Besides, I would see Harry and the sadness in her eyes was so deep, I couldn't bear to cause her any more pain. I kept an eye on her, as I know Abby would have wanted me to." Sighing, she walked over to the window and looked out at the sunset that was about to cascade the sky above with beauty beyond description.

"What about recently?" came her mother's voice from behind her.

Nicky turned around and leaned against the casement. "I planned to, I really did. Somehow, time rushed on and events crashed around us, and by that time, I didn't know what to say. I was afraid of what she would think of me. Then I got sick, and the last chance I had was gone."

Eden felt pity for her child. She had been wrong not to tell Harry, certainly at least by the start of the trip. Once they became lovers, if only for one night, the situation had become even more complicated. Nicky hadn't the experience to talk herself around that one, which led to misunderstandings and recriminations. "Harry thinks that you stayed away from Abby because of her, is that true, darling?"

"No! Absolutely not. I was in accelerated courses and all the holidays were spent on specialized field trips. I called the apartment once, about two months before Abby died. Harry picked up the phone…I panicked and hung up. I know, I was stupid. I could have spent some time with them and I feel so guilty about that now. Mom, it still hurts that I ran away from you and Dad at the same time Abby died." Tears fell as Nicky spoke for the first time about her cavalier letter to her parents five years ago as they reeled from Abby's death. Another reason she had decided never to go back in the field. *And look at me now. I'm running away again, only this time it's back to where I started.* "Please believe me, I didn't know at the time I sent you the letter."

"We knew that, darling. At the time, we all needed our own space. Time heals all wounds, remember? You and Harry need to talk. Think about it, Nicky, but don't take too long."

"I know. Harry said the same thing in a letter. With all the mystery surrounding our project, there hasn't been time."

"Make the time, Nic. You owe it to Harry and to yourself. If you let this pass you by, you'll never forgive yourself."

As she contemplated the advice, Nicky glanced out the window and saw her father ambling along toward the cabin. "Dad's coming."

"How about you go check with Abula? Some fine coffee laced liberally with Scotch would be a help. Your dad's going to need it."

"Good luck, Mom, and thanks for listening."

"Hey, baby, that's what moms are for. Maybe one day you might experience that for yourself."

Nicky smiled ruefully. "Perhaps, but don't hold your breath." She quickly moved to kiss her mother's cheek and hug her warmly.

"I won't," Eden said, returning the hug. "See you later," she called as her daughter left by the side door.

Chapter Twenty-three

Harry was grinning like a Cheshire cat as she waited for an audience with Guy Cole. He had wanted their meeting to be on his home ground, and he'd have it on home ground. An hour later, she was still waiting to be granted entrance into the great man's office. If she had been angry before, she was pissed off now. *This is the height of arrogance.* She drew a deep calming breath. *I can be patient; he's about to get his, no doubt about it. And I'm going to relish every moment.*

Cole's secretary gave a cold look as Harriet Aristides stood up for possibly the hundredth time and scowled at her. Then her intercom buzzed and she looked at the tall, intimidating woman who was bristling with pent up anger. "Mr. Cole will see you now."

"Damn straight he will," Harry bit out as she stalked into the office and slammed the door behind her.

Cole gave her a look that was cynical and calculating. "Harriet," he said in a condescending tone, "you decided to give in gracefully and come dance to my tune."

"Dance to your tune, Cole? By the time I've finished with you, your lawyer is going to be working out how you can sidestep a long term in jail!"

Guy Cole had kept an eye on Harriet Aristides for years. She was good, very good. The one thing he didn't knew about her was that she rarely said anything she couldn't support. "Then, my dear, please enlighten me to your newfound knowledge."

She pointedly ignored his motioning for her to sit. Instead, she towered over his desk, reminding him of a lion about to pounce. "One, you don't call me my dear; two, I don't sit with creeps like you; and three, read this and weep." She threw a folder at him that contained copies of her evidence, enjoying the shock and disbelief on his face before she marched out of the office, sneering at the secretary. As Harry punched the button for the elevator, she heard Guy Cole shout for his secretary to contact his lawyer and then find Eric Lasser. The doors opened and she stepped into the car. The weight of the world she thought she had on her shoulders was miraculously falling away as she descended to the ground floor.

Harry knew that the documents in the folder she had given Cole would be the saving of her company. They would be the ones to obtain the approval for the testing and sale of their revolutionary new drug. There would be no licensing for the product the Cole Company had submitted. As the floors quickly passed by, she pondered Jacob's words the night before. They implicated Eric Lasser and provided positive proof that he had been working for the Cole Company. Apparently heavy gambling debts and drinking problems had wiped out Eric's resources, and he had felt he had no choice but to resort to stealing his friends' work and selling it to the highest bidder. Eric's contact had been a Cole employee named Randy Allerdice, Jacob's father. Since Randy and Eric had met through Jacob, the young man was taking some of the blame onto himself.

Together she and Jacob had spent the night tracking down people who could verify the facts. When everything was confirmed, she seized the opportunity to arrange a meeting with Cole, discussing it with no one, not taking the chance of tipping her hand.

The details of her next move were racing through her mind when one made her heart somersault and stopped her in her tracks. *Nicky trusted me to handle the situation.* Nicky had known Eric for years and he was as close to family as one could get, without being a blood relative. "How could he be under suspicion?" could have been Nicky's logical question, but instead she had put the information into Harry's hands.

Harry's thoughts dwelled on the image of Nicky. A kaleidoscope of their time together floated in her thoughts, from the first day to the last minutes. *How I wish you had decided to come back here, Nicky. We could have shared some good memories.*

The bell on the elevator sounded the ground floor and the doors swept open. *Now we have a company that can move into the next decade under full steam.* In the process, she would make a few very important people rich and famous, even if they didn't want the accolades or the money. As Harry walked out of the Cole building, she could feel a tingle going up and down her spine and electricity coursing through her veins. There, before her, stood the vision of her heart's desire, and it astounded her. With a brilliant smile, Nicky walked up to her, enclosed her with loving arms and whispered, "I've come home."

"Excuse me, lady," said the brusque voice of a passerby.

It shocked Harry out of her haze and she realized she was standing in the middle of the sidewalk, looking like a goof. For a fleeting moment, she looked around, half expecting Nicky to actually appear. She did not.

She arrived back at her building and walked quickly into her office. She pressed the intercom button and buzzed her PA. "Sally, I need a line to the base camp. Can you arrange that for me? Good. Let me know when it's ready. Will you also call a meeting of the board and all the major department heads for one o'clock? Thank you."

Half an hour later, Sally notified her that the call was ready

"Hello, Eden?"

"Harry, it's great to hear your voice."

"It is good to hear your voice, too. I want you all to know that everything has been taken care of and we are back in business."

"Then you got Nicky's message and spoke with Jacob."

"Yes, thanks to Nicky. And, as far as I am concerned, nothing will happen to Jacob. I'm thankful he decided to step up when he did."

"I'm glad to hear that, Harry. Jacob is a good man."

"I agree with you, although we thought that about Eric, too. Is Nicky around?"

"Yes, I need to get her, can you hold on?"

"Sure, I'll hold on." Harry waited impatiently as the minutes ticked by. At last she heard the receiver being picked up.

"Harry, is that really you?" Nicky asked.

The sound of her voice made Harry feel weak in the knees. "Hi, Nicky. Yes, it really is me. How are you doing? Did your Mom tell you the news? When are you coming home? You haven't been sick again, have you?"

Nicky laughed at the rapid-fire questions. "Slow down, Harry…fine, yes, soon, and no."

It was Harry's turn to laugh. "I'm sorry about all the questions. I'm just so happy to hear your voice."

"And, I am so happy to hear yours, Harry, I've missed hearing it."

"Nicky, I wanted to thank you for encouraging Jacob to come here and help us save the company. You did that you know…you saved our company. If it hadn't been for you, I would be cleaning out my desk right now."

"Harry, I didn't do anything really," she demurred.

Harry smiled at Nicky's typically modest response. "Even if you think you did nothing, thank you for that nothing."

"You're welcome."

"Nicky, when are you coming home? We need to talk face to face."

"Soon…before you know it."

"Soon" was too indefinite for Harry. "Really? When do you think that will be?"

"I have a few loose ends to tie up and then I'll be on my way."

"I'll be counting down the days 'til then," Harry said.

"So will I. Bye."

"Bye." Harry's heart was singing as she hung up.

The private line in her office began to buzz. Picking it up, her smile was at the ready for the caller, for right now nothing could burst her happy bubble. At least that's what she thought. "Uncle Harry, what a surprise. When did you get into town?"

Harriet's face turned ashen as she hung up the phone in disbelief. *Did I really hear what he said? No it can't be!*

Chapter Twenty-four

Harry walked toward a spot that was as familiar to her as her apartment. Sitting down on the bench she'd had put in three years earlier, she sighed. "Six years, Abby. You left me alone six years ago and I still don't know if I can let you go." Harry dropped her head and contemplated her clasped hands. When she looked up again, she stared hard at the headstone. "My Uncle called recently Abby and I'm not sure how to tell you this. He told me some shocking news my love. A source he would not name told him there was the possibility that you, our baby, and Sam's death weren't accidental. I suppose meant well. How ludicrous can those allegations be after all this time, Abby? He wants me to meet the woman who abandoned me as if I didn't matter. He called her my mother. How can I forgive that? I'm not going to do what he wants and contact her or anyone one else related to her. As far as I'm concerned, she doesn't exist. Period!" The fact that the woman who gave her birth was lying gravely ill made no difference to her for she felt nothing for her but contempt. Her uncle's insistent suggestion that it was time to see her birth mother caused her to retch at the thought. "My mother could go to hell. The quicker the better I say"

Her thoughts veered back to the reason she was there.

"Usually James is here with me and you don't have to listen to me bore you with all the business nonsense. Today it's different. You would be proud...not of me this time, but of your parents. They've come up with a fantastic find and it's going to save lives, lots of lives."

She glanced around the cemetery. No one was nearby. She knew that anyone seeing her would have thought she was having a conversation with herself. She had never thought so. Abby had always been close to her spiritually.

"I've met your sister, Abby. She's nothing like you, quite the opposite. I like her, though."

As she said the words Abby's image, which had been fading as the year passed, disappeared altogether, and was replaced with Nicky's smiling face. She tried to summon Abby's face in her mind, but couldn't. Sitting silently, she wondered what life would have in store for her now. The company was on solid footing; the new medicine was close to production and testing, and Nicky... *What of Nicky?*

"Do you mind if I join you?"

The hairs on Harry's neck prickled as she immediately recognized the voice...*Nicky*. Sparks once again were charging the air around them. She looked up at the face that wasn't a fantasy this time and a small smile curved her lips. "Please, I'd like that. Abby would have been happy you came by, too. When did you get back?" The silver-flecked green eyes that she dreamt about gazed at her with an expression of compassion and warmth.

"Just a little while ago. I thought I might find you here. Harry, I have something to tell you and it wouldn't be fair if you didn't hear it from me."

Harry's heart, which had been beating hard when Nicky arrived, plummeted like a stone in water at those words. For just a moment, she couldn't speak, and then all she could muster was, "I see."

"I don't think you do, Harry. I've come for you. I told you I would come back to you." Nicky took the larger hands in hers, pulled them toward her lips, and kissed them reverently.

Harry was perplexed, surprised, and unsure what Nicky meant. The smaller woman had become confident and assured in the months they had been apart, so different but wonderfully so. "I don't..."

"You will, I promise. I need you in my life, Harriet Aristides, and I will make it work. I'll help you start again...if that's what you want." Nicky was playing every card she had and that wasn't many. All she knew was that she was in love with Harry, and if she had to wait for her to be ready to love again, she would. She was going to make sure that Harry knew she was waiting, and would for the rest of her life.

Harry looked at Nicky and felt the immensity of what the woman was offering. Her eyes tracked to the headstone and she mentally went over what she had lost and how she felt about it all. Closing her eyes against the welling up of emotion she felt, Harry knew that it was time for her to let go, to allow Abby to rest, and in doing so open her life to love again. *Abby, I don't know if I can do it though.*

Softly the wind spoke: *You're not lost and alone any longer, my love. It's time to love again, Harry, time to let go.* Then the gentle breeze ceased.

Holding out her hand, Nicky smiled in reassurance as Harry clasped it. She drew the taller woman closer to her as they embraced softly and tenderly at first. Soon they were lost in each other, the air charged with their feelings. They kissed feverishly, each trying to consume as much as possible, until the weather doused them with a short, sunny shower.

Laughing, they held each other close as the rain soaked them. "Are these the right conditions in which to learn how to love rain?" Harry asked drolly.

Nicky grinned, nodding. "Absolutely. I'll teach you all about rain and so much more. What would you say to us having a large yard full of flowers and plants?"

The short-lived rain stopped and the odd dark cloud turned to clear blue skies, and the sun beat down warm upon their faces.

Harry smiled as she ducked her head for another kiss, her emotions raging out of control with Nicky so close. Looking down into the green eyes, Harry smiled and wrapped Nicky more tightly in her arms. She looked up at the bright blue sky above them and knew the time was right to leave the past in the past and start living again. Sometime in the future, she would share with Nicky the conversation she had regarding her mother. Perhaps Nicky's insight might dissolve some of her own bitterness concerning the situation, and she might have some idea of what to do next. Whatever that might be, it would have to wait, because right now that particular moment was for them, allowing only brightness to pervade their thoughts and actions. "Let's go home."

Hand in hand, they walked toward the parking lot. Harry abruptly stopped and looked back at Abby's headstone. She was leaving Abby behind, but would never stop loving her or forget their life together. She felt a deep sense of sadness and loss, but knew Abby would approve of her relationship with Nicky.

"You okay?" Nicky asked softly, her own eyes filling with tears of gratitude that Harry was finally letting go of the past. And, if she needed help, she was going to be right there beside her with that helping hand, regardless of what it was or who might be involved; it was as simple as that.

Harry turned to the small, wonderful woman. "Yes," she said with a wistful smile. As a single tear rolled down her cheek, she heard Abby speak:

Be happy, my love...

About the Authors

JM Dragon

Born in England JM Dragon is and now a New Zealand citizen, living in the beautiful Canterbury countryside, JM Dragon loves to garden, travel and has a love of animals. Her animals, many of them strays, even the odd chicken, have proved a new focus in her life. Sharing her life with her family, two cats, two alpacas, and over forty bantam chickens in differing breeds; she's found a totally different focus in her life than when she lived in England.

Her writing is a long cherished release for the characters that invade her mind on many an occasion. Always having written stories from a child, she found the internet a place she could share her creative world with other readers. Having stumbled across venues on the net for her writing, she found new subjects to explore. She currently loves the creative, readership and friendship genre she has comfortably taken residence in for the last twelve years. A keen reader of sci-fi, crime/mystery, classic, and romance of course.

JM Dragon is here to stay and loves to experiment with storylines-who knows what she will tease us with next.

Erin O'Reilly

Erin O'Reilly resides in the Texas Hill Country on Lake LBJ for the last five years. Erin previously lived in various cities around the world. When not enjoying the lake she owns and runs a computer consulting business. A lifelong bird watcher, Erin also likes to cook, sew, read, and do various crafts in her spare time. Erin belongs to the Sapphic Readers, which is a lesbian book club in Austin, Texas.

First challenged by a friend to write a story, Erin has since written numerous online and publish works. Her story Deception was a GCLS Finalist in 2008. That book also garnered the Sapphic Readers Award in 2009. Story creation involving strong characters always seems to dictate the story and invade her mind at all hours. It always amazes here when the characters she is developing suddenly take on a life of their own and lead the story down a completely different path. She thinks that, when all is done, the characters make an impact on the storyline the story is better for it.

E-Books, Print, Free e-books

Visit our website for more publications
available online.
www.affinityebooks.com

Published by Affinity E-Book Press NZ Ltd
Canterbury, New Zealand
Registered Company 2517228

Printed in Great Britain
by Amazon